HIGHEST P
JOVE HOMESPU

"In all of the Homespun I've been very taken wit colorful small-town people doing small-town things and bringing 5 STAR and GOLD 5 STAR rankings to the readers. This series should be selling off the bookshelves within hours! Never have I given a series an overall review, but I feel this one, thus far, deserves it! Continue the excellent choices in authors and editors! It's working for this reviewer!"
—*Heartland Critiques*

We at Jove Books are thrilled by the enthusiastic critical acclaim that the Homespun Romances are receiving. We would like to thank you, the readers and fans of this wonderful series, for making it the success that it is. It is our pleasure to bring you the highest quality of romance writing in these breathtaking tales of love and family in the heartland of America.

And now, sit back and enjoy this delightful new Homespun Romance . . .

Winter Longing
by Christina Cordaire

Also by Christina Cordaire . . . her acclaimed
Homespun Romance *Forgiving Hearts*:

"Warm and wonderful . . . a valuable lesson of forgiveness and the power of love."
—*Romantic Times*

"A beautiful slice of Americana that captures the ecstasy of healing souls, the glory of redemption, and the beauty and purity of love . . . brilliantly and realistically done."
—*Affaire de Coeur*

"Consider this a must on your reading list."
—*Rendezvous*

WINTER LONGING

CHRISTINA CORDAIRE

JOVE BOOKS, NEW YORK

If you purchased this book without a cover, you should be aware that this book is stolen property. It was reported as "unsold and destroyed" to the publisher, and neither the author nor the publisher has received any payment for this "stripped book."

WINTER LONGING

A Jove Book / published by arrangement with
the author

PRINTING HISTORY
Jove edition / February 1996

All rights reserved.
Copyright © 1996 by Christina Strong.
This book may not be reproduced in whole or in part,
by mimeograph or any other means, without permission.
For information address: The Berkley Publishing Group,
200 Madison Avenue, New York, New York 10016.

The Putnam Berkley World Wide Web site address is
http://www.berkley.com

ISBN: 0-515-11811-7

A JOVE BOOK®
Jove Books are published by The Berkley Publishing Group,
200 Madison Avenue, New York, New York 10016.
JOVE and the "J" design are trademarks
belonging to Jove Publications, Inc.

PRINTED IN THE UNITED STATES OF AMERICA

10 9 8 7 6 5 4 3 2 1

To my daughter, Johanna,
who has inherited her great-great-grandmother
Henry French Richard's spunk and determination.
And yes, Jo, the story of how Henry French
got her name is true, but I've changed the
Ri-chard to Richards to protect the innocent.

Chapter One

M<small>ISS</small> H. F<small>RENCH</small> R<small>ICHARDS</small> held her head high and looked ahead with steely determination. There was no way she was going to let them know how much they hurt her, no way they were going to see the pain she felt at having all her bright hopes dashed like this! Chin elevated to the point that she was not even watching where she walked, she fought back the tears of humiliation that threatened to embarrass her even further and placed one foot firmly before the other on the rough railroad platform as if she fully intended them to leave permanent prints there.

The short, ginger-haired man walking close behind her kept up his steady stream of stinging vituperation. "You cannot possibly imagine that we would want the likes of you here. There is no way this town could ever tolerate a person of your radical persuasion." He knew Miss Richards might have taken some small comfort if she'd known with what reluctance he was sending her away, but of course, she did not. So he watched the sway of her hips, mesmerized, and fought a devastating sense of loss. He was all too aware that it wouldn't do to let anyone in the little crowd of people who'd followed them from Widow Salton's boardinghouse know how much—how *very* much—he regretted this departure of such a lovely

1

almost-member of his staff. Even now, even knowing what she was, he still got slightly dizzy when he remembered his first sight of her standing there in the door of his office this morning.

At the memory he stifled a sigh. Standing there in his doorway, she'd looked like some ethereal being who'd lost her way and was hoping *he* would be able to save her. He'd been struck dumb by her beauty and had only been able to stare for the first full minute she stood waiting. She'd piled her shining dark hair up under a hat that was supposed to look businesslike, no doubt, but he'd found it only succeeded in looking delightfully frivolous above so beautiful a face. In small, clinging curls the dark silk of her hair had been escaping down the back of her slender neck and beside her cheeks. Her lovely gray eyes, shining with intelligence, had captivated him on the spot. He'd almost swooned with joy when he learned that she was the Miss Richards he'd been expecting.

Then—ah, would that he had never done it—he'd asked her to tell him something about herself. When she had, the dreams she'd inspired as he ushered her into his office had gone crashing down like a house of cards. He'd been so appalled at her sweetly expressed opinions that he felt foully betrayed.

How could she have done this to him? Couldn't she sense all she had instantly meant to him? His indignation swelled again. With an effort, he pulled his gaze from her hips and lashed out at her, "You have deceived us all, Miss Richards." With satisfaction, he saw her cringe just a little, and knew that she hated being called a deceiver. His satisfaction was cut short, however, as he realized her attitude made her even more appealing to him. If only there could have been some way to keep this goddess in his life!

There wasn't, of course, she had overstepped the boundaries. Indeed, if stout Mayor Silas Townley, huffing along just behind him with Miss Richards's other portmanteau, had had even the smallest suspicion that he wanted to keep Miss H. French Richards in his employ no matter what, his own job would be forfeit. To guarantee further against such an intolerable possibility, he said to the lovely young lady, "Here comes your train back to Boston, Miss Richards." Drawing himself up to his full height, he puffed out his chest. His mustache trembled with righteous indignation. "I hope you have the grace to regret having come as a viper to our collective bosom."

There was an approving murmur from the small group of influential men and women of the community who stood behind him—all except Mrs. Salton, and the widow's softhearted championing of the girl would have no effect on the rest of them, he knew. Their all but unanimous support goaded him to add in ringing tones, "And I assure you, young lady, that I shall send notices of your perfidy throughout the entire state. No one"—he flung a pointing finger at her and shook it in admonition— "no one in all of Massachusetts will deign to give you a post when I am through!"

The young goddess fixed him with one direct, accusing look and lifted one perfect, winged eyebrow making him go weak in the knees. The slight trembling of her lower lip completely unmanned him. Then, she surveyed the rest of the assembled townspeople with quiet hauteur, and turned regally to mount the steps of the train. He jumped forward and plunked her first bag onto the steps she had just vacated as she swept into the railway carriage, head high. Mayor Townley added the second, and a porter snatched them up and followed her into the rail car. The conductor signaled the engineer, and the train chugged away.

Her tormentor stood there in the sunlight and felt as if his life had just ended. In a hollow tone he said to the mayor, "There. Good riddance."

"Yes, indeed," Mayor Townley agreed, removing his hat and swiping his handkerchief over his glistening pate. "This town is well rid of such a polluting presence." But his voice sounded every bit as wistful as his friend's.

Very late that same day Miss Henry French Richards was back in the bosom of her family. She felt that it was most unfortunate that she had had to be called for by her father.

Her short train trip back to Boston after leaving the pleasant little town that had so rudely rejected her had been uneventful. It was just happenstance that a parade for the right of women to vote was congregating right there at the station.

The spirit of women with a high purpose, the sea of Sunday hats, and the suppressed excitement of people doing something both important and daring had permeated the station, and she'd not been able to resist. Hastily paying a cabby to take her luggage home, she'd found herself marching in the parade.

When men along the streets took exception to the right of women to vote and began shouting, "Stay home where you belong!" "Let your husbands make your decisions for you!" and "Go home and take care of your babies!"—an admonition that drew blushes from the unmarried maidens in the group—the police had deemed it necessary to step in. That had spoiled everything. Her father had had to leave the bank of which he was president to come and collect his only daughter from, of all places, a police station, and the episode had done little to improve his disposition. Now, back in the luxurious mansion that had been her home all her life, she was paying the price for her political convictions.

"If you ever, *ever*, do such a thing again, Miss Henry French Richards"—her father shook his finger in her face, his own red with suppressed anger—"I promise you I will put you in a convent for the rest of your days!" He was clearly disturbed enough to shout, but her father never shouted.

Henry French Richards regarded her father with luminous gray eyes and refrained from answering. Somehow, she didn't feel as if this would be a good time to remind her father that the family was Methodist and that it had been for generations. Clearly her latest efforts to better the plight of womanhood had irritated him to a greater degree than usual.

All she had done, though, was join in a parade. And it was a parade for a very worthwhile cause. Her father, and, indeed, her mother as well, had always talked as if supporting causes in which one believed were one of the most noble acts in life. And they both knew she believed in the women's right to vote.

The sad truth was that she had joined the march to cheer herself up after having been fired from her first post. She'd desperately needed to do something significant to lift her spirits after her terrible experience in the lovely little town in which she had so wanted to teach.

"Answer me, French!" Her father's agitation was increasing in the face of her silence. "I refuse to have you stand there and stare at me as if you were the injured party here. It is your dear mother and I who have had to suffer the slings and arrows of your outrageous behavior. You, I can see, are in no way affected by it."

French sighed inside. How did one answer the charges of a parent like her father? He and Mama had reared her to care about others and to take up the cudgels against tyranny. Every story they'd read her as a child had been about heroes fighting to right wrongs. She would never have heard her first fairy tale unless it had been told to her by the nursery maid. Now that she'd grown up and was fighting to right wrongs, just as their stories had taught her, they seemed appalled that she was trying in her own small way to live up to those bedtime stories. It was all a trifle confusing — and, though she was reluctant to say it, even to herself, a little unfair.

Why, hadn't her mother been so concerned with keeping her own word that to honor that word she'd named her only daughter after a *man*? It had been Mother's cousin, of course, and he had certainly earned the privilege by taking such good care of Mama during all her confinements, but that hadn't made it any easier for *her,* her Mama's only girl child, to stagger through the first few years of the exclusive private school she'd attended with a name like Henry!

Her name had made her an outsider, and being an outsider had given her a deep compassion for the less fortunate of society, as she'd felt rather unfortunate herself in those years. She almost sniffled at the memories that rose up, even now — memories of cruel childish laughter directed straight at her.

Now, again today, for this wasn't the first time, it appeared that she'd displeased her parents by exhibiting the very traits they'd so carefully nurtured in her. What was she to do? It was too late to change, she was twenty years old, for pity's sake! And it wasn't her fault the police had arrested her and her fellow paraders.

She felt tears tremble on her lashes. She took a deep breath and willed them to go away. Her effort was too late, though. Papa had seen them.

"Ah, French." He called her by her middle name, as everyone did. He was as reluctant as all the rest of their world to call a girl "Henry" no matter what the official record of her birth might read. "Don't cry, child." He reached out a hand as if he would touch her in some comforting way, then withdrew it in embarrassment, unsure of just what he'd intended to do with it.

"Don't cry. Don't cry, child." He grasped the lapels of his coat to give his hands something to do that would not disconcert him and started for the door, thoroughly cognizant that he'd hurt his only daughter. Stopping on the threshold he looked back uncertainly. "Don't worry," he promised vaguely, "everything will come right in the end."

It was as close as he could come to comforting his child. Both of them knew it was not enough.

As the door closed quietly behind him, French threw herself on her bed and wept. She told herself that she was only permitting this little bout of weeping as a turbulent tribute to the fact that she *did* love her parents, no matter how they confused her, but it wasn't true. She couldn't have held back her tears if her life had depended on it.

After a while her sobs quieted, and she rolled over on her back and stared morosely at the ceiling. In addition to her grief at her parents' attitude, Henry French Richards was having a bad moment of self-doubt. Perhaps, she mused, she should try to be a little more circumspect about expressing her political views. Casting her mind back over her latest debacle, she had to admit that it might, for instance, have been better to wait a while to express her opinions to a new group of acquaintances. Maybe if she had ever learned to curb her enthusiasm for her beliefs, she would not now be back home again irritating her poor parents.

Bravely, she acknowledged that this wasn't the first time she'd regretted having expressed her strong views on one subject or another. It was just the first time it had cost her a position. Of course, it was her very first position, but it had certainly not been productive to state her opinions to her *ex*-principal the very day she met him.

If only she'd managed to hold her tongue, she might still be teaching two towns away, still be living in the delightful little room she'd rented from the comfortable widow who'd been so sorry to see her go. If she'd just waited until the staff at the school had all gotten to know her better, perhaps then they would not have been *quite* so quick to dismiss her from her teaching post.

She sighed again, full and freely this time since her father was gone.

"What am I going to do? Nobody in the whole state of Massachusetts is going to give me a teaching position now." The memory of her all but apoplectic recent ex-principal assuring her of that was still too painfully fresh.

She rolled over to stare up at the ceiling. Funny how she'd misjudged him. When she'd knocked hesitantly on the jamb of his open office door, he'd looked up, frowning, but his eyes had warmed as they swept over her person, and he'd invited her to come in with considerable enthusiasm. He'd been all interested atten-tion, fussing over her, finding her the most comfortable chair, getting her a lemonade. "Honestly," she allowed herself the unacceptable luxury of pouting, "I thought he was going to fall over his own feet, his attitude was so dratted warm in his welcome."

Lulled by his eager hospitality, she'd innocently responded to his invitation to tell him a little something of herself. It had been the biggest mistake of her life! When she'd made no more than a few mild statements of her belief in the rights of women, he'd looked as if he were ready to explode! She could still see him leaping to his feet as he'd shouted at her, "Miss Richards! Surely you do not think that I would permit someone of such radical views to teach children entrusted to *my* care!" Seizing her by the arm, he'd pulled her abruptly up out of the chair he'd brought for her only moments before. He'd been unable to get her out of his office quickly enough, and she'd gone back to her cozy little rented room to pick up her things with the outraged comments he'd been making to the other teachers ringing in her ears.

She hadn't even had time to spend one night in the pretty little chintz-canopied four-poster. She'd been rushed to the train and back to Boston as if she carried the plague, back to the cold ice-blue brocade and white silk wallpaper of her spacious and overly familiar bedroom.

She glanced around it now. There were her bookcases and her desk and the comfortable chairs by the fireplace. There was a lovely view of the garden from her tall, sunny windows, too. It wasn't as if it were an uncomfortable room. Indeed, it was not, it was just that it had been too many times an uncomfortable place for French. She couldn't help it, she wailed, "It's just that I've spent most of my life in this room!" And she had, too, either as punishment for some childhood sin, or when trying to steer clear of her dear parents who were made so acutely uncomfortable by the opinions and activities of their youngest child. Now she was in her room again and she'd probably spend most of her time here, for now she'd be stuck at home until her father married her off!

She shuddered. Married off—and to a man of her *father's* choosing. It was not to be borne, she hadn't even gotten a chance to try her wings, and now her father would insist that she settle down in a comfortable marriage. Comfortable. She didn't even like the word when it was used to describe marriage. Marriage should be . . . exciting . . . and deeply fulfilling, not merely comfortable. And besides, she had nothing but faint disgust for the self-assured, supremely opinionated young men her Papa found so suitable. At the very thought of them, she turned back over and allowed herself another bout of tears. This time it was for her, all for her. She could visualize her future. She could just see herself turning from an interesting, vibrant girl of some beauty to a washed-out, totally conformable creature married to some rich banker! She added six totally comfortable children to her mental picture, all of whom looked exactly like their stuffy father and, worse, thought like him, and didn't like *her* at all. That would be more than she could stand, for it meant that she was never to sample the life of freedom she craved . . . and never to meet the kind of man who . . . the kind of man who could take her breath away.

"Ooooh, I can't bear it!" She smothered her howl in one of the bevy of pretty pillows that crowded her bed and wept all the harder. This time she wasn't weeping for her poor, put-upon family at all, though, this time she was weeping for poor, trapped little Henry French Richards.

*   *   *

Evidently, however, she had misjudged her father's embarrassment over his only daughter's "antics," as he called her political activities, for it was then that the letters began.

❄

❄

❄

Chapter Two

Dearest Julia,

   You must help us. The situation about which I wrote you in my last letter has gone far beyond our control. Surely you can contrive something, you were always the clever one.

               Hopefully,
               your loving sister,
               Catherine

Dearest Catherine,

   I do not know how Charles and I can help. We are in the middle of nowhere out here in Colorado. Surely French would not leave the culture of Boston for life in the wilds. Surely things cannot be as desperate as your letter implies. After all, dearest, though I hesitate to mention it for fear of offending you, you were always the one of us with the best, and most dramatic, imagination.

               Lovingly,
               your devoted sister,
               Julia

Julia,

   Thank you for reminding me of my lamentable tendency to overdramatize things when we were chil-

dren. My dear husband, Clifford, assures me, however, that I have quite outgrown that tendency. He has promised to write you so that you and Charles will have another, masculine opinion on which to base your decision.

Love,
Catherine

Dear Julia,

Catherine insists that I write to assure you that she is in no way exaggerating the headstrong tendencies of your favorite niece. The girl is determined to ruin herself. The girl has been all but unguidable since your and Catherine's brother Jacob started sending her a share of the earnings of his silver mine out there.

Also, I fear she might come to harm over her constant interference in the affairs of others. Furthermore, Catherine and I are deeply embarrassed socially by her recent campaigning for the rights of women, whom she insists on calling downtrodden. Both of us would appreciate anything you and Charles might do to help us at this juncture.

Sincerely,
your brother-in-law,
Clifford Richards

Julia,

She has been arrested for marching in a parade for women's right to vote! Clifford had to go down to the police station to get her! I doubt that we will ever recover from the terrible stigma she has placed on us socially. She is the talk of every gossip in Boston, and everywhere I go I am subjected to titters behind hands of the mean-spirited, and such pitying looks of sym-

*pathy from the nice ones that I can no longer bear it.
If you don't do something, I shall never, never ever
speak to you again!*

Catherine

*Post Scriptum
I received your telegram telling us of the disappearance of our brother, Jacob. Very distressing. Is there
really no trace of him? French will no doubt be quite
upset, as she has enjoyed her correspondence with
him. Clifford and I feel, however, that she will be
easier to control without the allowance Jacob has
been in the habit of making her, so perhaps it is all for
the best.*

C.

"What?" Charlie Chambers stared down at his wife,
frowning. "Is that all she has to say about the loss of her
only brother?" His blazing eyes expressed the true depth
of the scorn he was making every effort to hide from his
precious wife.

He shifted to safer ground—to the matter about which
his sister-in-law did seem to care, even if it was for all
the wrong reasons. "What in tarnation does that silly
sister of yours think we can do about *her* daughter? The
woman must have finally gone round the bend."

Julia slipped an arm around her husband's waist.
"Poor, dear little French. They don't even care that she
loved Jacob. Really loved him. They haven't even
thought to comfort her. I can't even begin to imagine how
difficult it must be for an intelligent child of spirit to live
in the same house with Catherine and Clifford. See how
they call her 'girl' and 'she' as if she had no name at all."
She rubbed her cheek against his shoulder and sighed.

"Can't you think of some way we could bring her out here to stay with us?"

Charlie looked down into his wife's face and was overcome with the tenderness he never failed to feel for her. Pulling her more tightly into his arms, he rested his cheek on the top of her head.

Julia snuggled closer. "Just think, Charles. If I hadn't met you, I might have been in the exact same position French is in now."

He snorted, then pulled back to look down into her face. "And that's another thing." He scowled at the thought. "Henry French Richards. What kind of a name is that for a girl?"

Patiently Julia went over it again, though she was fully aware that her dear Charles knew the reason for her niece's odd name as well as she herself did. "Catherine promised to name her next child after our cousin, Dr. Henry French, who always moved into the house to attend her for the birth of each of her children. It was just bad luck that after five boys the sixth child was a girl."

"Well, why the hell . . . Sorry. Please forgive me, dear. But they could have told him to wait for the next boy child, couldn't they?"

Julia but looked at him for a long moment.

"Okay, okay. I know. Clifford and Catherine are sticklers for the idea that they must honor every word they utter. Seems to me like they could at least of named the child Henrietta." He cocked his head. "Come to think about it, I can't say that would have been much of an improvement."

Julia smiled and gave him another hug. Charlie drew a deep breath, savoring the scent of roses that Julia wore.

"French is such a delightful girl, Charlie." Julia's face lit with the memory of her last visit to Boston, and the lovely girl with whom she'd become so close. "She's so bright and beautiful. Can't we think of some way to help her? Never mind Catherine and Clifford. Couldn't we devise some way to bring her out here where she could be herself? Where she could be free? Can't we help her escape the restraints of Boston . . . and her parents?"

Charlie looked down into the eyes of his wife. The tears he saw sparkling there finished any objections he might have had about taking on Catherine's problems with her daughter. His lean frame shook with the force of his sigh. "I'll go ride into town an' talk to Kyle. Maybe he can come up with an idea." He patted his wife awkwardly on the shoulder and said gruffly, "At least we won't call her 'the girl,' and there aren't any police stations out here for her to get carted off to."

Julia gave him such a fierce squeeze that the air went out of him with a whoosh.

Kyle Devereaux shoved a hand through his heavy mane of chestnut hair and glared at his rancher friend. He had to shout over the sound of the saw shrieking its way through a fresh log. "Dammit, Charlie. I have my hands full with the mill. I don't have any idea what the devil to do with Julia's favorite niece."

The crestfallen look on Charlie's face got to him. "Let's go over to Mike's Place and talk about it!" Maybe he could cheer him up by buying him a drink.

At least his shouted invitation brought a smile from his old friend, and they left the office and started across the yard, shoulder to shoulder, tacitly leaving conversation for the relative quiet of the Irishman's saloon. As they neared the huge pile of sawdust from the working mill, they saw two boys digging frantically in the golden pile.

The sight galvanized Kyle. Fear gave him added speed

as he sprinted in their direction. There was no doubt in his mind that a child, sliding down the great pile of sawdust, had been caught and buried in an avalanche of the stuff. Suffocation by the clinging sawdust was a very real threat if he wasn't dug out in time.

As he neared, the boys pulled their companion, a girl of about five, gasping and sputtering, free of the sawdust. "Stop crying, Jesse. You'll only make it worse," one of the boys told her as they began dusting her off.

The other boy looked up in time to see Kyle running toward them. "Look out! It's old man Devereaux!" His warning sent the three floundering through the soft sawdust in a panicked race in the opposite direction, the girl still coughing as she flew along, towed by her two slightly older companions, until they disappeared into the forest.

Kyle stopped, cursing weakly with relief. He was shaking all over.

Charlie stomped up just then, and threw an arm around him when he saw Kyle's pale face. "You all right?"

"Yeah. Yeah, I'm all right." This time. He was all right this time, because now the child was all right. But memories of the other time were crowding him, and that time it hadn't been all right.

Charlie's arm hung loosely around Kyle's shoulders and he eyed him askance as they continued on over to Mike's Place. A short walk from the mill to the edge of town, and they entered Main Street. Both men, deep in thought, turned down the street, away from the two churches, Catholic and Protestant, and the flocks of houses that nestled around them like chicks around their mother hens, and headed for the row of businesses.

As they passed Holt's Mercantile, both men tipped their hats absently to a woman just coming out the door and they went on across the street to the saloon on the opposite corner. Pushing through the double swinging doors, they headed across the sawdust-strewn floor and bellied up to the bar.

Kyle muttered, "Whiskey." He knocked it back and signaled for a refill.

"This isn't like you, Kyle." Charlie's face showed his deep concern. "What's got into you?"

Kyle turned to face him. "That child. She could have died in that pile, Charlie, and it would have been my fault. I should have had it fenced." His voice strengthened. "I will have it fenced."

They walked over to a table and sat, and Kyle went on. "There was an incident like that when I was working at my first sawmill." He shook his head and downed a single swallow from his glass. "I've never forgotten the face of the dead boy I helped dig out. His eyes . . . the sawdust. I can still hear his mother sobbing when I think about it."

"That's hard, Kyle." Charlie knew he wasn't much good at consolation. He let a brief silence do the job for him, then said softly, "Glad the kids were safe this time."

Kyle's mind was still on the children. "Wish to hell I could keep 'em out of the sawdust hill for sure. A fence will help, I know, but somebody'll climb it one day. I wish I could be sure."

Charlie looked thoughtful. "Yeah, it would be a tragedy if one of the little ones came to grief." Suddenly an idea struck him. "Kyle!" He spoke with such a force of enthusiasm that his friend twitched.

"What?" Kyle was annoyed that he had flinched.

Charlie reined himself in a bit. Better to work up to the grand solution carefully. He didn't want to botch it. Better to go real slow.

Taking a deep breath he ventured out, "My Julia says that you have to educate people to danger just like to anything else. You know, like a baby has to be taught not to pick up a rattlesnake?"

"Yeah." Kyle watched him closely, frowning. "Makes sense."

"Well, you got to do that about the sawdust pile and about all the other dangers around a mill for the children of all your workers."

"Charlie," Kyle's voice held a neat balance of irritation and concerned frustration, "I've talked till I'm blue in the face. If their parents can't tell them, how the blazes do you think I can?" He looked at his friend in disgust. "Hell, I can't even get 'em in one place long enough to tell 'em anything. They just run wild through town, you know that."

"Yeah," Charlie said slowly, his hand rubbing at his chin as he seemed to give the matter his full attention. "Still, it seems to me there might be a way."

"Yeah? Well, spit it out." A frown drew Kyle Devereaux's brows so low that his blue eyes darkened under their shadow.

Charlie knew he'd have to work carefully to bring his plan off. He'd have to work it carefully from both ends. Fact was, he needed Julia's good mind to help him figure this one out. For now, he'd stall Kyle. He'd keep on stalling him until he had everything in place, then he'd spring it on him. "Well, there just might be a way to get them children together, teach 'em about the dangers of the sawmill, and even keep 'em penned up for most of the day."

Interest lit Devereaux's eyes back to a clear, sunny blue. "Yeah?"

"It'd cost you a bit, though."

"Anything within reason would be well worth a considerable expense to me, Charlie." Then he frowned again. "It would have to be something the parents couldn't object to, you know. We can't just kidnap the little dears and lock 'em up."

Charlie looked at the hopeful expression on his young friend's face and knew that he'd just set his hook. Striving to hide his jubilation, he rose from his chair. He had the feeling that he was about to solve both Kyle's problem and his own, and please his Julia in the bargain. "Let me get back to you, Kyle. I think maybe I have a plan that'll work real good."

Back at his ranch, Charlie Chambers felt as if he would burst with pride in himself. He'd found a way to help his wife solve her sister Catherine's dilemma and to give Julia her fondest wish as well. It didn't take a genius to figure out that she was hoping with all her dear, sweet heart to get her niece to come out here to stay with them, and if that was what Julia wanted, then that was what he was going to get for her. It was one of the few sadnesses of his life that he and Julia couldn't have the children she had so desired, and he'd failed to be heartened as he'd watched her pour all her frustrated mother's love onto her sister Catherine's brood.

He hadn't thought much of the boys, himself, pompous little reproductions of their father that they were, but he shared her enthusiasm for bright little Henry French. He'd watched her grow more beautiful, in mind and spirit as well as in physical grace, with every visit he and Julia had made back to her home in Boston. The girl was something special.

Come to think of it, so was Kyle Devereaux. An additional plot formed, unbidden, in his mind as he rode home. He lit off his horse and left the reins trailing to ground-tie him. Storming across the wide veranda he tore open the front door and bellowed, "Julia!"

She came hurrying from the back of the house where she'd been chatting with her housekeeper-friend, Mary Wells. He gave her a quick bear hug, dragged her into the parlor, and told her what he had in mind. "What do you think of my idea, Julia?"

"It's wonderful." She smiled up at him radiantly. "You're wonderful." Julia looked as if he'd just given her the moon. "It's splendid of you to get Kyle to do it."

"Whoa, now. I didn't say I'd gotten Kyle to do it, you know."

"But you will. The idea of a school to keep the children out of trouble at the mill is inspired. And the fact that it will better their chances in life is bound to appeal to their parents as well as to Kyle."

"Yeah, but . . ." His voice held a heavy reluctance Julia was quick to pick up on.

"But what?"

"But I don't think Kyle is going to go for your niece teaching the kids."

Julia was clearly disappointed. "Why not? French has all the qualifications anybody could want."

"Yes, honey, but a lumber camp—and that's pretty much what this town is, just a glorified lumber camp—is a mighty rough place for a lady from Boston. Especially a beautiful, *young* lady from Boston."

"Oh, dear. I suppose you're right." Her face betrayed her feelings. "I am so disappointed. I'm afraid I was already looking forward to having Henry French with us."

"Too bad," Charlie said with mischief in his eyes, dropping his pretended reluctance, "that she isn't the boy her name makes her out to be. Then you could start airing out the spare bedroom." He pulled her into his arms, and she rested there a moment with her head on his chest. He waited patiently until she figured it out.

Suddenly, Julia twitched once, then slowly, with infinite care, she pulled back and shifted to look into her husband's face. Her eyes were alight with joy, and the sight filled him with laughter. They stood and gazed at each other in complete accord while wide grins grew on their faces.

"Surely you wouldn't do that to poor Kyle?" Julia finally asked.

Charlie bent and gave her a quick kiss. His grin became wicked as he answered, "Wouldn't I?"

The next day Charlie rode back into town, bursting with his plan. At the sawmill, Kyle went for it like a trout rising to a fly.

"A school. That's a great idea, Charlie." Kyle ran his long fingers through his hair, concentrating intently, instantly planning. "Shouldn't take more than a few days to decide how many children we need space for." His blue eyes crackled with purpose as he looked across his desk at his friend. "I'll have to ask the men how many children are in their families." He dragged a sheet of paper across the clutter on the broad surface in front of him and made a brief note.

"Don't forget to get the ages, too."

"Yeah, and to get a schoolhouse built." He grinned at his friend. "Charlie, this is one fine idea. The children will be locked up over their books all day. I can stop worrying about whether or not they're getting in trouble around the sawmill. I can stop sweating that one of them might meet with some accident." He stood up and thrust out his hand. "How can I thank you?"

Charlie fumbled with his hat and pretended not to see Kyle's hand. After all, he was getting ready to pull a deliberate trick on his best friend, he needn't complicate the burden on his conscience by shaking Kyle's hand.

As his abused conscience prickled, he blushed a little at the thought of accepting his friend's thanks. Then he steeled himself against his clamoring mind. Henry French would do a fine job, he knew it, and her presence would mean a lot to Julia. All he'd have to do would be make himself scarce until Kyle cooled down.

There was no doubt in his mind that Kyle would need cooling down when he got an eyeful of French. Boy howdy, would Kyle need cooling down. There was no way the curvaceous little beauty was going to look anything like the *Mister* Henry French Richards that Kyle was about to be led to expect he was hiring, that was dang sure.

Well, Kyle would just have to get over it. Charlie was pleased at the way his plan was falling into place, in spite of his misgivings about what he was sure Kyle's initial reaction would be.

Julia would be so happy to have her niece with them that Charlie decided he could bear Kyle's anger. It was just that, in common with all the rest of the men who knew the lumber baron's temper, he didn't look forward to incurring it. Not by a long shot. He guessed it would be small payment for the scurvy trick of sneaking French in on Kyle, though, and it would be no less than he deserved, so he cleared his throat and said, "You're welcome," as if he hadn't a care in the world.

His conscience thus bashed into submission, he went on to compound his sins. "The way I see it, it's a mighty fine thing for all concerned. You won't have to worry as much, the kids'll get some learning, and the schoolmar . . . aster can stay with Julia and me."

Kyle looked at him sharply, his blue eyes narrowed, assessing. Charlie wondered for a heart-stopping instant if Kyle had picked up on his slip. "That's a long ride in from your ranch, Charlie," Kyle offered reasonably, "he can bunk with me. I've got plenty of room."

"Ahhh . . ." Charlie didn't know what to say to that one, so he left it alone. Taking a deep, steadying breath to try to control the guilty blush he felt creeping up his sun-bronzed neck, he managed, "Plenty of time to decide that when . . . er . . . *he* gets here." The last words came out a little too fast, but there wasn't anything Charlie could do about it.

Before he got in any deeper, he decided to run. Jamming the hat he'd been turning round and round in his hands down on his head, he beat a hasty retreat.

Chapter Three

"DAMN AND BLAST! What the devil . . . ?" Kyle Devereaux scowled at the letter in his hand. Incredulous, he reread it.

Dear Mr. Devereaux,

Assured by your mother that you will be a good influence on your young nephew, we are sending the boy to you there in Colorado by tomorrow's train. The correctional institution here in New Orleans has had no success with the child who continues to embarrass your sister and mother by his behavior.

Only your willingness to take him keeps us from making a more permanent arrangement to stop him from his harassment of two such charming ladies.

> *Standing in admiration of*
> *your forbearance in*
> *taking him in, I remain,*
> *Josephus Caney Peabody*

Kyle still stared at the letter. What nephew? Which sister? What could the boy have done that was so awful that this Peabody jackass wanted to put him in a penitentiary? That was the only provision present society made for true incorrigibles.

Kyle was even at a complete loss as to the identity of the child. Except for the generous checks he sent to his mother, all ties with his family had been broken before any of his sisters had been fully grown, and he had no idea that any of them had married.

And who the hell was Josephus Peabody? Clearly some boy was in trouble with this pompous, presumptuous letter writer. "No. Be fair," he admonished himself aloud. "The man is obviously just another victim of Mother's famous charm." So was the boy, it would seem. Just as he had been. His jaw hardened at the memory.

He looked at the date on the letter, and fell to cursing under his breath. Peabody had neglected to give him any itinerary for the boy, but by the date, Kyle knew that he had to have arrived by now. So where the devil was he?

"Well, Mother, you've done it again." He fought the bitter sea of emotions that threatened to swamp him. His mother was rearranging another boy's life with no regard for either his safety or his comfort, just as she had done with his own.

He wondered what her excuse was this time. That she was not old enough to have a grandson, no doubt, just as she'd felt she had to get *him* out of the way because she "wasn't old enough to have a hulking son around."

Her lack of motherly instinct had sent him from the cloying, sweetly scented society of New Orleans to the rough, pine-scented north woods of Vermont to work for a harsh, distantly related man he'd never seen before. While his mother could not have cared less how he fared there, it had been a godsend for Kyle.

By his departure from Louisiana, he'd been denied the decadent lifestyle of most of his friends. There had been no obliging quadroon mistress in a discreet *garçonnière* for him, no opulent lifestyle. In the end, as he'd developed the strength of body he'd needed to hold his own in lumber camps, and the strength of morals and mind he needed to guide his course through life, he'd grown to believe he had cause to thank his mother for her heartless abandonment of her only son.

That hadn't led him to forgive her, though, and to this day the only woman for whom he could find the faintest respect and affection in his heart was Charlie's wife, Julia. Other women had learned to their dismay that he could withstand all their charms. His only forays into the feminine world were visits to women of a certain reputation.

Now his mother had done it again. She'd somehow saddled him with a boy that he'd never even heard of, and who was obviously lost somewhere between New Orleans and Sunrise, Colorado. Concern for an unknown nephew, he told himself sarcastically, was just what he needed with a school half-built and the schoolmaster already en route from Boston! And the blasted school-master was en route from Boston straight into the center of the lumberman's equivalent of a range war!

Now that the railroaders were trying to put him out of business, he couldn't even offer the schoolmaster a reasonable guarantee of safety. The way things were shaping up, it looked like every phase of his operation was going to come under fire from Kendal Abernathy, the railroad's newly arrived troublemaker.

"Rafferty!" He heard his shout echoed outside as others in his employ passed it along to Kyle's foreman and right-hand man.

A minute later Rafferty, his wild red hair practically standing on end, thrust his head in through the door. Intense disappointment filled his face when a quick glance around Devereaux's office showed no signs of trouble. "What's up, Mr. Devereaux?"

Kyle shot him a venomous look.

"Okay," Rafferty surrendered with a grin. "What's up, Dev?"

"A boy is being sent here. Seems he's in need of a new home."

Rafferty shook his head. "Could have picked a better time. Those railroaders in town are here to make real trouble, Kyle."

Kyle cut to the heart of the dispute. "You think I should break my contract with the miners for the timbers they need and cut lumber production for the builders in Denver to do as the railroad asks?"

"Hell, no. I know as well as you do that them wanting us to make our entire production be ties for them is only a trick. If you did do that for 'em, they'd just come up with something else to ruin your business." He scowled. "They aren't after railroad ties, they're after the mill— and that for next to nothing—so's they can make them ties themselves. Yeah, and lumber for building their stations and warehouses, besides. They're too damned cheap to pay anybody."

Kyle stood considering. Finally he said, "Looks like we're going to have our hands full, Rafferty."

"How so, boss?"

"Well, in addition to keeping the loggers safe while they work and guarding the mill against sabotage, we have to build the new school and protect the schoolmaster from any harm."

"Sounds like a big job, all right."

"Yeah." Kyle let a moment pass before he changed the subject. "I could use your opinion on something. I have another little complication." He glanced at the letter.

"Anything I can help with?"

"I don't know yet. I may need you to help find out where this boy is. I'm worried about him."

Rafferty shook his head again. "Life sure gets complicated."

"Sure does," Kyle said under his breath. He dumped the letter concerning the boy his mother was abandoning into the clutter that was his desk drawer, reached for his wide-brimmed black Stetson, and left the office to go with Rafferty into the mill.

As he went, he tried to shake off his worry about the whereabouts of the abandoned boy.

Henry French Richards was beginning to feel rather abandoned herself. First the loss of her beloved Uncle Jacob, then her family, and now this. The woman her father had arranged to accompany her on her journey west had gotten tired of the train's coal smoke and jolting rhythm, and was threatening to get off in St. Joseph, Missouri.

"I simply cannot bear another instant of this primitive travel, Miss Richards. We shall have to disembark here and rest until I can recover sufficiently to escort you back to Boston."

French stared at her.

"I shall wire your father immediately. Such a civilized man, your father. I am completely certain he will understand and sympathize with our plight."

French didn't think so. In fact, French was absolutely certain that her father had no desire to be subjected to his only daughter's company if there was any way to avoid it. By sending her west, he had devised a way to avoid it. Mrs. Welby was mistaken to think he'd be happy to have her return home again.

"Come along, come along. We barely have time to disembark before this disgusting train starts out again."

That got French moving. She reached for her companion's carpetbag and handed it to the woman.

"Hurry! Get your own."

"No, Mrs. Welby. I have no intention of returning to Boston. I have signed a contract with Devil-Oh Lumber to teach in Colorado, and I shall honor the terms of that contract."

Mrs. Welby fell back against one of the seats. She stared at the beautiful girl in front of her, incredulous. "You cannot be serious. You cannot intend to travel more than a thousand miles still on these wretched trains alone. Do not be foolish."

Gray eyes regarded her calmly. "Yes. That is exactly what you are forcing me to do."

Mrs. Welby regarded her fiercely for a long moment, then she folded her hands primly together at her waist and told French, "Very well. So be it. Whatever comes, it will be on your own head."

French didn't answer. Most of her life, things had been falling on her own head, and it didn't look as if the process was anywhere near an end yet.

Mrs. Welby compressed her lips, gave a loud sniff, and muttered, "I never. I simply never." Having expressed herself in a manner she thought adequate, she left the train and her charge without a backward glance, and went to wire Mr. Clifford Richards that she had resigned her chaperonage of his daughter. The girl was impossible, and she would tell him so. *Not,* she thought, *that there was the faintest chance that he didn't already know it!*

Shortly after Mrs. Welby made her departure the train pulled out of St. Joseph. Before long, French gave up trying to take an interest in the passing scenery, and looked around at her fellow passengers. At least, she looked around at those she could see without craning her neck in an unladylike fashion. Almost immediately, one of them caught her attention. He was a slender boy of about twelve, and he was watching her from across the narrow aisle. There was a mournful quality about him that touched her heart.

Reaching into her carpetbag, French drew out a round, handsomely decorated tin. She'd purchased it in Boston as a gift. It was full of her Aunt Julia's favorite candies. She knew that her aunt would approve of this sacrifice of her gift in a good cause. Smiling invitingly, she held the tin out toward the boy.

His eyes, a smoky blue, seemed to fill his face. He looked at her unblinkingly for a long moment, then he swallowed hard and reached cautiously for a candy.

French had the oddest feeling. It was almost as if he expected her to snatch her offering back at the last minute. She stretched toward him instead, holding the tin closer for him to make a choice.

"Take two, why don't you? They aren't very big," she invited.

Solemnly he took a second piece, and she watched as he tried not to wolf the sugary confections. *The child must be hungry!* She was trying to discover a way to question him that wouldn't drive him away when a large man in rough clothing pushed his way into their car.

The man lumbered up the aisle, lurching with more than the unsteady motion of the train. His gaze fell on French, and his entire face lit up. "Well, now." His voice was hearty with alcoholic goodwill. "What have we here?" He leaned down over the seat next to her, breathing whiskey fumes toward an apprehensive French.

French leaned away from him, her eyes wide. She tried hard not to cringe.

"Is this here seat taken, pretty little lady?" He leered at her, swaying on his feet.

Then the boy she'd given the candy to was there. "Yes! It's my seat." He shoved past the man and plopped into the place beside French. "She's my sister and she don't talk to strangers, mister."

"Oh?" His brow furrowed in a frown of intense concentration. "Z'at so?"

"Yes. It's so. It has to be, because her future intended is as big as a house and has a temper that nobody can control, not even him. We don't want no trouble, so we just don't let her talk to strangers."

The drunk scowled down at him, striving to make a decision from the information he'd just been given. The effort was too much for him, and he left them, shaking his head. Halfway up the car, he sagged into a vacant seat. Almost before his body settled, he was snoring.

French took her first deep breath for minutes. Turning to the boy she said, "I don't know how to thank you. I would have had no idea how to handle that man." She smiled tremulously. "He was inebriated, wasn't he?"

The boy's eyes lit. The pretty young lady didn't know a souse when she saw one. Finding himself more knowledgeable than she was made him swell with pride. Manfully he told her, "He was drunk. You already thanked me. You gave me that candy." The boy started to rise.

"Please"—French grabbed him by the sleeve—"sit here with me. I should feel ever so much safer." She smiled softly at him. "A lady traveling alone needs a brother to protect her."

He looked at her intently, as if he were looking for

sarcasm in her words. Finally he decided that she wasn't trying to trick him and sat down again. The movement was gingerly this time, as if he were taking his place on a hot griddle. It was in stark contrast to the carefree plunge into the seat he'd made in her defense.

French sensed that he was poised for flight and that the wrong remark or a string of questions might send him flying. She'd have to go at making this child into a friend very carefully. Extending her neatly gloved hand, she said, "I'm Henry French Richards. Please call me French." She grinned at him impishly. "I refuse to answer to Henry."

"Well, I should hope so!" His eyes narrowed. "Are you joshing me? You ain't really named Henry, are you?"

She sighed heavily. "I'm afraid I am."

"Jehoshaphat," he said wonderingly.

French let her gaze flick the length of the railway car. She found it unsettling that no one seemed to be taking the least interest in the boy. "Everyone calls me French, however," she assured him hastily, noticing the maturity in his eyes, and offered, "I hope you will, too."

"I don't know whether I can do that, Miss Richards. You are a lady after all."

"But I am a lady in need of a friend." She saw him hesitate, and pushed a bit. "You have already been my knight in shining armor."

His face glowed at that. "Knight to the rescue? I like that." He grinned suddenly. "I guess I could call you Miss French, since you want me to."

"Thank you, I do. I hope you'll act as an escort to me, as well. I'm certain I shall be much less open to advances from strangers if I have my 'brother' traveling with me."

He thought about that. "Yeah, I guess that's true."

French sealed their bargain by offering her aunt's

candy again. The tin was half-empty by the time she felt it was safe to ask the boy any questions. Even then, she sensed she had need to be circumspect, so instead of asking a question she said, "I'm going to Colorado."

The boy looked at her carefully. "So am I," he admitted after a long moment.

French pretended not to notice his reticence. She offered the candies once more, and when he refused any, packed them away again. "I'm going to teach school there."

This time the boy spoke with patent disbelief. "Naw. You're too young and too pretty to be a schoolmarm."

French laughed. "Why, I thought from the penny magazines that all schoolmarms in the West were young and pretty."

"Not as pretty as you."

That brought a blush to both their faces, and French hastily changed the subject. "Where are you going in Colorado?"

For a minute he just stared at her and she was afraid that he wasn't going to answer. Then he said, "I'm being bundled off to live with my uncle in the wilds of Colorado."

His tone was so desolate, she was filled with sympathy. Forgetting that she'd intended to be shrewd in her dealings with the child, she asked softly, "Don't you like your uncle?"

"Don't know. Never seen him."

"Oh."

The boy looked up into her lovely gray eyes and saw pity there. He didn't much like pity. "Aw, it ain't so bad. Least I've got a place to go. Think of all those orphans on the orphan trains after the war. They ended up just anywhere. I'm not like that. I got me a real-live uncle, my mother's older brother, who's going to take me in."

"What about your mother? Is she . . . ill?" French held her breath. Suppose the boy's mother had passed away?

He hung his head. "No," he said so low that his companion could hardly make out his words, "she just doesn't want me anymore."

French clamped her lips closed against the tide of sympathetic words that welled up in her throat. Instead, she reached over and took his hand in her own. She was glad that he made no move to take it back from her, for she didn't think she could have borne it. Feelings of rejection and loss washed over her in waves. She felt his pain as keenly as she had so often felt her own. He was a kindred spirit. He was someone else whom nobody wanted.

Quiet as two mice, they sat holding hands as the train rolled on into the setting sun.

Chapter Four

JULIA RAN DOWN the stairs, unaware that she was trailing her fashionable hat by its ribbons, the bright straw bumping on the steps behind her. "Charlie, Charlie! Where are you? Are you ready? Oh, Charlie, we must go or we will be late. Where is my parasol?"

Charlie put down his paper and rose from his favorite chair. "Here I am, Julia. Steady there, old girl. We have plenty of time."

Julia shot sparks at him. "Don't call me old girl. And don't say 'steady there.' I'm not a horse." She snatched her parasol from the credenza and looked at her reflection in the hall mirror. "My hat! I've forgotten my hat."

Charlie grabbed her arm as she whirled around to run back upstairs. Holding her loosely in his arms he raised her hand to his cheek, kissed it, and then disentangled the ribbons of her hat from her fingers.

"Oh!" Startled at having forgotten she had her hat, she watched him place the little confection on her head and tie the blue ribbons that exactly matched her eyes in a bow at the side of her face. Watching his calm movements in the mirror relaxed her. She laughed softly and turned to plant a kiss on his weathered cheek. "I think I'm a bit excited, don't you?"

"A bit."

"Oh, Charles. We are to have French with us." Her eyes glistened with tears. "It will be almost like having one of our own, won't it?"

He pecked her on the cheek and said gruffly, "Come on, we'll be late meeting the train. We still have to stop for Kyle."

They weren't late, however, even though Kyle delayed them momentarily while he read a telegram he'd just received from somebody in the East named Peabody. The depot was still twenty minutes from town, but there was plenty of time. "Can you believe this?" Kyle thrust the telegram toward Charlie.

Charles scanned it briefly. "Refuses to be in any way responsible for your *what*?" He spoke reproachfully. "You never told me you had a nephew." *In fact,* Charlie mused, *you didn't tell me you had any family at all.*

"Didn't know I did. Now the boy's lost somewhere between here and New Orleans." He said N'awlins, like a native, and Julia's interest was piqued.

"Kyle, dear, are you one of the New Orleans Devereauxs?"

Kyle almost scowled at his only female friend. He certainly didn't count himself a New Orleans Devereaux. "One of their castoffs, more like, Julia."

Julia raised an inquiring eyebrow, but got no response. Evidently this was a matter into which she would have to inquire at a later time. Her handsome young friend was obviously too concerned with the fate of his young kinsman, as well he should be, to satisfy her curiosity.

Truth to tell, her own mind and heart were so full of her niece's coming that she scarcely cared right now, anyway. But she filed it away for further consideration. Like her husband, she'd been unaware of Kyle's having any family. She had every intention of looking into his past, reluctant though Kyle seemed to divulge it, at a later date. Right now, however, she knew they had the little matter of Kyle's first sight of Henry French Richards to make it through safely. She sighed. Kyle was too much of a gentleman to lose his temper in front of a young lady. She hoped.

Charlie shepherded the two of them out to the surrey he kept for special occasions. When Julia begged him to ride with them, Kyle led his horse to the back of it and tied him on. Then he lifted Julia effortlessly up to her seat and sprang in behind her.

Charlie glanced back over his shoulder at Kyle. Satisfied he was settled, he lifted his hands and said, "Giddup."

Kyle tried to find a comfortable position for his long legs. Sitting like a parishioner in church had never been his favorite posture, but the surrey allowed for little more. For Julia, however, he'd endure any discomfort.

He watched her fidget and smiled. She sure was excited about the new school, but then Julia, bless her, was one who always had the good of others foremost in her mind. She was so caring. If there had been any women like her in his young life . . . he cut that thought off. It was too late for him. Far too late. Kyle Devereaux's personality had been molded by the masterful hand of a completely selfish woman. It was all done and over for him. That was a fact that he'd accepted long ago.

The day was pleasant, warmed by the dying Indian summer. Because it was still only late autumn, the road to the rail spur was smooth enough from the frequent use of wagons hauling freight into their little town. Come winter, the rains and the freezes would make it downright dangerous because of the ruts from those same wagons slogging freight up the hill to town from the new rail spur.

Kyle scowled at the thought of the railroaders. They'd been pressuring him for some time, and he didn't like it. Not one blasted bit.

As if he'd picked up on Kyle's thoughts, Charlie asked, "You still getting a lotta lip from the railroaders, Kyle?"

"Just the same old things." Kyle made his answer vague, not wanting to upset Julia.

Charlie nodded. He heard the guarded tone in Kyle's voice and let the subject drop for the same reason.

They could have talked about a brothel, however, had they had the inclination. Every fiber of Julia Price Chambers's being was focused on the road in front of them and the prospect of seeing her niece again after two years of nothing but her delightful letters.

Julia straightened just then, and both men wondered if they'd been indiscreet, but she was only pointing ahead to the rough shed that served as a warehouse and the long platform that, with it, made up the railway station. Excitement bubbled from her.

For an instant the depot looked completely deserted, then the figure of the stationmaster stepped out of the low shed and walked toward the east end of the platform. Stationmaster might be a title too grand for the tiny whistle stop, but not for the man who wore it. Phinehas Faraday was a small man, but his dignity was immense. His competence matched his dignity, and he was the only person connected with the railroad that Kyle had any use for. Phinehas saw to it without fail that Kyle received any freight he ordered from the factories and sawmills in the East in spite of his employers' standing orders to see that he did not.

As a result, when Phinehas came into town, every lumberjack from topper to camp cook treated him with respect. They'd have had to answer to Kyle if they hadn't, and nobody really wanted to find himself in the position of having to face an angry Kyle Devereaux. There weren't many men who would.

Charlie drove them to a spot of shade close to the platform, got down, and tied the horses to the rough log hitching rail. Reaching up he lifted Julia down. "Think you might last a little longer if you walked off some of that energy?"

Julia smiled at him and nodded. "I can hardly wait. It's been so long since I've seen Henry French."

Kyle felt a pang of pure jealousy. A rival for Julia's affections wasn't exactly his idea of a treat.

Phinehas came over, interrupting Kyle's thoughts. Even as he turned his attention to returning the taciturn stationmaster's greeting, he wondered just why Julia was so eager for the arrival of the new schoolmaster. Maybe he should have taken more of an interest in the hiring of the man she'd recommended. A quick perusal of the teacher's excellent qualifications was all he'd had time for though, with the railroad situation worsening.

The railroaders were getting to be a real threat to his peace of mind. It was the presence of a group of hard cases they'd sent into town that had made Kyle all the more anxious to get the school set up and the children safely in it. Clearly, the men were out to make trouble for him, and he expected it to start anytime now.

His jaw tightened as he thought of the railroad's demands that he all but give them the finished ties to continue their spur on into town, and the rails on farther west. He'd have sold to them in a heartbeat if they'd offered a fair price, but that wasn't their way. They'd rather spend the money to pay thugs to threaten him. And he'd be damned if he'd knuckle under to threats.

It was going to get mighty interesting before it got better, that was for sure.

He stretched his cramped legs and jumped down to follow Julia and Charlie. Julia fairly vibrated with excitement, and he smiled, shoving his jealousy out of his mind.

There wasn't much interesting that went on out here for the womenfolk. It was nice to see her so fired up about a new member of the community. If the schoolmaster decided to stay out on the ranch with her, he guessed the company would do her a world of good. He'd not press the man to bunk in with him, in spite of the fact that it would be more convenient for the teacher. If there was a chance having him out at her place would make Julia happy, then he'd keep out of it.

The schoolmaster could probably use the exercise of riding in from the ranch, anyway. Teachers were a damn sight too sedentary to his way of thinking. Time enough to offer the man his hospitality when the blizzards came.

Smoke on the horizon sent Julia into raptures. "Oh, Charlie, there she is! There she is!"

Charlie squeezed her arm in warning. He didn't want Kyle figuring things out and starting a row. Once French was on the scene, Kyle might all but choke, but his good manners would keep him from exploding when he saw the school*master* he'd hired was a school*marm*. "Julia, dear." Charlie filled his voice with meaning. "Ships may be called she, but I don't think trains are."

Julia was instantly contrite, her blue eyes full of anxiety. "Of course, you are perfectly correct. I *do* apologize!"

Kyle frowned down at her. You'd have thought Julia

was afraid Charlie would take her home and beat her, the way she was kowtowing to him. What the blazes was going on?

The train puffed up to the platform, having slowed from its dazzling speed of thirty-five miles an hour while it was still almost half a mile out. Soot and coal dust settled around them in a cloud as white steam hissed from the boiler and enclosed them in its fog.

Kyle and Julia, both from large eastern cities, stood and endured, Julia secure under her frilly parasol. Charlie, raised in the western territories, cussed and stomped and flapped at the steam with his Stetson. "Godamighty! What a filthy beast!"

Kyle grinned in silent agreement, but Julia didn't even hear him. Julia was following Phinehas Faraday to the passenger car from which the conductor of the train had descended and was carefully placing the steps.

An instant later a young woman appeared at the top of the steps and hesitated briefly. And in that brief moment of time, Kyle was struck dumb at the sight of her. She was breathtaking! She was as curvaceous and delectable a morsel as he'd ever seen. Desire tore through him like a thunderbolt.

In a daze he turned to Charlie. "Damn, Charlie, what a little goddess. If she's come to set up for trade here, she's gonna be the richest little soiled dove in Colorado." He grabbed his friend's arm. "I wonder if she'd consider a private contract?"

Charlie groaned like a wounded buffalo. He pried Kyle's fingers off his arm and backed off to a safe distance. He choked once as Julia started toward the vision that held his lusty young friend entranced, then managed to gasp, "She's already under contract to you, Kyle."

He eyed the puzzled Kyle as if he were a coiled rattlesnake and headed for the baggage car just as Julia threw her arms wide and sang out, "Henry French, dearest girl, you are here at last!"

Chapter Five

KYLE DEVEREAUX HAD never felt so foolish in his life. He knew his mouth was literally hanging open, but he couldn't gather his wits enough to close it. He'd just told Charlie that he would have liked to put this little beauty under contract as his mistress, and here Julia was greeting her like a long-lost friend!

If Charlie told Julia what he'd said, Kyle's worries would *all* be over. He'd be a dead man. Julia'd kill him!

Shoving that thought out of his mind he looked around for the teacher. But wait. Hadn't Julia just called the fantasy-inspiring little goddess Henry French?

Henry French! Damn and blast. The schoolmaster's name was Henry French Richards. Hell! The schoolmaster was a girl. This girl!

And Charlie. He'd known! And Julia! They'd done this. They'd done this to him on purpose. Julia and Charlie together had done this to him. They'd bamboozled him into sending for this little vest-pocket Venus. *They* had recommended Henry French Richards.

His head was spinning with the difficulty he was having taking in the perfidy of his two best friends. They'd had him to dinner and they had led him to believe he was getting a school*master* for his lumber-camp children, and all the while they'd known that the schoolmaster was . . . that he was . . . that she was . . . that *he was a she*!

Best friends, ha!

He finally fought his mouth closed. It closed with a snap like a steel trap. Anger jetted through his mind removing all reason. His eyebrows snapped down to meet over the bridge of his nose, and he felt that if he spoke, he'd bellow steam to rival that of the engine that had just arrived.

Julia was extending a hand to the boy who had followed the vision from the train, and had waited patiently beside the incredibly lovely creature to be introduced. Charlie gave them both a hasty wave and, with a wary eye cocked toward Kyle, continued his rush down the platform, ostensibly to see to the school*marm*'s trunks.

Kyle started after his former friend like a charging bull elephant. His boots struck the floor of the platform like gunshots.

Julia left off reaching a welcoming hand to the waiting boy and grabbed Kyle's arm as he charged past her. With the firm purpose of protecting her husband, she swung him around to meet the newcomer.

French stared, her own mouth opening. He was the handsomest man she'd ever seen. Tall—he must be at least two inches over six feet—with a lithe form to rival that of the most superb of athletes, the man had the face of an angel. An avenging angel. She looked at the blazing blue eyes under their full, well-drawn brows, saw the way a muscle jumped in his clean-shaven, square jaw, and almost thought she could see flames issue from his arrogant, aristocratic nose.

When he ripped his hat from his head as if he would throw it at her, she saw that he had thick, wavy auburn hair that curled at the nape of his neck in a way that made her fingers absolutely itch to touch it there.

All of a sudden French found she was having difficulty getting her breath. Remembering the wish she had long held and long thought would be denied her, she felt the world around her spin. There really was a man who could take her breath away. Here he was. He actually existed. He was not merely a girlish fantasy, he was real.

Everything around her took on a rosy glow and without even realizing that she did so, she smiled radiantly at this man who had taken her breath away.

"French, may I present Mr. Kyle Devereaux." Julia's voice was full of pride. "Kyle, this is my niece, *Miss* Henry French Richards."

Kyle glared at Julia. How could she have done this to him? How could Julia have so deliberately deceived him?

Suddenly another concern wiped that question from his thoughts as if it had never been. Real fear shot through him. Ah, God, he prayed she wouldn't hear from Charlie how he had seen and immediately lusted after her niece.

Dammit! The little goddess was a blasted school-teacher! With those heavily lashed, luminous gray eyes and that cloud of dark hair, and those . . . he groaned inwardly and fought down another tide of horribly inappropriate, simple male desire . . . those delectable curves that were designed to drive a man wild, she was going to run around a lumber camp trying to teach a lot of half-savage children?

Sure she was! Clearly, she was only here for the express purpose of driving *him* out of his mind! And just when he needed all of it to keep his sawmill out of the hands of the railroaders.

How the devil was he supposed to survive this latest attack on his peace of mind? How the hell was he supposed to feel about Julia, whom he just about worshiped, doing this to him? Most importantly, there was Charlie. He had masterminded this whole fiasco. How was he going to kill Charlie without upsetting Julia?

Eyes blazing, lips compressed in a firm line, he bowed slightly to the exquisite visitor and ground out, "Miss Richards," in a tone that was far from welcoming.

Too bad. It was the best he could do.

Then he turned bleak eyes to Julia and said, "Since you seem to have a full load, I'll be getting back to the mill." He replaced his hat on his head, tipping it as he did so, and marched off to untie his horse from where he had trailed the surrey from town.

He mounted in one practiced, fluid motion and was gone before French could stop regretting his having covered his thick, dark auburn hair with his hat. She'd been so pleasantly mesmerized by the fires that had burned in that magnificent mane in the sunlight that even after his horse's hoofbeats faded away, she still stood smiling vaguely in the direction he had taken. With him gone, she felt a strange, poignant sense of loss.

Beside her, the boy murmured, "So that's old Devil-Oh."

Wondering what her young friend had said, French was drawn back to the present, her dreams of tall, strong men with fire in their hair went flying. She closed her mouth by a conscious act of will, then opened it again to say, "Oh, Aunt Julia, I do apologize. This is my friend and escort, Jamie Waring. Jamie, dear, this is my wonderful aunt, Mrs. Chambers."

Jamie doffed his soft cap and took the hand Julia

extended for the second time. "Pleased to meet you, ma'am."

"You escorted my niece?" Julia looked a little bewildered. She turned to French. "But . . . I thought that your father had arranged for a lady—a Mrs. Welby, wasn't it?—to escort you."

French looked disgusted. Even disgusted, she was lovely, Julia thought. She remembered the effect her niece had had on Kyle and was quite pleased. She strove to keep her mind on the matter at hand, and, with an effort, refrained from daydreaming about her favorite bachelor and her precious French. Having French with her was so overwhelmingly marvelous that everything else paled by comparison, even the blossoming thought of getting the recalcitrant Kyle to the altar.

That idea brought with it some very serious matters that must be attended to, however. Except for the fact that she adored him and he was Charlie's best friend, what did she know about Kyle Devereaux? Very little. It was going to be necessary to find out a great deal more. When it came to her beloved niece, no precaution was going to be neglected . . . even investigating her dear Kyle's past.

She heard her niece's well-modulated voice telling her of her chaperone's desertion and of how Jamie had come to her rescue when the drunk had accosted her, and was immediately and immensely grateful. "My dear young man. How absolutely splendid of you. We are so thankful that you were there to take care of French." She beamed at Jamie. "Please tell me you will stay with us for a while. A break in your journey must surely be welcome if you have come all the way from the East, and we would love to have you as our guest."

Jamie hesitated only an instant. He had a pretty good

idea from what he'd just seen of his formidable uncle that he'd be a lot more comfortable with his Miss French and her Aunt Julia than he would be with the redoubtable Kyle Devereaux.

His Uncle Dev looked like a real fire eater, and he wasn't certain he wanted to trade the casually cruel tyranny of his mother and grandmother for that of a fire-breathing uncle just right yet. Smiling his best smile, he bowed and said, "Why, thank you, Mrs. Chambers, I'd be mighty delighted. I'm not sure my uncle wants me, anyway."

Kyle Devereaux was back at the sawmill before Charlie got his happy little group back to the Lightning Double C. Seeing the long wagon in front of his office, he was glad that he'd come so quickly.

"Rafferty!" His bellow caused his big chestnut gelding to pull back from him as he wrapped the reins around the hitching post. "Steady, Daumier," he said in a soothing tone, and the big horse stood quietly. Kyle patted him on the neck, glad he'd cooled him a bit on the way into town now that he had to leave him standing.

He covered the distance to the spacious, one-room building that served as his office with long, impatient strides. The scene that met his gaze when he slammed the door open did nothing to cool his temper. Five men from the railroad stood with their backs to him, while Rafferty, his mill boss, stood protectively over Kyle's desk with a heavy, short length of lumber in his hand.

"What the devil's going on here?"

Abernathy, the leader, turned to face Kyle. "Nothing at all, Devereaux. We were just waiting to see you, and Rafferty burst in on us with that club in his hand and started calling us names."

Kyle looked at the disorder of his records, files were spilled everywhere, desk drawers snatched out onto the floor and rifled. "Unless he used 'sneaking, cowardly snake,' he missed you by a mile, Abernathy."

Abernathy's face lost its false friendliness. "Now, see here, Devereaux. You've got no need to go calling us names, too. We're here to make you a fair offer for this mill so we can turn out railroad ties at a price that we want to pay for them. Neither you nor Rafferty has any business getting upset and insulting about it."

Kyle cocked his head, his face impassive. His gaze roamed assessingly over his open records again. The big rolltop desk he used to keep track of his files was empty. The table in front of it that served him for a desk was swept clear of papers. The files littering the thick carpet that covered the floor told him somebody was mighty eager to learn more than they'd any right to know about his business. Or maybe they were just hoping to scramble things up so that he'd have a tough time conducting it. He knew it wasn't Rafferty, and if it were, as it obviously was, the railroaders, he knew it sure as blazes wasn't with an eye to helping Devil-Oh Lumber. His eyes were steel-blue when he looked back at Abernathy.

"Dammit, Devereaux, our offer is a fair one, made in good faith."

Rafferty snorted, fought to keep his mouth shut, and failed. "Fair? Fair? You blasted thieves don't know the meaning of the word fair. A third what the operation's worth would be twice what you want to pay, you lying snake!"

Kyle decided he'd had more than enough irritation for one day. Now it seemed to him that a merciful God was providing him with a perfect way to work a little of it out of his system. He put all his frustration caused by the advent of the schoolmarm insultingly in a single word. "Out."

They outnumbered Rafferty and him almost three to one, and he hoped they'd oblige him with a good fight in light of the odds. He needed, really needed, to smash something just now, and suddenly the natty Abernathy and his four thugs looked like the perfect target. "Rafferty, get rid of that club."

Rafferty sensed his boss's mood with an unfailing confidence that rivaled that of a faithful hound. With a wide grin, he sent the club sailing out the window and balled up his huge fists. When he did, one of the thugs raised his own fists in a threatening gesture, and Rafferty laughed his joy out loud.

Savage expectation surged through Kyle, and he stripped off his coat and tossed it over a chair. The hope of imminent battle lightened his mood.

Abernathy, however, wasn't going to be so obliging. With a derisive smile at Devereaux, he said, "Come on, boys. We're leaving." They pushed past Kyle, some of them as disappointed as he that there wasn't going to be a brawl. Tromping down the path to the hitching rack, they climbed into their wagon and drove off.

Kyle's shoulders sagged. Some days nothing went the way he wanted it to.

Chapter Six

"IT'S LOVELY, AUNT Julia. I know I'll be so happy here." French turned and gave her aunt a quick hug. "Thank you for not making it blue." Her words were heartfelt.

Julia hugged her in return, then drew back with a startled expression on her face. "What a clever child. You have found me out."

French chuckled and looked around at the pink and white prettiness of the room. "You gave yourself away every time you visited us in Boston, Auntie."

Julia was so amazed her voice squeaked on the word "How?" She'd been so certain that she had always been the very soul of discretion.

She'd always been careful never to let the smallest sign escape her that might have been construed as a criticism. She knew that if she had, her sister Catherine would have ceased inviting her to visit, and she would have had nothing but her letters from French then. "How?" she repeated in a stronger tone.

"You always rubbed your arms as if you were cold whenever you were in my room." She rushed on when she saw that she had distressed her aunt. "The decor did give the impression of cold. All that ice-blue and white and silver. And everything tailored like some hotel room, with never a girlish ruffle in sight." She rubbed her own arms. "Brrrr. I still feel the chill of it when I think about it."

She threw her arms wide in a gesture that embraced her new room. "This is warm and ruffled and just what I have longed for as long as I can remember."

She went to the dressing table and picked up the gold-backed brush of the toilette set there. As she did, she caught sight of her face in the mirror and was startled. Never had she seen herself looking so happy, but that was to be expected, for she never really had been. What surprised her was that she didn't look merely happy and relaxed, as she expected to—for she'd known all along that she was going to be happy once she was here with her Aunt Julia—she looked excited. And she knew the reason.

Softly, radiantly, she was glowing with the happiness that she'd been experiencing from the very first moment she'd seen *him*. He was . . . magnificent. Seeing him there on the railway platform had supplied her with a face to put on the figure that had always haunted her maidenly dreams. She blushed at the thought of the fantasies she was already weaving around the breath-taking—literally breathtaking, for she was again having a little trouble catching her breath, just from the thought of him—Kyle Devereaux.

She sighed. Teaching children from *his* lumber camp and mill was going to become her life's work if she had anything to say about it.

All through her teens, while surrounded by gray-suited, solemn-faced prospective bankers, and even into this, her twenty-first year, she'd dreamed of a man capable of sweeping her off her feet. Now that she had found him, she'd never let him go.

Then, like lightning striking, the thought that he might

already be taken hit her. She spun away from the mirror in a panic. "Aunt Julia!"

"Oh, my dear, what is it?" Julia's mother-heart responded to the girl's distress, speeding its heartbeat. She moved quickly to her niece and took both of her hands to hold.

Shyness overcame French. She dropped her lashes to cover the embarrassment she knew would show in her eyes. What would her aunt think? No matter. She had to know. Even though she knew she would learn her employer's marital status very quickly from the children she was to teach, she couldn't bear not knowing immediately.

Bravely, she met her aunt's concerned gaze, striving to appear only politely interested in her aunt's friend. But it was in a breathless whisper that she asked, "Mr. Devereaux, Auntie. Is he . . . is he spoken for?"

Julia could have laughed aloud with relief. She held a tight rein on herself, however. It simply wouldn't do to seem to take her niece's question lightly by exploding, as she felt like doing, with the joy the question engendered in her. "No, dear. Kyle is a bachelor still."

She closed her lips firmly on all the hopes she harbored for her niece and Kyle, knowing they must never be spoken until they came true. Instead she asked the question she knew would naturally follow if she hadn't been knee-deep in machinations to bring the two young people together. Quietly she said, "Why do you ask?"

French's face flamed. Julia saw her struggle to keep from grinning, and found she was having the same difficulty. Her precious niece's lips trembled with the effort to control her smile, but she couldn't hide the lovely light that filled her eyes.

Julia began making plans for the wedding. She didn't even slow her planning when French lowered her luxuriant lashes to hide the telltale glow behind them and said with hard-won nonchalance, "Oh, no particular reason. I was . . . merely curious."

After they had changed for dinner, the two women headed for the stairs. In the wide upper hallway at the top of them, they met Jamie. He nearly barreled into them as he rushed from his room. "Oops! Excuse me!" He turned crimson. "I guess I'm in too much hurry to get down . . . to the dinner table." His last words trailed off to a whisper as he realized he was being rude.

Before he could say any more, Julia eased his discomfort. "Of course, you are, dear. All growing boys are constantly ravenous, that is only to be understood."

Jamie stood transfixed. To have met two gentle, caring women in a row was almost more than he felt he could believe. His only knowledge of the fair sex having been his selfish mother and his equally self-centered grandmother, he was momentarily stunned. Chiding himself to recover, he managed a heartfelt, "You're beautiful. Both of you are beautiful."

The women accepted his compliment graciously, murmuring their thanks. They moved toward the steps as if he had only told them they were lovely to look at.

Jamie smiled a soft smile and followed them. It was just like this pair of extraordinary females to think he meant they were merely pretty in their dinner gowns. It was probably one of the things about them that had made him realize they were truly beautiful—inside, where it was really important. They were beautiful underneath, and he thought himself the luckiest boy in the world to have discovered two such women after having spent all his young life in the stifling, picture-perfect society that frequented his grandmother's house.

Julia and French went down the wide staircase together, arms linked. When they reached the spacious foyer, Charlie, resplendent in his best dark suit in honor of French's first night at his dinner table, met them.

"What is one poor old rancher to do with two such beautiful ladies?" He leaned down and kissed each on the cheek in turn, beaming. "Come along, boy," he told Jamie. "Unless I miss my guess, you should be about half-starved by now."

Jamie grinned and followed the three adults toward the dining room.

Julia told her husband what he was to do with the ladies on his arms. "Feed us, my dear. Just feed us if you love us. It is our fondest wish just at present."

"And here I'd hoped that your fondest wish would be for my company. I'm crushed." He seated Julia and nodded approval when Jamie moved to help French with her chair.

French looked from Charles to Julia and a warm feeling stole through her. There had never been any such loving banter at the dinner table at her home in Boston.

There, the dinner hour was inevitably spent reviewing the events of the day, and the review had been inevitably followed by her father's suggestions on how to improve one's performance. The memory saddened her.

"French, honey . . ." her uncle said.

"French, dearest . . ." her aunt said at the same time.

"Are you all right?" They finished their question in unison, the expressions on their faces anxious.

French looked from one to the other. Her own expression was incredulous. Here she was at the dinner table with two family members, and they were worried because she was quiet and just a bit sad. She could hardly believe that anyone cared so much for her feelings.

Maybe this was going to be an even more wonderful place to be than she had hoped! She felt as if a great weight had tumbled from her shoulders. Here she was going to build a new life. A happy life. She took a huge breath and said, "I'm fine, thank you. Just fine."

In town, at the office of the sawmill, Kyle was a whole lot less than fine. "What the blazes can I do, Rafferty? I have to find out what happened to my nephew, and I have to be here to get this school set up. Not to mention guarding 'Devil-Oh, Colorado' from the blasted railroad. Abernathy and his thugs aren't going to leave it at this." He swung an arm wide to indicate the stacks of spilled papers he hadn't gotten back into order. "We have to get the children corraled before those snakes come around starting trouble."

Rafferty looked up from the papers he was stacking. "No answers to all those telegrams you sent?"

"No good answer." Kyle's eyes were dark with concern. "One said a boy got put on the train out of New Orleans, all right. Another said a lone boy was still on it at Saint Joe. After that, no trace. There hasn't been a single lone boy on any train since." He cursed helplessly. "Of course, my mother hasn't bothered to respond, and it would help a helluva lot if I knew his name!" He slammed his fist down on his table desk. "Dammit, Rafferty. What kind of people send a twelve-year-old boy across a continent all by himself?" He glared at his friend and right-hand man.

Rafferty ran a hand through his hair and deliberately failed to meet Devereaux's gaze. He had plenty of answers, most of them unsuitable for polite company, that in any other circumstances he'd have shared with his boss.

Not now, though. Not when they both knew that it was the women of the Devereaux family who had put that boy on the train to Colorado with less care than they would have sent one of their pet cats.

Rafferty thought hard for a minute. "Send somebody else to look for the boy, Dev. That's legwork. Here you got a bad situation. Abernathy will do all he can to shut you down now he's found out that he can't bully you into doing things his way. You got the brats to get out of the woods and off the streets and safe for when the rough stuff starts." He slanted a wary glance at his friend and boss. *"And you got another headache here as well."*

Kyle straightened up from the pile of files he was gathering and fixed his friend with an inquiring stare.

Rafferty met it without a qualm. "You got a problem with that new schoolmarm."

"How the hell do you know about *her*? She hasn't even been to town, yet!"

Rafferty grinned at him. "I sent Moses out to the depot to see if that new saw blade had come in. From that last hill he saw what people got off the train and he saw the way you pokered up.

"When nobody but her got off here, he damn near killed his horse getting back here with the news. It was all over Sunrise minutes before you tore in and found me in here with Abernathy. Wasn't long after that one of the other men said some fellow named Jamie Waring went off to the Chamberses' with her."

Kyle used an impolite word.

Rafferty bought time by going over to light against the oncoming darkness the lamp that hung in the center of the room. Then he just kept gathering up Kyle's papers. Almost a minute passed before he spoke. "I could go."

Kyle snapped his head up. His brows drew down into a frown as he considered the possibility with all its ramifications. It would be a real handicap, staving off the railroaders without Rafferty to guard his back, but his lost nephew was more important than the mill, as Rafferty knew.

If worse came to worst and the mill was destroyed, Kyle knew he could always relocate the men he had working here to some of his other sawmills. That was a possibility, at any rate. His stubbornness argued that to do that would be accepting defeat. But his coolheaded-ness assured him it was a good plan to have to fall back on. He was grateful to Rafferty for forcing him to come up with it. A long moment passed as he looked into the eyes of his friend. There was no one he'd trust more to do the job.

Finally he told him, "Go find the boy."

Chapter Seven

SEVERAL DAYS LATER, a sleepy Julia snuggled closer into her husband's embrace. "Charlie," she announced, "I do believe French has noticed Kyle."

"Huh! Not in half the way he's noticed her, you can bet."

"No, I'm not talking about Kyle. I don't care about his being angry that she wasn't a man. I'm talking about the fact that French was positively *anxious* to learn whether or not Kyle was unattached. Isn't that wonderful?"

Charlie thought a moment. Julia was happy. He decided this might not be the best time to tell her that her favorite bachelor had mistaken her favorite niece for a fancy piece. Nope. Not the right time at all. In fact, he decided, there wasn't gonna ever be a right time. So instead of saying anything, he pecked her on the forehead and started to roll out of bed. Just then the cock crowed again. "Time to get going."

The high four-poster made it easy to hit the heavy carpet standing. Not for the first time, he grinned as he reached for his pants. His home might be rustic in appearance from the outside, there was no doubt about that. A gigantic, two-story log cabin, its only claim to fame was that it sprawled over quite a bit of ground. Inside, though, in spite of warm tan log walls, it had every luxury Julia had been accustomed to in her Boston home. He'd made durn sure of that.

He had to admit he thoroughly enjoyed it, too. Like now. Julia's fancy Oriental carpets sure beat the hell out of bare floors in the cool dawn of a morning.

All in all, in every way, Julia Price Chambers was the best thing that had ever happened to him. Yes, siree! He chuckled and reached for the shirt Julia had laid out for him last night.

Julia smiled at the sound and pulled the covers up around her chin. "Must you go right now? In fact, must you go at all? It's Sunday."

He resisted the urge to rejoin her in the bed. "Yep. Gotta go check on the boys up on the north range. They should be getting about ready to move them cows down to settle 'em in a warmer pasture."

"Those steers," Julia corrected automatically, nuzzling her pillow.

His eyes twinkled. He was long-used to the way she corrected his cowboy talk. He was careful never to use it when company who came from her side of things was around the place, but it was natural to him, and he knew she didn't mind it, so he repeated. "Yep. Gotta go see about those cows," he said, in spite of the fact that they were, beyond a doubt, steers he'd raised for the meat packers in Kansas City. "I'll just have a cuppa coffee with the boys and be back in plenty of time for your citified breakfast."

He was dressed and gone before Julia wondered dreamily about the tone of voice he'd used earlier. Remembrance of it brought her back awake. Just what *had* Kyle said to Charlie about her darling French?

True to his word, Charlie was back in time to clean up for Sunday breakfast. Afterwards, he allowed as how it

would be tiring for French if they were to drag her back
to town for church on her first Sunday on the ranch.

Julia let him get by with it without commenting that he
didn't seem too disappointed at missing the sermon,
himself, because she knew that Kyle was going to ride
out to the Lightning Double C for dinner around noon, as
usual. She waited until about an hour before he was due,
enjoying the quiet companionship they shared in the
cozy family parlor, before she told French.

French looked at her as if she'd announced the sky
were falling. "Oh, Aunt Julia! What shall I wear?" She
sprang to her feet, startling Charlie out of a doze.
Gathering the skirts of the perfectly lovely day gown she
was wearing, she headed for the stairs at a dead run.

French wasn't the only one upset by the news that
Kyle was coming for Sunday dinner. Jamie felt more
than a little threatened by the thought of facing his uncle
across the dinner table after not having identified himself
right away as Devereaux's nephew from New Orleans.
He wasn't worried about the "now" part. He was scared
stiff about the "then." The day was not too far distant
when he'd *have* to admit who he was to his uncle. If Kyle
saw a whole lot of him now, he was sure going to wonder
about it then, and except for the fact that he didn't want
to leave his new friend Henry French Richards just yet,
Jamie didn't have much of an excuse to offer him.

Jamie decided it might be a good idea to play
least-in-sight for Sunday dinner. "Is it okay if I ask Miss
Mary for a picnic lunch, Mrs. Chambers?"

"Why yes, Jamie," Julia answered after a brief moment of consideration. "I suppose that would be all
right." She smiled. When she did, Jamie breathed a huge
sigh of relief, and Julia chuckled. Obviously the boy had
a pretty good idea of how long adults with guests for

dinner could sit around the table. Better to let him go than to have him impatient and uncomfortable.

Mary would be delighted to fix him a picnic lunch. Julia's housekeeper-cook-dear-friend had taken Jamie into her heart right along with French the instant they'd arrived and been introduced. Julia smiled again to think how lucky they all were to have Mary with them.

Mary Wells could have gone back to her family in Baltimore after her husband's death in a mining accident. They still wrote and invited her at least once a month. Julia had used to wonder about why Mary hadn't gone, but then she'd seen the way her own dear brother Jacob had looked at Mary Wells, and thought maybe she understood. Mary was certainly quieter since Jacob's disappearance.

Julia wished that Mary would confide in her. Shared burdens were always easier to bear, but Mary was a large, competent woman well able to keep her own counsel, and Julia refused to pry.

Jamie clattered out to the kitchen to find the Chamberses' indispensable housekeeper-cook, and Julia folded and put away her needlework. As she rose to follow her niece upstairs at a more leisurely pace, sad thoughts were pushed resolutely to the back of her mind. Before she even got out of the parlor, she was smiling like the proverbial cat with canary feathers showing between its teeth.

Charlie was still musing over French's precipitate departure. "What in tarnation's got into that girl?" Charlie shook his newspaper to a more readable shape. The Denver paper was, thanks to the newfangled trains, not even the best part of a week old, and he was determined to enjoy it. Between catnaps, of course.

"Nothing, dearest. Just read your paper. We'll be back

down directly." Julia noticed that he didn't question Jamie's behavior. How like a man.

Charlie shook his head and watched his wife walk sedately toward the stairs up which his niece-by-marriage had just flown. Women. He'd never understand 'em. All that bustle about no more'n Kyle coming to tie on the feed bag. Oh, well, what the hell. He'd get to read his paper in peace anyway.

He shook his head again. That niece of Julia's could sure move when she'd a mind to, she'd made it upstairs in record time. He watched appreciatively until his neat-figured Julia was out of sight, then went back to his reading, letting his eyelids drift closed.

Upstairs, Julia found French tearing clothes out of the clothespress in her room and muttering to herself. "Can I be of any assistance to you, French?" She waited in the doorway.

"Oh, yes! Please come in." She turned eagerly toward Julia. "Do you know his favorite color?"

Julia didn't bother to play games by asking, "Whose favorite color?" She was pleased with her niece's desire to do all she could to attract Kyle Devereaux. It went so well with her own plans. "I believe Kyle's favorite color is blue, dear."

She watched as French hung everything that was of another hue back in the wardrobe. How lovely the girl was, and the warm anticipation that filled her face made her lovelier still.

Kyle would never be able to resist her, Julia was sure. Then her own earnest desire for his well-being would be realized. She had every intention of getting Kyle Devereaux safely married off to someone who could spend the rest of her life proving to him that there were at least *two* caring women in the world.

With great bitterness, she knew all about Celeste Devereaux now. She'd pumped Charlie mercilessly until she was in possession of every fact he knew about Kyle, which, manlike, hadn't been much. Then she'd wired a detective in New Orleans offering an irresistible bonus for speedy information. Two days later she'd known all about Celeste Devereaux-Martin . . . the woman had remarried and hyphenated her new name to that of Kyle's socially superior late father . . . and the selfish cruelty with which she'd cast off her only son.

The retired Pinkerton man she'd hired to spy for her had added that Celeste Devereaux-Martin, according to her friends, had shown neither remorse nor the first motherly feeling since. In fact, it had been the recent repeat of her callous behavior, this time with her grand-son, that had set New Orleans society buzzing afresh about her treatment of her only son, Kyle Devereaux. That gossip had made the detective's job much easier and more swiftly done.

Julia had made an adjustment in her thinking as she'd finished the man's lengthy telegram. She'd moved Kyle from his status of favorite bachelor friend to adopted family member. She'd had to claim the despicable Devereaux-Martin woman's son for her own from that instant. She was determined to see to the healing of some of the wounds *that* woman had inflicted on Kyle's spirit. Henry French, she decided, was just the one to help with the job.

"Will this dress do?" French interrupted her thoughts, looking up at her hopefully as she pushed forward one of the two dresses she held.

Julia saw immediately why French liked one more than the other she'd unconsciously put behind her. The other blue dress French had was the same silvery blue in which the dear girl's room back in Boston was decorated.

Julia tussled with herself. Finally she decided that the occasion was too important for anything but a completely honest answer, no matter what, so she said quietly, "The other will make your eyes even lovelier, French dear."

French sighed and hung the sunny blue dress back with the others. "I know. Mother always said that I should wear this shade for that very reason. Thank you."

Julia was pleasantly surprised to learn that her sister Catherine had taken so great an interest in her daughter's appearance. She felt a little more kindly disposed toward her sibling to learn of it. She'd thought Catherine took interest only in her fine, handsome sons. She was happy to have this to remember instead. She told French quietly, "The other dress you should wear to your first day of school. The children will find it nicely bright and cheery . . . and I'm sure Mr. Devereaux will stop by then to see how you are faring." She let her niece see the twinkle in her eyes.

French didn't pretend to be embarrassed by her aunt's perception. Smiling suddenly, she rushed across to her and threw her arms around her. "Oh, Aunt Julia. It is so nice to be here."

"It's wonderful to have you, dear."

They pulled away from one another and looked into each other's eyes. Both dissolved in tears of happiness.

Julia laughed first. "We are going to have a lovely time, aren't we, French?"

French smiled tremulously and gave her aunt another hug. "Yes, I do believe we shall, Aunt Julia. I simply can't imagine there being any doubt about it."

Kyle loped his horse toward the Lightning Double C trailing Rafferty's after him. He'd put Rafferty on the train yesterday and was sorely missing his presence already. He guessed that was why he was bringing Rafferty's big gelding along to be turned out to pasture in his absence instead of leaving him at the livery stable in town. It was a small payback for Rafferty's kindness in offering to go look for the boy. There was, after all, no one else he'd trust to do the job, and it meant a lot to him. If Rafferty hadn't volunteered, he'd have had to go. That would have meant leaving the mill to the nonexistent mercy of the railroad . . . and leaving Henry French Richards.

Today wasn't like all the other Sundays he'd spent with the Chamberses. Always before he'd looked forward to a good meal, congenial company, and the loving attention he'd given up denying that he craved from Julia Chambers. Today, he rode toward the sprawling ranch house with mixed feelings. His affection for Julia Chambers was deeper than any he'd ever felt for any woman and he knew she loved him in return. Because of that, his stomach was in a knot. How would Julia feel if Charlie had told her what he'd said about her niece? It was obvious Julia loved the girl like a daughter.

He groaned aloud, and Daumier's ears flicked back toward him. "It's okay, boy." He reassured the horse out of habit, he didn't feel anything was going to be okay, himself. If Charlie had told Julia that he, Kyle Devereaux, had been all but panting to offer her niece the position of being his mistress, Julia was gonna skin him alive.

"Whoa, boys." He pulled the big horses down to a walk. "Let's just cool you down a bit."

His mount snorted and flung his head impatiently.

"Yeah, Daumier. I know you're eager for that deep bed

of fresh straw, but I'm just a might leery of riding full tilt into Julia Chambers's guns."

He eyed the house carefully, as if he could somehow sense any inner turmoil there. All seemed tranquil and well. Surely Charlie would have found a way to warn him if Julia were on the warpath? He was banking on it, anyhow. "Okay, Daumier. Go on, boy." He let the horse move forward of his own accord, and arrived at the hitching rack in front of Charlie's sprawling log house with a flourish.

He smiled crookedly in approval to see one of the hands was already coming up from the barn for the horses. Pointing to Rafferty's horse, then the pasture, Kyle acknowledged the friendly nod the cowhand gave him and turned toward the house.

"Kyle! Welcome, boy." Charlie, alerted by the hoof-beats, was waiting at the door. As he came out and crossed the porch, the two women moved forward to look out.

French heard her uncle say, "About time you got here," then everything but the man he greeted simply faded away.

He looked even taller and more incredibly handsome in his well-tailored black broadcloth suit than he'd looked in his more casual attire at the station the other day. She saw the blaze of his hair as he swept off his hat, then saw it turn a rich dark brown again as the shade of the porch dimmed it. His eyes, bright blue and slightly squinted against the sunlight, opened in the shadow of the roof, and the crinkles at their edges disappeared. He strode across the wide veranda to clasp Charlie's hand as she watched, fascinated.

What in the world was happening to her? Before he even looked her way, she was wondering if Aunt Julia had pulled her stays just a little too tight when she'd helped her into her blue dress. Whatever the reason, she seemed to be having the same strange shortness of breath she'd experienced the last time she saw him. She felt Julia squeeze her hand and hung on for dear life.

"French," Julia said, "you remember Mr. Devereaux, of course."

"Of course," she heard herself murmur. She hoped she didn't look as dazed as she felt. Kyle Devereaux, as he moved forward to receive Aunt Julia's kiss on his cheek, absolutely overwhelmed her with his presence. From him, she caught the faint scent of pine woods after a rain and another that she was sure was his own, and wondered when she'd received the ability to smell everything around her so sharply. Even her sight seemed to be magically enhanced, and she saw the white flecks in Mr. Devereaux's eyes as he returned her calm greeting.

"*Miss* Richards, I hope you are comfortably settled in?"

She smiled then. Having had her uncle's skillful trickery explained to her as they'd driven home to the ranch from the train depot, she certainly didn't miss the emphasis Kyle Devereaux placed on the feminine form of address. With her usual directness, she said, "I hope you have forgiven my uncle, Mr. Devereaux."

It was Kyle's turn to murmur a cool, "Of course." He shot a glance at his host. He hadn't forgiven him. He'd get Charlie back later. For now, though, he'd no intention of ruining one of Julia's fabulous Sunday dinners.

French was unaware of the underlying tensions between the two men. "Oh, I am so glad. I think Uncle Charles felt that I would do as creditable a job as a man, and he knew I was anxious to be with my aunt."

Kyle didn't have as much trouble returning her smile

as he'd thought he might. Especially when he heard old Charlie called "Uncle Charles" in that sweet, soft voice. He cast an amused glance over his shoulder to where "Charles" stood with his wife. Meeting Julia's fierce glare, he hastily returned his attention to the delectable Miss Richards.

Making conversation was difficult when his mind wasn't on talk, but he tried. "I hope teaching lumber-camp children won't prove too difficult a task for you, Miss Richards."

She turned the full battery of her lovely gray eyes up to him and smiled. He almost lost her reply. Deep in her eyes, he saw light like polished silver and the sweetness of her nature reflected there. *Dammit!* She even had dimples.

"I love children, Mr. Devereaux. While some are difficult, I've never met one I'd say was impossible." The softness of her smile melted something way down deep in him. Even from Julia he'd never had such a tender smile.

Suddenly he wanted more than anything in the world to protect her. Not like the protection he'd wanted to offer her as she'd stood on the railroad platform in all her delectable, curvaceous splendor. No, not like a woman under his protection because she was his . . . his . . . the word wouldn't even form in his mind now about this gentle creature. Besides, he was even ready to protect her from himself. More than that. Now he even wanted to protect her from the cares and troubles of the rough world into which she'd placed herself by coming here to Colorado. Now he wanted to wring the neck of every child that might even think of making trouble for her when she taught. Hell, he even wanted to keep the wind from blowing on her too hard.

He must be losing his mind!

Striving to keep his thoughts coherent, he concentrated on the conversation. He wanted to tell her she looked too young to have had wide experience with children of any sort. He wanted to tell her she'd never been in a lumber camp before and that she had no idea what she was facing in the half-wild children spawned by his men.

Instinctively, he knew that if he did tell her, the dimples would disappear, so he didn't speak. He wanted to enjoy them a while longer.

For the life of him, however, he couldn't see how she expected to control a bunch of lumber-camp brats with a voice so soft and breathy that he had to lean toward her to hear it. He guessed he'd better show up at the schoolhouse early tomorrow morning to see to it that she managed. He pledged himself to do so. If he was there, nobody'd give her a hard time. Not with him ready to lean on them.

Charlie came over to them with a smirk on his face. He managed to turn it into a smile for French. "May I have the pleasure?" He offered her his arm to take her into the dining room.

Kyle wanted to hit him. Instead, wearing a grimace that he hoped would pass for a smile, he stormed across the room to where Julia waited.

Julia watched him come and was delighted. She smiled as she put her hand on his arm. How very nice it was to see her valued friend Kyle ready to punch her beloved husband out over the escorting to dinner of her dear French. How beautifully all her dreams of the future were falling into place.

She sighed a contented sigh and gave Kyle's arm a gentle squeeze by way of apology. She was, after all, hoping to turn his safe and sane—and rather rough—

world completely upside down by introducing French into it permanently.

Loving them both as much as she did, it was the very least she could do.

Chapter Eight

SUNDAY DINNER PASSED more pleasantly than any French could ever remember. Her Aunt Julia and Uncle Charles were still so obviously in love, even after twenty years of marriage, that it was a pleasure to watch them together. French hoped with all her heart that someday she would be blessed as they were. She and whomever she married.

She blushed as her gaze traveled unbidden to Kyle Devereaux. Goodness! Did this man engender thoughts of marriage in her? Her honesty attacked her. Of course he did.

She went all breathless at the thought, and a tingle came up from her very toes. Oh, dear, she'd have to be careful not to let anyone see how he affected her. She had no wish to make a fool of herself.

Kyle saw the delicate blush that warmed the lovely face opposite him and wondered what had caused it. He felt one corner of his mouth turning up in an appreciative smile. The little darlin' was having an effect on him all right. It must be because she was Julia's niece. Maybe it was because she was so gentle and biddable, as well. Clearly, she was nothing like the headstrong, autocratic women of his own Devereaux family.

Thank God for that. And while he was thanking, he added heartfelt thanks for good old Charlie's discretion.

He was certain, now, that Charlie hadn't told Julia he'd wanted to take this delectable creature to bed on a regular and continuing basis the minute he'd seen her. If Charlie had told Julia, she would no doubt have thrown him out as soon as he'd ridden up.

Feeling safe again, he relaxed to enjoy his perusal of Miss Henry French Richards. She was really something. Soft and vulnerable, not in the least like the tall, icily elegant—and inhumanly cold—women of his own illustrious family. He watched her toy with her food, saw the affectionate glances she gave her aunt, and felt the same hunger he'd experienced when he'd first caught sight of her rise in him again.

Fortunately for all of them, though, the idea that she needed protection of another sort, not the possessive, arrogant kind that a man gives a mistress, welled up in him even more strongly. She was such a quiet, delicate little thing. It was obvious she had no idea of how rough things were out here in the man-dominated territory west of the Mississippi.

His thoughts soared off into uncharacteristic flights of fancy. She was like a rose that had bloomed in an enclosed garden and had never felt the strength of the wind. He took a deep breath and silently pledged himself to look after her.

"Well." Julia had watched the play of emotion on the faces of the young people and was ready to take a hand. "Why don't we take French down to the barn and show her the surprise Charlie has for her? Then you, Kyle, can take French down to the river for a stroll. It would do you both a world of good after one of Miss Mary's dinners."

Kyle grinned at her. "I'd like that very much, Julia." He wiped the grin from his face and turned to French. "That is, if you'd care to go for a walk, Miss Richards?"

"I should love to, thank you."

Again she spoke in that breathy little voice that made him want to rise half out of his chair every time she spoke to hear her. What a dainty, completely feminine little thing she was. He helped her from her chair as if she would break if he wasn't careful, and gave her his arm to guide her to the front door as if she'd never make it there without him to take her.

Julia threw her husband a triumphant look as he pulled out her chair.

Charlie returned one of utter disgust. Kyle looked like some moonstruck calf.

Julia swatted his arm before she took it in imitation of the young couple ahead of them. She regulated her wide smile to a polite expression of interest in case one of them turned around to see if she and Charlie were with them. Not much chance of that, however, she saw with smug satisfaction. French and Kyle were completely absorbed in each other.

Kyle had taken his hat from the rack beside the front door, and now, instead of putting it on as they descended the porch steps, he held it so that it shaded French's face from the late-afternoon sun. She would have to have a broad-brimmed hat of her own so that the sun would in no way harm her lovely rose-petal complexion. He made a mental note to bring her one when he came to the schoolhouse to see to it that all went well for her tomorrow.

Tomorrow she would be in the schoolhouse he'd had built for her. Suddenly, he wished he'd used finer lumber, and that he'd had the men put in more finishing details. He glanced down at her hand where it rested lightly on his arm and worried that she might get a splinter in one of those delicate fingers. The men had merely roughed out the interior of the building, thinking that the children would probably make a mess of it anyway. He'd send a crew in to sand the place overnight, he decided.

French walked looking up at the wonderful highlights the sun struck from his dark auburn hair. She didn't have to worry about where she walked, because she was floating along beside Kyle Devereaux. She didn't want to look away from him for even an instant. He was handsome, but it was the caring quality she sensed in him that drew her gaze.

Somehow, from all her family had said about the West, she'd expected all the men to be rough, and yes, she had to admit that she'd expected to find them a little uncouth, as well. In fact, she'd thought, from his abrupt departure from the rustic little train depot, that maybe Kyle Devereaux would be one of those "men of the West."

His manners were excellent, though. Not one of her very proper brothers had better table manners, and she was secretly thrilled at the way he shielded her face from the sun with his hat. On a less commanding man, the gesture might have seemed somewhat affected, but on Kyle Devereaux . . . it . . . it fitted somehow.

French thought he was larger than life. Easy self-assurance enveloped him like a princely mantle. Surely he was the embodiment of all her girlish dreams. She smiled a secret little smile to realize it. Then she admonished herself sternly to keep a pleasant, neutral expression on her face. *Don't drool over him, for pity's sake.*

Julia called out from just behind them, "Wait at the barn door, please, you two."

"Yeah," Charlie added. "No peeking. We wanna be there when she sees her surprise."

Charlie left Julia standing with the two young people

and moved forward to swing the big double doors of the barn's center aisle wide. Stepping into the shadows of the barn aisle, he gestured for them to join him. "Come on in. See what you think of this."

"This" was a neat little gig with shiny yellow-painted spokes in its wheels. Kyle propelled French gently forward. All three of them awaited her reaction.

She stood silent, staring at the smart little equipage.

"Well." Charlie's voice was impatient. "Do you like it?"

"Like it? Oh, yes. Oh, yes, I do. It's beautiful." She looked around at them in pretty confusion.

"Do you really like it, dear? We weren't sure you liked to drive." Julia was watching her carefully, trying to read her expression.

"Oh, yes, Aunt Julia. It's grand." Her face clouded. "But . . . I don't know how to drive."

There was a collective sigh of relief. "It's easy," Charlie said.

"I'll drive it for you." Jamie Waring startled them all by popping out of the dimness at the back of the barn.

"Oh, Jamie. You startled us." Julia smiled and held out her hand to draw the boy forward. "Kyle, this is the young man who escorted our French safely here for us. Jamie Waring, this is Mr. Devereaux."

Jamie stumbled through his part of the introduction, scared witless that his uncle was going to recognize his name. He needn't have worried though, old Devil-Oh hardly looked at him, he was so busy staring at Miss French.

"I'll be happy to teach you to drive." Kyle's voice was a low, almost intimate rumble. His eyes were locked on French's face. He looked as if he'd go get the moon for her if she would just condescend to ask him for it.

Julia brightened and took over. "How nice of you, Kyle. I'm sure you will make an excellent teacher. Thank you."

French turned back to him. "Are you sure it won't be too much trouble?"

"No trouble at all." His gaze caught and held hers a long moment, and she found herself out of breath again.

Charlie grunted. He'd had about all he intended to take of this sloppy mooning around. If this kept up he'd lose all his Sunday afternoon chess games with Kyle. He changed the subject. "You can ride her, too. Here's your saddle."

French didn't see the saddle, all she saw was the dainty head of the mare with the star that Charlie had indicated when she'd said French could ride "her."

She had to work at approaching the mare slowly, she wanted so badly to run to the stall door. She looked at her uncle when she reached it. "Are you saying she is mine to use while I'm here?"

Charlie exploded with indignation. "Hel . . . Heck no, French. I'm saying she's yours, period."

French put her arms around the mare's neck and buried her face in it to keep them from seeing the quick tears that came. The mare whickered softly and rubbed her chin on the back of the girl's dress.

Charlie started forward to keep her lovely blue dress from being soiled, but both Kyle and Julia grabbed an arm to detain him. Neither wanted him to spoil the moment the girl and the mare were sharing.

Julia said softly, "We knew you'd need a way to get to school, dear. A gig seemed a nice solution for days that are not nice enough for you to ride to town."

French sneaked a hand to her face to be sure she wouldn't embarrass anyone with her foolish tears, then turned around to thank her aunt and uncle. "Thank you. Thank you both. It's the nicest present anyone has ever given me." She smiled tremulously. "I shall do my best to learn to do everything properly." She looked a little ashamed. "I'm only an indifferent rider, you know. I wasn't allowed to ride with my brothers in the park very often." She smiled apologetically. "And I'm afraid I've never ridden astride at all. Not even once."

"Well, that doesn't matter. I'll teach you all you need to know." Kyle looked a little surprised that he'd volunteered so strongly. He put it down to the rosy blush that colored French's cheeks, then smiled at her. "I'm sure you'll be a very quick pupil."

Charlie started scowling and his eyes narrowed. The eager look on Kyle's face put him in mind of his friend's first reaction to French at the depot. Maybe having Kyle Devereaux teaching French to ride was a little like having the fox guard the henhouse.

He started to voice his objections, but Julia gave him a hard pinch and said, "That would be wonderful, Kyle. I shall have one of the boys drive French to school in the morning and for as long as she needs him, and the two of you can work out a time for you to begin her lessons."

Jamie Waring stepped into their circle truculently. In his eagerness to get to drive the gig, he'd completely forgotten that he'd deliberately missed a really great dinner to stay clear of Kyle Devereaux. "I said I could drive her, Miss Julia, and I really can. I learned a lot from the cabbies back at home. I spent a lot of time with them when my mother didn't want me around, and I drive pretty good. Besides"—he made the ultimate sacrifice— "I guess I should go to school while I'm here anyway, shouldn't I?"

"Of course you should, Jamie. That will work out just

fine." Julia was appalled she'd been so careless of the boy's feelings in her eagerness to promote Kyle's teaching French as a way to bring them together.

Charlie and Kyle exchanged a glance. They understood one another perfectly. Both wanted confirmation of the boy's abilities before they turned him loose with French.

Charlie reached up for a shiny patent leather trimmed harness. "Why don't you just try her out while we're all down here raring to see what she'll do?"

"Good idea." Kyle went to get the mare. "I'll help you harness her up."

French stepped back to stand out of the way with her aunt. "Oh, Aunt Julia, this is like being in a dream. I can't imagine a more perfect day."

Julia smiled and squeezed her arm. It was turning into a perfect day for her, too. French and Kyle were obviously taken with each other, and now Kyle was volunteering to spend time teaching French to ride and drive. She couldn't have wished for better if she'd had the powers of a fairy godmother.

Julia was well aware Kyle would have to steal time from important business matters to teach French. She felt a little pang when she thought of that. But it was only a little pang. She was sorry about his business, but she had her own priorities, and Kyle's lumber operation's problems took a poor second place to them.

Besides, if what Charlie told her was correct, Kyle was rich enough already. Fighting the railroaders over this mill was just another example of masculine foolishness.

"Just think," French invited them to join her plans, "with this lovely little mare to ride, I shall be able to take long rides into these lovely woods." She gestured to the tall trees scarcely a mile away.

Alarm shot through Kyle, yanking his attention back from where the boy was doing a creditable job of driving. The woods weren't a safe place for a lady alone at any time, not with cougars and bears. With his men there they were worse, and with the railroaders looking for ways to spike his operation, they were downright dangerous. Worry was thick in his voice when he told her, "Maybe you need to wait on the woods for a while, Miss Richards."

French turned a face with more strength in it than he'd noticed there before. "I won't want to wait long, thank you." She smiled at him, certain of his understanding. "I'm sure you realize that I'm eager to investigate my Uncle Jacob's disappearance. Every minute counts, as I imagine winters are severe here." She stroked the dainty mare's nose when Jamie brought the gig back to them. "It will be so much easier now, with this lovely mare to take me farther afield than I could possibly have walked."

Investigate? The word hit Kyle like a rock. This dainty little morsel was taking it into her head to *investigate* some Uncle Jacob's disappearance? The idea was ludicrous. Besides . . .

Then it hit him. She was Julia's niece, and old Jake Price had been Julia's brother. The sharp twinge of alarm he'd felt when Miss Richards had said she wanted to ride in the woods grew to lightning-bolt proportions.

Old Jake had found a silver mine that was worth plenty. Whoever had caused him to disappear would be playing for keeps. There'd be no way a sweet bit of fluff like Miss Richards could hold her own against men of that stamp.

He found himself using a phrase he'd vowed would never pass his lips. "*Now see here*, Miss Richards. You can't take up an inquiry into old Jake's disappearance just like that." He cast about for a reason—any reason—that might keep her safe at home. "The sheriff wouldn't take it well to have a woman interfering in his business."

He heard a gasp from Julia, and a muttered "That's done it" from Charlie. Jamie Waring popped his head around the gig, eyes wide, to watch what was going on.

None of that registered with Kyle. Kyle was too busy adjusting his thinking, rearranging all his plans made just this afternoon, and trying to understand the change that was taking place in the delectable Miss Richards.

Her soft gray eyes flashed and narrowed. The luscious, rose-petal soft lips he'd wanted to kiss since the first moment he'd seen her thinned into a firmness he'd never have expected them to be capable of attaining. She lifted her chin challengingly toward him. When she took a step nearer him, she seemed to grow several inches taller.

While he stared, she demanded in a voice that contained none of the breathy softness he'd so admired, "Are you saying that I have not the intelligence to investigate my uncle's unexplained absence because I am a *woman*, Mr. Devereaux?"

Kyle Devereaux stood stock-still and concentrated hard on keeping his jaw from dropping. Without any warning, his rose had developed thorns.

Chapter Nine

THE NEW SCHOOLYARD was a seething, screeching mass of children by the time French and Jamie arrived. Dust flew in clouds as the boys chased and teased and tussled. Squeals of delight and promises of mayhem reverberated with equal enthusiasm from the rafters of the newly built schoolhouse.

Jamie pulled the mare to a halt and sat staring, a very still French beside him. "Jehoshaphat, Miss French. What are you going to do with that mob?"

French took a deep breath, swallowed hard, and told him with a calm assurance that she was far from feeling, "It's just excitement on the first day of school, Jamie. They'll quiet down once we're in the schoolroom." Ignoring his doubtful expression, she touched her hat, as if settling it more firmly for a battle ahead. "You put Midnight in her stall, and come in as soon as you have made her comfortable, will you?"

"Sure, Miss Fr . . . Richards." He shot her an anxious look as he guided the mare to the gate of the schoolyard. "I'd better call you Miss Richards while we're here at school, don't you think?"

French rewarded him with a smile. "Thank you, dear. I'm grateful you thought of it. It wouldn't do for me to show favoritism."

Jamie glowed. He held the mare still with a deter-minedly gentle hand and watched the graceful way French got down from the gig. Nobody at home would have said that. Heck fire, nobody at home would have waited for him to figure it out. They'd have ordered him around and told him exactly what to say before he'd even had a chance to offer to do the right thing.

He sighed as he flicked the driving reins to signal the mare to move off toward the shed that would shelter her for the day. It occurred to him that maybe he should be feeling guilty. He didn't, though. He knew that soon enough he'd have to report to the person to whom he'd been shipped like a package. His conscience wouldn't permit him to avoid his duty too much longer. But who could blame him if he lingered just a mite to enjoy such wonderful, caring companions as those he had at the Lightning Double C?

"Nobody, that's who!" The words erupted out of him. He was surprised to hear them, but he grinned and held on to his warm glow as he led the dainty mare to her makeshift stall.

French in the meantime walked with dignity toward the schoolhouse steps. With a pleasant expression, but carefully without smiling, she went up them. On the small porch at the top of the steps she turned with great deliberation and quietly surveyed the noisy crowd of children scuffling in the yard.

One by one, the rest joined the few who had gotten quiet when the gig arrived. Her stare passed from one face to the next until she had looked directly at every child who would meet her gaze and the schoolyard became hushed.

French let the silence spin out for a full minute. During that time, some of the boys began to squirm. She spoke before they became too restless. "Please come quietly into the schoolhouse and take your seats when I ring the bell." All over the yard there were mesmerized nods of agreement. French held them with her calm gaze an instant longer, then turned unhurriedly and entered the school.

As she closed the door behind her she sagged back against it. "Whew!" She pressed a hand to her stomach to quiet the butterflies there, then reached up to remove her hat with hands that shook a little. "So much for the first hurdle. Now if I can just manage all the rest."

She had to stop herself from adding that at least coping with her pupils would keep her from dwelling on the awful ending to what had been a perfect Sunday. And it had been a perfect Sunday. For the first time in her life, she'd seen what it was like to spend a day with a loving couple. She'd watched the affection that passed between them, seen their gentle teasing at the table, and their warm concern for their guests, and it had been an experience that warmed her heart.

It had been like a dream come true for her, for it was something she'd thought, after growing up at her parents' table, only existed in dreams. The dashing lumberman, Kyle Devereaux, too, had been the stuff of dreams. Meeting him had supplied a face for the man who had long haunted her own.

Everything had been so wonderful, so completely wonderful . . . until . . . She sighed as she remembered the way Kyle Devereaux's handsome face had closed when she'd merely *implied* her views on the equality of women with men by insisting on her right to go look for her Uncle Jacob.

Not for the first time, her scruples had cost her her dream. This time the most important and poignant dream of all, and she felt the pain of its dying afresh. Suddenly she muttered plaintively, "Oh, when will you learn to keep your mouth closed, French Richards?"

But she wouldn't. She knew she wouldn't. When you believed in something, you just couldn't. Why, it would be like a preacher's wife or daughter sitting silent while someone reviled God. There was simply no way she could have stopped herself from challenging Mr. Devereaux as she had. No, and no reason she should have had to. But, oh, she wished with all her heart . . .

After all, Kyle Devereaux was the handsomest man she'd ever seen. He'd captured her—she forced herself to say "imagination," because she refused to say "heart"—from the first moment she'd seen him. More than anything, she'd wanted to get to know him better, but she'd driven him away as surely as if she'd used a gun.

Funny, though, that as she let her mind dwell on him something in the center of her chest ached at the thought that she might have alienated him. Clearly, she admitted, it wasn't her *imagination* that was suffering this strange sense of loss.

Fortunately, right now it was necessary to pull herself together for the sake of the children she was to teach. Pining over her employer had no place in this first day of school. She was amazed that the mere glimpse of him as she passed his office could affect her so.

"There's no time for that now," she told herself sharply. "Get the children in and seated, French Richards, and stop mooning over Kyle Devereaux."

She did have to get the children in before the spell she'd cast over them wore off and they turned back into rambunctious little hooligans. They wouldn't stay awestruck by her calm, commanding demeanor for long. She must get them in, take their names, and get them seated and busy in a hurry, or she'd have trouble on her hands.

She reached for the precious bell she'd bought in Boston the very day she'd become a certified teacher. Reverently she lifted it out of the small carpetbag she'd brought. She ran her fingers around the cool, smooth rim of the bell, taking comfort in the memory of choosing just this one from the several she'd been offered. Taking such care to choose had made it special. She smiled. And this day and these children were going to be special, too, she knew it.

Straightening to her full height, she went to the door. Assuming a stern, confident expression she was far from feeling, she opened it, stepped outside, and began to ring the lumber-camp children in to the classroom.

Kyle Devereaux sat at the large, flat table he used as his desk and stared at the pile of papers that clamored for his attention. He hated paperwork.

His eyes were heavy from lack of sleep. Last night he'd been over at the schoolhouse directing a crew of his men to sand and smooth the interior of the large, airy room.

After he'd spent the day with Henry French Richards, he'd had to see to it that the rough surfaces of the walls, windowsills, and doorjambs were sanded as smooth as satin. He had to . . . even if she *had* changed before his very eyes into a . . . What was it that was eating at him? That she'd become so confident? Self-sufficient? Julia was all that and he certainly didn't mind it in her. Surely he wasn't becoming the kind of weak man who had to have his women mindless clinging vines! What was it about Henry French Richards that he found so damn disturbing?

Last night it had been concern for her that had kept him at the schoolhouse until dawn. The men had thought he was being overly careful to keep the children from picking up splinters, and he'd let them think that was his reason for paying them double their usual wages to do the job.

He'd let them think that was his reason. The truth of the matter was that he had no intention of letting French Richards hurt herself even slightly if he could do anything to prevent it. In spite of the change in her last evening at the Chamberses' barn.

He wondered how he'd become such a fatuous fool in one short afternoon. At least he hadn't bought the little beauty a broad-brimmed hat, he told himself with satisfaction.

He heard the rattle of wheels and went to the window in time to see Jamie doing a very creditable job of driving the schoolmarm to the new schoolhouse just down the hill. She was in blue again, and the little chip of a hat she wore exactly matched her outfit.

Suddenly he was sorry he hadn't gotten Nate Holt to open the Holt and Son's Mercantile and find him a pretty, wide-brimmed bonnet. He turned from the window with an impatient sound. "Blast it, I have work to do."

He cursed himself for a besotted fool. Things were at a pretty pass, indeed, if he had to tell himself to get busy. He shook his head. French Richards was proving too damned distracting.

If he didn't get the orders on his desk straight and going out on time, the railroad wouldn't have to put him out of business, he'd do it himself. Gritting his teeth, he applied himself to the task.

Five minutes later he pushed aside the papers he was working on when he heard the ringing of the bell. He could tell by the rhythm that it was being rung by *her* hand. If she'd given it to one of the children to ring for her, it would have pealed with a quicker cadence as the child strove to get the most noise from it before it was taken back or passed on to one of his companions.

In his mind's eye, he could picture her standing there in the sheltering porch he'd had built at the top of the schoolhouse steps. He tilted his chair back to the point of peril, put his booted feet up on the corner of his desk, and gave himself over to seeing her again in his imagination.

She'd start out neat as a pin, he knew, but he'd bet that that rebellious hair of hers would be slipping from its pins with every shake of her arm. He could envision the tendrils framing her face.

He wondered whether or not she'd still have on the saucy little hat she'd been wearing when she passed by his office. Then he wondered if she'd like the huge airy room he'd designed and had built. He was glad he'd done his best to make the room pleasant. He'd done it for the children, of course, his lumber-camp kids and the town and ranch kids who'd been schooled at home or not at all. Now that he'd met the schoolteacher, he was elated that he had. His mind jumped to wonder if such a sweet little thing would be able to control the children he'd saddled her with.

He'd found she wasn't the dainty rose he'd so poetically called her in his stupid flight of fancy the day before. He still felt as if that knowledge had robbed him of something infinitely precious.

Maybe, somewhere in the deep recesses of his mind, he'd thought that if she were that soft and yielding, she might have found a place in her heart for a man like him. A man whose own mother hadn't even wanted him.

"Hell," he growled under his breath, chair legs slamming to the floor. "What the devil did you expect? If she'd been the perfect woman you'd thought her, what the blazes do you think she'd have to do with you, Devereaux? Your own mother couldn't even stand to have you around."

Running a hand through his thick wavy hair distractedly, he eyed the stacks of papers that needed his attention. They failed to overbalance the scales in their favor.

Miss Henry French Richards might not be the timid flower he wanted her to be, but she wasn't a tyrant, either, and he thought it might take at least that to manage the brats he'd seen running through the town for the past year or so. No woman, however odd her ambitions, should have to face a mob single-handed.

It was all the reason he needed. He snatched up his hat and shot out of the office.

Chapter Ten

By Saturday the class was whipped into some semblance of order, but French was just plain whipped.

"Honestly, French, dear, you do look exhausted." Julia gave her a quick hug to take any sting out of her words, and surreptitiously touched her niece's forehead to see if the girl was just tired out, or if there was something worse to worry over her about.

"I'm fine, Aunt Julia. Really I am." She gave her aunt a smile. Then her voice took on a note of eagerness. "I'm pleased, too. By the end of the week, the children were showing some real interest in learning."

"Well, good for you, dearest." Julia smiled to see the glow that came over her niece when she spoke of the children. Any reservations she might have had about sticking her nose in Kyle's business when it came to selecting a teacher for the children of his lumber-camp school left her. "I'll bet Kyle will be pleased."

"Huh." French rolled her eyes skyward. "I'll bet Mr. Kyle Devereaux will be *amazed*." She frowned at her aunt. "He didn't expect me to be a success, you know. He even left a bully in charge of frightening the children into behaving."

"How awful." Julia frowned. "Was the bully necessary?"

French smiled ruefully. "I hate to admit it"—she looked at her aunt sharply—"and I probably wouldn't to anyone but you, but he did make those first few days easier. You know. Until I could get everybody sorted out and could properly assess their levels of learning."

Julia nodded. "Yes, I can see that you might need a little help until you could get the ball rolling, so to speak. Now that it is rolling, whatever will you do with your bully?"

French turned away to tie her hair back. "Oh, Teddy Harper's a rather nice sort after you get to know him. His strength seems to lie not so much in his physical power to pick on the others as in the fact that they respect him. He's done nothing to frighten anyone since the others have buckled down to their studies. I think it'll all be just fine."

She turned from her mirror, satisfied with the way the blue ribbon she'd been tying held back her hair. "They're good, bright children, Aunt Julia. It's a crying shame that they've had so little chance to receive an education."

"Well, the West is rather a rough place still. The women here are so busy working right alongside their men that they have very little time or energy left to teach the children."

"That's another thing. I've certainly been surprised to see that women here in the West seem to have a great deal more to say about what goes on than they do in the East."

"Well, dear, there are simply not as many people here. All of us are more closely involved in everything that occurs as a result."

"I like that. At home, women are engaged in a battle to get to be treated as the intellectual equals of the men."

"Little reason for that out here. Until there's a much

greater population, I think women will find themselves able to express their opinions right along with the men. Wyoming even gave women the vote a few years ago."

French looked thoughtful. "Hmmm. 1869, wasn't it? Bet the East is way behind that."

Julia said with a wide smile, "I doubt, too, that there are many people out here who even use the words 'intellectual equal,' to be perfectly frank."

French laughed. "In that case, I must suppose that I am currently without a cause. What splendid news that will be for my poor parents."

Julia chuckled. "Will you be bored, dearest?"

French saw the twinkle in her aunt's eyes and knew she meant Kyle Devereaux. "Oh, I suppose I shall be able to find something else to engage my interest."

Then she became serious. "Besides, I do have a cause. I have my children. They are fine enough to make one want to do one's best for them and I intend to prepare them to enter any university in this country if they should want to go."

Julia, filled to bursting with pride in her niece, patted French's arm. "What are you planning to do with your first free day, my dear?"

"I thought I'd see if Middy is as easy to ride as she is to drive. Jamie has let me drive her enough to see that she really is a dear. It's made me brave enough to see if my meager riding skills will keep me out of trouble."

"Well," Julia reminded her, "don't forget that Kyle volunteered to help you with your riding."

"If I find I have any difficulties, I'll apply to him for instruction the minute I get back from my ride."

"Promise?"

"I promise."

"Good. I'll go ask Miss Mary to pack you a lunch."

*   *   *

The trail French chose to follow into the woods was well defined. It slanted off at an angle from the road that led into town, and climbed gently up toward the mountain. Midnight seemed as eager as French to explore the inviting dimness of the forest after the bright, unseasonably warm sun of the broad valley that held the Lightning Double C. Before they had gone far, however, French heard voices.

"Got a right good stand of lodgepole pines up about a mile, Mr. Devereaux."

"Good. Send the men there, Haislip. I'd like to keep as many of them as we can away from the area the railroaders are patrolling."

"Hell, Mr. Dev. Meaning no disrespect, but our boys are more'n ready to take on those railroad thugs."

French heard Kyle Devereaux laugh. "I'm sure of that, but I'll get a lot more work out of men who haven't been busted up in a brawl. Keep 'em logging here for the next few days."

"Yes, sir, Mr. Devereaux."

There was a creak of leather, and Middy whinnied to the horse she knew was just ahead.

"Oh, drat," French whispered. She wasn't interested in being caught in the woods by Kyle. Too vividly she remembered that day he'd warned her about riding in the woods unescorted. *And* she remembered what a ninny she'd made of herself. She looked around for a place to take Middy off the trail before they could be discovered.

Middy's whinny had precluded a clean escape, however. She heard Devereaux tell the man he'd been talking to, "I'll be right back."

French gave up looking for a safe trail and simply rode on.

Rapid hoofbeats were muffled by the heavy pine needles that covered the trail. An instant later, Kyle Devereaux rounded the curve that had kept French hidden from him. He rode as if he were part of the horse under him. French had to sharply remind herself that they were not currently on the best of terms.

"Miss Richards." He lifted his hat to her. "What a pleasant surprise. I hadn't thought to see you before tomorrow."

French had to think for a minute why he expected to see her tomorrow. Sunday dinner of course. Hadn't Julie told her he always came? Why did this man have to rattle her so? Her voice didn't betray it, however. "Good morning, Mr. Devereaux." She kept her expression cool and her voice crisp. She didn't want to encourage him to join her. She wasn't in the mood for a scold, nor had she forgiven him for the high-handed way he'd dealt with her class Monday morning.

He chuckled. "I see you haven't forgiven me for interfering in your classroom."

"Actually, Mr. Devereaux, I must thank you for putting Teddy Harper in charge of my class." She glanced sideways at him from under her lashes and was pleased to find that he looked startled.

Seeing Kyle Devereaux disconcerted was all the encouragement she needed. "I'm certain it was a kindly intended *interference*, and I am equally certain that *your interference* did hasten the time when the children found that the acquisition of knowledge is more than just an intolerable burden."

Kyle shifted in his saddle to get a closer look at her. There was no way he'd missed the cool emphasis she'd slathered all over the word "interference." Her message was clear. He fought down an admiring smile. She had spunk. "I think I understand what you're saying, Miss Richards." A grin tugged at the corner of his mouth at that, but he knew better than to let it happen. "While you appreciate my interference because it helped you settle your students more quickly, you would just as soon that I minded my own business in the future. Am I correct?"

French rewarded him with a radiant smile. "Yes, Mr. Devereaux. You have caught my meaning exactly."

"Oh, I'm a good student, Miss Richards. I learn fast."

They rode on in silence for a long moment. Finally French said, "Haven't you business to attend to, Mr. Devereaux? I should hate to keep you from it."

Kyle was torn between replies. Obviously, Miss Richards was still smarting over the way he had *"interfered"* in her classroom. Sulking or not, the woods still weren't a safe place for her. Even though the railroaders were busy harassing his loggers over to the north, there were still the everyday dangers of the forest to consider.

Bears and cougars could be as dangerous as men, if not as vile. She was in need of watching over, but she had just clearly dismissed him. He reined Daumier to a halt and tipped his hat. "Very well, Miss Richards. I'm sorry to have intruded once again. I hope you enjoy your ride."

He spun Daumier on his haunches, and dashed away from her to rejoin his men. He had to take comfort in the fact that his men's movements in the area would no doubt have frightened any wild animals deeper into the woods and made them safer for the schoolmarm. Still he had the uneasy feeling that he should have accompanied her, but damned if he could figure how to do it short of knocking her in the head!

French ate all she could of Mary's delicious picnic, and there was still enough food left over for two more people. She spread it out on a large flat rock for the little forest creatures to enjoy. That way Mary wouldn't feel her efforts were unappreciated. She'd liked Mrs. Wells the moment her aunt introduced them, and she wouldn't hurt her feelings for the world.

Carefully folding the napkins her lunch had been wrapped in, French tucked them neatly away in her saddlebag. Mrs. Wells was as particular about the laundry as she was about food.

She looked around the little clearing she had discovered. There was certainly nothing anywhere near like this in Boston. She took a deep breath, savoring the crisp, clean smell of their needles, and listened intently to the song the wind sang in the tops of the Colorado pines. What a wonderful place this was for her picnic.

She recalled the only other picnic she had ever been on with a repressed shudder. That had been a stuffy, formal picnic her family had once eaten in one of the Boston parks. The servants had laid out a linen cloth, placed cushions around it for the family to sit on, and proceeded to serve a banquet. The family had endured more than enjoyed the outing, she remembered.

She took another deep breath, drawing the fresh, pine-scented air deep into her lungs, and sighed in appreciation. If she had her way, she'd never return to live in Boston.

She turned to her mare. "Are you thirsty, Middy? Would you like a drink before we start back?"

She gathered the reins that the little mare had been trailing as she grazed. She was glad Middy hadn't stepped on them. French didn't know whether or not she would have looped them up in some way, but she guessed that it was all right not to, as western horses were trained to ground-tie, after all. Surely they must be trained to look out for their reins, too. She made a mental note to ask her Uncle Charles.

There was so much to learn about this country. She felt a burgeoning eagerness to learn it all. Everything was so fresh and new. She felt as though there were a good chance, if she tried very hard to hurry and learn it all, that she might become a part of this wide-open country that sprawled so vastly under its big sky.

At home, she'd always felt as if she were merely one more of a long list of names added to the roll of those who came after the Pilgrim fathers. Here everything was so new and the land so sparsely settled that she felt as if she could make a difference somehow. A difference that would be counted. It was a good feeling. She was glad she had come.

Middy nudged her and brought her back to herself. "All right, girl. I'll take you to get some water." She led the way toward the lively stream that flowed at the edge of the clearing, the mare picking her way daintily after her.

They'd almost reached the stream, when suddenly, Midnight threw up her head and slammed back on her haunches. Her ears quivered rigidly forward. Then her eyes rolled, the whites glaring, and she reared, tearing the reins from French's grasp. Whirling, she screamed shrilly and plunged away at a gallop back across the clearing and down the mountain.

"Whoa! Whoa, Middy." French ran a few steps after her horse, then stopped as the futility of her actions hit her. The mare was gone, leaving only the echo of her hoofbeats.

Immediately, French felt very much alone. "Oh, drat," she murmured. Her voice sounded forlorn to her. Fighting the feeling of unease she felt at being left so far away from the ranch without a mount, she looked around to discover what had startled Midnight so.

She found the source of the animal's terror instantly. Her own heart quailed. There, under a low-hanging branch just across the stream from her, it crouched. Through narrowed eyes it watched her, ready to spring, its lips drawn back over glistening fangs!

French shrieked and turned to run. Fear sent strength rushing through her. She sprinted away from the danger. A root caught at her booted foot. She went sprawling.

Shaking with horror, she twisted to look over her shoulder. She had to see where the beast was. It was still there, snarling at her, every hackle raised! Saliva dripped from its fangs.

Almost sobbing with fear, French tried to claw herself away from it, desperate to free her foot from the springy root that held it. Her effort was in vain.

No matter how violently she yanked and pulled, the root simply stretched to accommodate her every movement, retaining her as a captive. Nothing she could do would free her foot. The root would not let go.

All French could do was lie there overcome with terror, waiting for the beast to attack.

Chapter Eleven

CRINGING FLAT AS she could press herself against the ground, French lay there certain the animal was about to spring. In abject, bone-melting terror, she waited to feel its claws tearing at the flesh of her back, its fangs at her throat.

Her eyes were tightly shut. Pure fear flowed down the back of her neck from the base of her skull in waves, each more debilitating than the last. A sob broke from her as the waiting became unbearable. She dug her finger-nails into the soft earth of the clearing to hold her shaking hands steady. Another few seconds stretched by as long as an eternity.

French could bear the waiting no longer. She eased her eyes open, fearful she would see the slavering beast hovering right over her, but it hadn't moved. What was it waiting for? Why didn't it pounce?

She'd seen, in her one horrified glance at the animal, that it was huge and lean and hungry. The image of it crouching there was imprinted on her brain forever. The beast was starving! Surely it would devour a helpless human, sprawled just a few feet away from it?

French fought down a whimper. What *was* it waiting for?

Another moment crawled by. She could bear the awful

suspense no longer. Shaking uncontrollably, she pushed herself up until she was half sitting. Still no attack came.

Fearfully, she turned just enough to see the beast from the corner of her eye. It was exactly where she'd first seen it.

They stared at each other. Yellow eyes met gray. Neither blinked.

French was afraid to. She was afraid that if she did, the animal would pounce. Her eyes burned with the strain of keeping them fixed on the animal only a few yards away across the stream. Finally, she had to blink. When she did, the animal threw back its head and howled piteously.

French's eyes popped open again in a flash. Over her shoulder, she stared at the large gray shape under the tree. Still the animal didn't move.

She couldn't just sit here and wait any longer! French fought and won over her trembling. She took her first real look at the animal.

It was a large gray dog. A dog! She could have wept with relief. She loved dogs. No dog would ever hurt her. Neither would this one, even though this one was a very big dog—a sled dog, she thought.

Relief flooded her. Surely a sled dog would be used to humans? Even if it wasn't a particularly friendly sled dog, surely it wouldn't attack her. She slid slowly around until she was facing the dog.

The dog regarded her fixedly.

"Oh, no!" Sympathy wrenched her heart. She saw why the dog didn't move. Its paw was caught in a small steel trap, the kind she had learned about from reading books on the settling of the Hudson Bay area. Trappers, she'd read, often set such traps beside streams to catch fur-bearing animals.

French looked at the trapped dog closely. She should

go for help. It would take quite a while now that Midnight had run off and left her on foot, but the dog needed to be freed, and she could hardly expect to handle such a great beast alone.

The paw was bloody and swollen. French knew it was causing the poor dog a great deal of pain.

Suddenly, as if it wearied of waiting for her to help, the great dog dropped its head to its paw. Even as French watched the dog began to gnaw its leg just above the cruel teeth of the trap. It was going to sever its very paw from its leg in a last bid for freedom.

"No!" French could not hold back the cry. She flung her hand out toward the dog as if the simple gesture would stop it from mutilating itself. "No, you mustn't. Wait! I'll free you."

There was no time to go for help. By the time she could reach any, the poor animal would have maimed itself to win its freedom.

The dog stopped gnawing and watched her. French forgot her fear of the animal. She was frantic to help the poor beast get out of the trap.

"French, you must be insane," she heard herself mutter, but the voice had nothing to do with her resolve. She knew she had no choice. She had to get that trap open before the sled dog chewed off its own foot.

To do that, she had to get her own foot loose first. How was she going to do it? She'd nearly wrenched it off pulling at it already. She slid herself nearer to consider the problem.

"Oh!" As she moved closer to the root to inspect the grip it had on her booted foot, the springiness of the root relaxed. French saw with deep self-disgust that she could have been free all along if she'd just stopped pulling against the root. If she'd just let the dratted thing relax, she could easily have slipped her foot out. She did so now, deeply ashamed at the way her own unnecessary panic had kept her trapped before.

The dog watched her impatiently. It truly looked half-starved. Possibly the only reason it was still alive was that it had had the water from the stream to drink.

Food. The dog needed food. Her fear gone, French was beginning to think again. There was plenty of food left from her lunch.

French scrambled up and limped over to the large flat rock that held the remains of her picnic. Gathering the bread and meat, she went back toward the dog.

Great yellow eyes narrowed at her approach. "Nice doggy," she murmured soothingly, feeling all kinds of a fool. "Good boy. Nice dog. Here's something to eat."

The dog's ears pricked forward. It eyed the food avidly. Cocking its head, it let go an anxious whine.

French came as close as she dared, and tossed a bit of ham from one of her sandwiches toward the dog. It never hit the ground. With a snap of strong jaws, it disappeared in midair.

Bits of roast beef from her other sandwich met with a similar fate, and then chunks of bread, until the dog accepted them with less desperation. Finally, there was nothing left but a pair of drumsticks Miss Mary had sent along from last night's fried chicken.

French knew chicken bones splintered very sharply and could kill a dog that swallowed them. She crossed the stream to be nearer the dog, and sat down very slowly and very quietly just out of its reach.

"We have to get you out of that trap, you know."

The dog looked at her.

"I'm not quite sure how to do it."

The dog looked at her with bright interest.

"I think I'll have to hold the trap open and you'll have to pull your foot free yourself." In her middle a tight knot was forming. She would have to use both hands on the metal of the trap. In addition to having no way to lift the dog's injured leg out of the trap, she'd have no way to protect herself. Her face would be very near the dog's own. There was no way she would be able to shield her face from the shining fangs that would be inches from it.

She looked at the dog, her gray eyes wide. "I guess the real question is, will you attack me when you're free?" She shuddered a little. "Will you even know that I am trying to help you? Or will the pain in your paw cause you to bite me when I try to open the trap?" They really weren't questions she wanted to consider, but she could only get rid of them by voicing them aloud to the dog, and Heaven knew that she needed to get them out of the corners of her mind. They were playing havoc with her courage there.

So she spoke aloud to give herself more courage, and the big gray animal regarded her as if it were trying to understand. With every word, she slid a little closer to the dog.

French could no longer look at the animal, her eyes were fastened instead on the trap and the poor, savaged leg caught in it. Better to keep her eyes on the trap, to focus on the job to be done rather than to look up at the magnificent dog and see those teeth that could tear her face to pieces as she struggled with the cruel steel trap. Teeth that *would* tear her face to pieces if the dog didn't understand that the pain she was causing it was for its benefit.

She was close enough for the dog to grab her now. It made no move to harm her. "I don't suppose I could ask you to just tear off my arm and leave my face alone, could I?" She tried to speak whimsically. It didn't quite come across the way her voice thinned and shook.

With hands that shook as well, she reached for the trap. The dog growled and moved back a little as if its courage—or perhaps its trust of her—had failed.

She took a deep breath and slid a little bit closer. "Steady now. Easy now." She made her voice as soothing as the wind that sighed in the pines above them. "Good doggy."

Her hands were on the two arches of the trap now. The dog's growl rumbled deep in its chest. She closed her eyes and tried to think of the crusted blood under her fingers and the pain the poor dog had suffered and how she was about to set it free. Anything but the paralyzing fear that was seeping into her spine again.

As she did, she was assailed by a brief vision of the dog blinding her. She rejected it with a gasp, and prayed instead. "Please, God. Give me the strength to open this trap . . . and the courage to do it." The dog snarled and snapped at the air in front of French's face when she began to put pressure on the two steel arches, striving to force them apart. "Dear God, please don't let him bite me. Please, God."

She'd never been so afraid in her life. She could feel the animal's hot breath on her cheek. No sound existed for her but its whimpering, snarling indecision.

She pressed down harder, and the dog yelped as the arches separated a little. "It's coming, dog," she gasped. "It's coming loose."

She saw the cruel teeth of the trap ease out of one side of the dog's leg. Suddenly she was overwhelmed by a need. She had to have a name to call this huge beast. She needed it desperately for her own courage, so she wouldn't be so terrified.

The dog whined, then whimpered with the pain she was causing it. But it didn't bite her, and she *had* to have something to call it. "Rover," the name sprang to mind. It was a stupid name for a magnificent, beautiful, huge sled dog, but it was the only thing that came to her through the scrambled emotions in her half-frantic mind.

Her stomach ached with the tension that filled her. She talked to the dog, attempting to ease its distrust of her, to distract it from its pain. "It's going to be all right, Rover. You'll be free in a minute."

The dog yipped as the teeth of the trap came out of the other side of its leg, but it didn't savage the face so near its own. As if it understood, it didn't retaliate for the awful pain she was causing it. With a final thrust of effort, French bore the arches of the trap flat to the ground.

The dog didn't move. French could feel the strength leaving her hands and shoulders in quivering waves. "Hurry, Rover. Move your foot!"

Desperate, she lunged forward and shoved her shoulder against the great shaggy gray one beside her, and the dog moved. Its bloody leg came free of the trap. With a snap that sent it jumping two feet into the air the trap closed again. The dog snarled viciously at the snapping sound of the trap closing.

French burst into tears. She sat rubbing her aching hands and crying like a hysterical child.

She'd done it! It had been the hardest thing she'd ever done in her life, but she'd done it. She'd been so frightened, and so weak, and so terribly, terribly afraid that she would fail. So terribly afraid that she wouldn't be able to free the great dog.

Now it was done, and she felt as if she would never be able to get up from where she sat, covered with the blood of the dog, thanking God for answering her prayers, and feeling, for the first time in her life, as if she had done something that really mattered.

With no regard for sense or safety, she threw her arms around the sled dog and hugged it with all the strength she had left. For a miracle, the dog didn't pull free and run away.

That sobered French. She sat up straight and tried to think what the dog wanted of her. Was she required to perform some further heroic act? Was it waiting for her to do something more? *Surely* it couldn't be hoping she would clean and dress its leg?

Then she saw where the dog's eager yellow eyes were focused. She still had the drumsticks from her picnic in her lap! Slowly, fighting an hysterical urge to laugh, with fingers that trembled, she began to peel the meat from the bones. Without hesitation, without fear, she held the first bit out to the big dog.

Without hesitation and without fear, the big dog took it carefully from her fingers. They continued until the last of the chicken legs had been picked clean, then the big dog turned and limped off into the woods.

Just before it disappeared from sight completely, it turned and looked back at her. Tears came to French's eyes. She felt as if she had just been given a very special gift.

Softly she whispered, "Good-bye, Rover. Good luck."

Kyle Devereaux turned Daumier down trail to get back to the office, half smiling as he looked around him. He loved the woods, especially the pine woods, where the trees always seemed to be sighing and murmuring secrets to each other—deep, age-old secrets.

He was listening to the pines when he heard the

hoofbeats. A horse was coming down the trail behind him with a lot less caution than a sensible rider would require of one. He put Daumier across the trail at a point where it was straight for long enough for the approaching rider to see him and stop in time.

As the horse came into view, he saw there was no rider. The saddle was empty, the stirrups flapping. It was the little black mare that French Richards had been riding!

Kyle hardly waited for the mare to slither to a stop on the pine needles of the blocked trail before he caught up her reins and snatched her around to gallop back the way she had come. He had to find French.

He had to see to it that she was safe. Julia would never forgive him if she came to harm when he was in the same woods with her. Hell, in the same country! And he'd never forgive himself.

He should have found a way to accompany her. He should have *made* a way to accompany her. She had no business in these woods alone! What the blazes had happened to her?

Spurring Daumier and dragging Midnight, Kyle Devereaux charged up the mountain like someone demented.

French finally got up from the edge of the stream. She moved in a gingerly fashion. She was stiff as a result of her fall, and stiff from sitting so still beside the dog.

After one look at the westering sun, she determined to be on her way. If she was going to get back to the ranch before dark, she'd better start walking. Quickly.

To bolster her courage, she said aloud, "Obviously Midnight isn't going to come back for you, Henry

French!" Leaving the clearing with one lingering backward glance, she started down the trail.

It had been a very trying day, not at all the restful time she'd planned to ready her for another week of teaching. As she walked, she realized that she didn't regret it, though.

She had only to remember that last look the big gray dog had given her before it disappeared into the trees to feel a wonderful sense of elation and accomplishment. There in her clearing, she, Henry French Richards, had done a really worthwhile and courageous thing. She felt ten feet tall.

She felt a little weepy, too. It wasn't because the ankle she'd twisted when she'd fallen with it caught in the tree root was hurting her, though it did throb a little. She was weepy because she knew that if she hadn't found the dog, it would have mutilated itself and been forever lame—if it didn't bleed to death. Her tears were tears of gratitude. She'd saved a life, and because she had, she felt so very privileged.

Limping on down the mountain, she smiled and began humming to herself. All in all, even if it had been a little scary, it had been a wonderful day.

Chapter Twelve

KYLE SAW FRENCH before she saw him. Relieved, he reined the panting horses to a walk. Henry French Richards was standing in the middle of the trail looking up at the trees over her head with a strange smile on her face.

First he noticed how beautiful she was standing there in a shaft of sunlight against the deep velvet green of the pine forest. Then, as he came closer, he saw that her clothes looked as if she'd been thrown to the ground and there was blood on her hands. The dazed expression on her face galvanized him into action. He would have killed both horses to get to her.

Storming up the trail like a madman, he slammed his mount to a halt and threw himself out of the saddle as he reached her. In his mind his voice clamored, *French! Oh, God, French, are you all right?* but he didn't let himself utter the words.

With every fiber of his body he fought to keep himself from sweeping her into his arms, resisting the strong urge to run his hands over her perfect little body to be sure nothing was cut or broken. Only the scars left on his spirit by a mother who'd despised any show of caring saved him from making a fool of himself. Instead, in an agony to hear her answer, he asked with cool courtesy, "Are you all right, Miss Richards?"

French was torn by his precipitant arrival from her happy contemplation of the kaleidoscope of blue patches of sky and glimpses of white clouds through the canopy of trees above her. She stared at him blankly for a moment.

This was the first time in her life she had ever been alone outdoors, and never had she been in a place like this, where the vast sky seemed to hang on the tops of the tall trees and splendid views were everywhere. She was reluctant to give up the wondrous discoveries she was making of the wild beauty around her—and the new strengths *in* her—even for Kyle Devereaux.

Kyle Devereaux's voice grated when he spoke again. "Are you all right?" He moved toward her a long stride and stood towering over her. "Has anyone hurt you?"

"No!" The reply was startled out of her by his intense regard, causing her to answer his question backward. "I mean, yes." She shook her head, plummeting out of her dreamy communion with nature and back to the present. "What I mean to say is that I am perfectly fine, and that no one has hurt me."

"Then why is there blood on your hands?" He couldn't help himself, he took her hands and inspected them for damage.

French watched him, embarrassed that she hadn't thought to wash her hands off in the stream. She'd been too eager to get started down the mountain to give her appearance a thought. No doubt she'd remember to do practical things once she was more used to this grand, wild country.

In her mind she heard herself chuckle. *No, admit it, French Richards. You were too frightened by what happened there in the clearing. You were completely out of courage and were running back to your Aunt Julia, heedless of anything else.*

Kyle Devereaux seized her by the shoulders. "Are you sure you're all right?"

French was perfectly sure she was all right. The quiet beauty of the mountainside had worked its calming magic, and the walk down the trail had cleared her mind. She even felt it had restored her courage.

The touch of Kyle Devereaux's hands sent tingles of pleasure through her heightened senses, though. French found she wasn't above encouraging him to keep his hands there on her shoulders.

The deep concern in his eyes spoke to some hidden yearning. With a soft smile, she surrendered herself to the tensions of the day, letting them come flooding back in to bear down on her.

She concentrated on all that the mountain's magic had healed . . . Midnight's shameful desertion and the hurt she'd felt when the little mare had refused to stop for her when she'd yelled "whoa," the cowardly way she herself had tried to flee the snarling beast half-hidden under the low-hanging pine bough without ascertaining first whether or not it was a real threat, the ignominious way she'd fallen flat on her face, and the terrible, unnecessary fear that she'd let overcome her then and as she tried to free the poor dog. Deliberately, she let it all combine to bring tears to her eyes. The result was quite satisfying.

Kyle Devereaux saw her lip tremble and the tears that trembled on her lashes sparkling like tiny diamonds. With a groan he swept her into his arms. He couldn't have stopped himself if his mother and a dozen like her had stood there beside him crying "shame." His left arm held her safe in its circle while his right hand stroked her hair soothingly.

French felt something crumble inside. Tears began to slip down her cheeks. She bit her lip, hard, to stop this silly behavior. She was ashamed, now that she had deliberately tricked him with her tears, but it was no use. The tears only came all the faster, and the reason for them came, too, to devastate her. Nobody had ever held her in their arms to comfort her before. When she'd been hurt as a child, whether suffering a blow to her feelings or a minor bump or scrape, and she'd sought refuge in the embrace of a parent, she'd always been held at arm's length and talked to firmly instead of hugged.

Now, ashamed and guilt-stricken or not, there was no way she could stand up to the tender kindness Kyle Devereaux's embrace offered. It was the first *physical* comfort she had ever experienced. She buried her face against his chest and began to sob her release of the day's tensions and her past lonelinesses into the front of his shirt.

Kyle was shaken to the core by her sobs. All he could think of was that he had to get her home to Julia without delay. Scooping her up in his arms, he mounted Daumier.

After one startled gasp, French clung to him tightly. She began to sob all the harder.

Kyle, more shaken than he'd ever been in his carefully controlled life, had to remind himself sharply that he'd have to take the trail at a sober pace with his horse carrying double. His every instinct urged him to send Daumier flying down the mountain as fast as the big gelding could go in order to bring the distressed girl in his arms to her loving aunt as quickly as possible.

The trail seemed interminable. He knew it well from his many trips up the mountain. Hell, he'd spent weeks up here planning his logging to preserve the beauty of the woods he loved. How the devil was it, now, that he'd swear in court that the trail had somehow lengthened?

His arm tightened around French. He whispered into her hair, "You're all right now. I've got you."

Even through her quiet sobbing she heard him and was filled with anxiety that she was causing him undue worry with her dishonest behavior. She wasn't, after all, crying for the reasons he believed; she was crying because she was unable to stop. Floodgates had opened deep down inside her because she felt cherished at long last.

She made a great effort to pull herself together. When she had herself back under control, she pushed away from his chest and looked up into Kyle Devereaux's face. The tenderness she saw there made her suddenly shy.

She could feel the words rumble in his chest as he said, "I'll have you home as soon as I can safely get you there . . . Miss Richards."

She wondered at the hesitation in his words. What had he been about to call her? Could it be that he had begun to think of her as French? She felt a small tingle of elation. How nice that would be. Especially since he'd been haunting her dreams so frequently of late. She felt a blush steal into her cheeks at the thought of the way he had haunted some of her dreams.

It wouldn't do to dwell on that! Quickly she told him, "I'm all right, really I am. It's just that it's been such a strange and stressful day . . . and then you appeared so suddenly . . ." She had to let her sentence trail off, she couldn't find a way to finish it . . . not a truthful way. To say "like a knight to the rescue" would have sounded foolish.

"You really aren't hurt?" When she shook her head, he

demanded, "Then what is the blood on your hands?"
Now he was scowling down at her.

Fortunately, the nerves she'd stretched to the breaking
point as she released the big gray dog chose that moment
to give way under the strain. Before she could stop
herself, she'd reburied her face in his damp shirtfront and
was sobbing again. "You just . . . don't . . . understand. You simply don't . . . know."

The last word came out in something that reminded
French of the howl the big dog had given. She thought
she'd die of shame right there in his arms. Gulping back
her tears, she pushed away from him again, ignoring his
stroking of her back, ignoring the calming murmur of his
voice.

What a strange man. Angry one minute, then crooning
to her as if she were a baby the next. Her father had never
been so mercurial. Neither had her brothers. The thoughts
annoyed her.

She glared up at Kyle. "I'm perfectly fine." She tried
to keep her voice firm. To her dismay, it quavered.

"Of course you are," he soothed.

French attempted to look him purposefully in the eye
and explain the series of events that had somewhat
unnerved her. She had no intention of having him
discover that it was his kindness that had unleashed the
deluge of her pent-up childhood longings. "Midnight ran
away from me, you see."

"Oh?"

He was attempting to be attentive and kind. She wanted
to kick him.

"Yes. She spooked because when I led her to the
stream to drink, there was a big dog caught in a trap on
the far side."

His gaze snapped from the trail to her face, his eyes

narrowed. "What kind of a dog?" His expression was no longer indulgent. Now he was tightly alert, she could feel the tension in his body where her own touched it.

French didn't bother to wonder what had gotten into him. She ignored the edge his voice had taken on. She felt completely out of charity with him just now. "A sled dog. You know. Long and lean and gray with big yellow eyes."

Kyle was so still for a moment that French wondered if he was listening. "You know," she prodded, "a sled dog. It must have come down from the north. It came to drink at the stream and got caught in the trap."

Kyle was still silent.

"You do know about sled dogs, don't you?"

"Yes," he said slowly. "It had a long tail that curled over its back, right?"

"No." It was her turn to frown. What had the dog's tail to do with it? "This one carried its tail straight and low behind it."

She felt his heartbeat quicken against her shoulder.

"And it was caught in a trap." His expression encouraged her to go on.

French thought it was a rather tense look, but continued without worrying about it. "Yes. And the poor thing was about to gnaw its paw off to get free."

The thunder of his heart increased. "And did it get free?"

French sensed that she was upsetting him, and now she wondered why. She waited awhile, carefully considering her answer. "Yes," she finally said half truthfully. At that, she felt the beat of his heart slow back to normal.

Then she felt it give an additional little lurch as he asked, "Without its paw?"

Kyle experienced a phenomenon he'd always believed

was purely a female prerogative. He had an awful premonition about what her answer was going to be. Suddenly the blood on her hands took on a clear meaning to him. His whole being cringed as he realized what the slender girl in his arms had dared.

French looked off toward the trees. "Nooo." The word was drawn out far longer than she'd meant it to be. She was buying time to think what she would answer next, for she was afraid Kyle Devereaux was going to ask her another question, and it was going to be a difficult one.

It was. It was more than difficult, it was downright disconcerting! Grabbing her by the shoulders, he forced her to look directly at him. His expression was thunderous. His voice frightened the birds out of the trees around them. "Henry French Richards! Do you mean to tell me you *helped* that animal out of that trap?"

French gasped at having him shout at her from a distance of six inches. She'd never had a man shout at her before. It certainly had a tarnishing effect on his armor!

He gave her a little shake, which moved him a little lower in her esteem, and demanded, "Did you?" Another shake as she held her silence. "Answer me," he roared. "Did you?"

She sniffed and said primly, "Of course I did. There was no one else to do it." She looked directly at him and fought back new tears that threatened to humiliate her. Firmly she told him, "If I had come back down the mountain for help, it would have been too late. The poor dog would have chewed off its paw."

She blinked again and again until all the tears were gone and she could begin to put Mr. Kyle Devereaux in his place. "Besides, as I've already informed you, I didn't have a horse. Middy had run away." She waited for him to acknowledge her logic. As she waited, she lifted her chin defiantly.

But Kyle Devereaux didn't seem to know he even had a place in which to be put. Nor was he in any way mollified by her logic. French, unable to read the expression in his eyes, began to feel a little apprehensive.

Kyle's thoughts were running riot. Never in his life had he had so many emotions bashing about in his mind. She was so brave to help an animal caught in a trap. Even a domesticated dog would be half-wild with pain and likely to savage her as she tried to help it. His heart skipped and thudded with relief that she had come through the incident safely. She was so stupid, rage rose in him at the thought, to risk herself so. How could anybody as lovely and intelligent as French Richards behave as if she were dumb as dirt?

And just look at her right now. She was so appealing and innocently desirable. How the devil could she sit there all but in his lap and thrust her little chin out at him as if it were a weapon with which she would defeat him? Dammit! Didn't she know how she offered her mouth to him by doing that?

His head spun and his heart thundered like the hoofbeats of her runaway mare. What the blazes was he expected to do with her? At this rate, she was truly going to drive him out of his *formerly* well-ordered mind!

Finally, he did what he had always done in a situation he couldn't get a grip on. He did nothing. They rode back to the ranch without another word.

Every now and again, French would sniff or murmur "hmmmpf," but he pretended not to notice. If he could only get her home without shaking her head off for taking such a chance or . . . He'd just turn her over to Julia to take care of before he kissed the fool out of her and created a situation in which they'd all be damned uncomfortable.

Once he got her safely home, he'd have a serious talk with Charlie about her safety. Something had to be done to keep the little idiot safe from herself until she learned that this wasn't Boston.

Whatever else had happened to Henry French Richards today, Kyle Devereaux wasn't going to add to her burden by telling her the truth. He was just going to offer up fervent prayers of thanksgiving for her safe escape. That ought to please a deity that seldom heard from him. Maybe it would even go a long way toward keeping her safe in the future. God knew he hoped so.

What he wasn't going to do, however, was to inform the precious, incredibly brave, beautiful woman in his arms that there were no sled dogs in this part of the country. He shuddered as his mind shied away from forming his next thought. There was no way he could avoid it, though. Clearly and simply there was only one explanation for what had happened in the woods today. God in his mercy had protected her, for the animal French Richards had described to him could only have been a wolf.

Chapter Thirteen

FRENCH AWOKE SUNDAY morning feeling a little stiff and sore from her adventure the day before. She'd managed to survive the guilt she'd experienced at all the fussing and coddling that Aunt Julia and Uncle Charles had done when she came up to the house last evening riding double with Kyle, resting against his chest, with her own mount quietly trailing behind. Her aunt and uncle had been truly concerned, and her heart warmed as she let herself remember.

She owed Kyle Devereaux her heartfelt thanks for having stopped and washed her hands before they reached the house. She'd felt really awful to have caused her aunt and uncle so much concern, and it would have been even worse if she'd come back to the ranch with her hands stained with blood. Heaven only knew how upset Julia would have been then.

Kyle had washed it all off, though. French still thrilled at the memory of the way Kyle had washed her hands in his own as if she were a helpless child. She could almost feel again his long-fingered hands, callused and strong and hard, gently rinsing the dog's blood from her own soft skin in the stream that ran beside the road to the ranch.

She sighed, then went over and looked at herself

critically in the mirror. Her fears were confirmed. Her gray eyes were misty with the memory. She was enjoying letting herself be too much affected by Mr. Kyle Devereaux.

She admonished herself to gather her wits and behave sensibly. "He'll be here soon," she told herself softly. She hoped she could make it through Sunday dinner today without melting away into silly, moonstruck feminity-at-its-worst this time.

A smile flitted across her lips. But, oh, that first Sunday had been truly magical. She sighed to remember the effect Kyle Devereaux had had on her. She'd truly never expected to feel that way about any man . . . *she had only hoped.*

Not that she still felt quite the way she first had about Kyle Devereaux, of course. She'd merely been mistaken about him then, when she'd tailored him to fit her girlish fantasies.

Kyle wasn't anything special to her, after all. She'd just been momentarily carried away by his masterful manner and his devastating good looks. Now that she knew him better, she could see the chinks in his armor.

"That's all behind you now, French Richards," she scolded her reflection. "You just keep that in mind."

And it was all behind her. Really it was. Since that day, that lovely, dreamlike first Sunday on the Lightning Double C, she'd learned how interfering and high-handed Mr. Devereaux could be.

It was absolutely infuriating to recall the way he'd sauntered into her classroom and judged her incapable of controlling the children without help from him. She still smarted under the humiliation of it. Even if his interference *had* gotten things into order a little more quickly than they might have been without his putting his nose into her business, it was still not his place to have done so. It had been very wrong of him. *So why did she keep thinking of him in terms that depicted him as a knight right out of a fairy tale?*

Stifling that idea, and holding firm to the thought that he had, after all, been interfering, she went downstairs. By remembering how aggravating the man could be, she excused herself for misleading him on the way down the mountain.

He was such a very unpredictable man. Soothing one moment and scolding the next. Yesterday, he'd held her so gently, and his soothing and kindness had been so very comforting, his behavior had caused her to put him back on the pedestal of her girlhood fantasies. Hard on the heels of that inclination, however, came the belated memory that he'd also practically ranted at her. Evidently, she was finding, women must guard their hearts against the tendency of their minds to indulge in selective remembrance.

It was a very good thing she didn't intend to put her particular mind to the task of understanding him, she told herself. She was here to teach children, after all, not to try to fathom a man like Kyle Devereaux.

Besides, she didn't have time to. She had to get busy finding out what had happened to her Uncle Jacob. Time was of the essence. The crispness of the last few mornings clearly proclaimed that winter was about to sweep away the last pleasant days of the Indian summer they'd been having, and she knew from all her aunt and uncle had told her that exploring the woods and mountains would be impossible once the snow fell. She would have to make a plan and hurry to get it in motion.

Julia looked up as she entered the family parlor. "Why, French, you're frowning, dear. Is something the matter?"

"Wha . . . ? Oh, no. I was just thinking that I'd like a map of the area, that's all." She kissed her aunt's cheek. "I was just having a serious discussion with myself about trying to find Uncle Jacob."

"Oh, dear. I doubt that there is a map. Unless Kyle has made one for his logging . . ."

Hoofbeats sounded on the road in from town, and both women turned to look out the tall windows beside the front door. *Speak of the devil,* French thought.

Julia said unnecessarily, "It's Kyle." She drew French back from the window. "Well now, it won't do to have him catch us hanging out the windows waiting for him, then, will it?"

Holding French's hand, she walked quickly into the more formal visitors' parlor. "Here, come and see these old daguerreotypes. I've been meaning to show them to you. Your mother gave them to me when I left Boston to come west."

She led French to a glass-fronted cabinet that held Julia's collection of family memorabilia. "These are various items that belonged to members of the family. I've collected them whenever your mother decided to clean her curio cabinets to add more recent acquisitions."

"Mother does have a habit of discarding any and every thing to make way for something new." French forbore saying "whether or not it has sentimental value." Aunt Julia knew that without her saying something critical about her own mother. Her mind was half on listening to the hoofbeats nearing the house.

Julia nodded. "Yes. Well, since your mother gave me these"—she reached for the tooled leather cases that held the pictures—"before you were born, I'm sure you've never seen them. They're of your Grandmother and Grandfather Price and several cousins."

French found herself interested in spite of Kyle Devereaux's imminent arrival. "Oh, how handsome he was." She held the daguerreotype of her grandfather, staring down at it an instant longer before reaching eagerly for the one of her grandmother. "Why, she's absolutely beautiful." Her interest was completely caught now by her first sight of her grandparents' faces. She didn't even notice Kyle riding up to the house.

Julia smiled at her indulgently. "Yes, she was. Everybody who ever saw her said so." She watched her niece's face a moment, basking in the girl's obvious enjoyment.

Charlie interrupted them. "Hey. Are you two gonna hole up here in the fancy parlor and leave me to entertain our company all by my lonesome? Come on, Kyle's here."

Julia smiled and led the way out of the best parlor. With her first glimpse of Kyle, she began congratulating herself. Her little diversion had been successful. French hadn't been caught waiting for Kyle like a baby bird for a worm. The eager anticipation for their meeting was just where she wanted it to be. Thanks to her having French out of the way on his arrival, it was on the face of her favorite bachelor.

Just then Jamie Waring thundered across the porch and erupted through the front door. Seeing Kyle Devereaux's tall figure in the foyer, he skidded to a halt and blurted, "Oh, golly, you're here. I forgot."

It was Julia's turn to frown. "Jamie. That sounded a little impolite."

Jamie gulped. He was well aware his words had sounded a lot more than just a little impolite, but it was like his worshiped Julia to take him to task gently. He looked up into ole Devil-Oh's face. It was full of amused tolerance. Jamie felt his own cheeks begin to burn.

"Sorry, Mr. Devereaux." He dug a toe into the rich Persian carpet that covered the floor of the foyer. Apology was a skill he'd been well drilled in all his young life. "I apologize for my unforgivable lack of manners."

Kyle's brows snapped down.

Julia wondered if this day was destined to be full of frowns and said, "What is it, Jamie? You look as if you were about to explode."

"Nothing, Miz Julia." He shot a glance at Devereaux.

Kyle saw the boy had news—news that he evidently considered important, but that he thought wasn't for feminine ears. He narrowed his eyes at the child to show he understood the gravity of the situation and said, "Would you mind taking Daumier down to the barn for me?"

Jamie hesitated only a second before he nodded and ran out to the big gelding at the hitching rack.

Kyle smiled. "Nice boy." He added casually, "Maybe I'd better go help him. Will you excuse me for a few minutes?" He bowed and followed Jamie out the door.

Julia looked at Charles, but he just shrugged and put an arm around each woman and started for the dining room. "Good. Now I have my two girls to myself. Let's go tie on the feed bag."

Julia gave her husband a mildly reproachful look. "Indeed," her tone was dry, "by all means let us go and tie on our feed bags. Kyle and Jamie will just have to come to the trough when they get here."

Charlie had the good grace to refrain from further comment, but he couldn't resist rolling his eyes at French. French laughed, and Julia said, "Don't encourage him, dear. He's bad enough already."

*   *   *

Outside, as they walked to the barn, Kyle questioned Jamie. "All right, Jamie. What's up?"

The boy's voice was troubled. "There's a gang of men in the woods. Looks like they followed you from town, Mr. Devereaux."

"How many?"

"I counted six."

Kyle cursed softly under his breath. Six were about twice as many as he felt like taking on bare-handed. He called himself all kinds of a fool for leaving his six-gun at home. He'd never worn it to Sunday dinner out of respect for Julia's abhorrence of firearms. Now it looked as if he was about to be paying the price.

Jamie's eyes glowed with admiration of his uncle's ability to cuss. No wonder people called him Devil-Oh sometimes, just like the sprawling lumber interests Kyle Devereaux owned. The man could sure swear! None of the cabbies who'd befriended him could cuss like that, not half that good. "Whadya think those men want, Mr. Devereaux?" He led Devil-Oh's horse into the stall prepared for him, and began loosening his cinch. His uncle lifted the heavy saddle off when Jamie got it undone, and took it out to the saddle rack built beside the stall door.

Jamie couldn't stop worrying that the group of toughs he'd spotted in the woods had come to do mischief that might upset Miz Julia or Miss French. He couldn't allow that to happen.

Kyle weighed the situation carefully. It looked to him as if the men in the woods had followed him out here to get at him when he was away from his own men. It was a good strategy on their part. God knew he'd have less than a poor chance against six thugs.

The idea of taking a beating sure as hell didn't appeal to him, but he didn't know this boy well enough to tell him that was probably their intent. He couldn't judge which way Jamie'd jump if he knew the hidden men were probably sent by the railroad to "persuade" Kyle to see things their way.

If he told him so, how did he know the boy wouldn't go to Charlie for help for him? He didn't want any of Charlie's men hurt because he was having a difference of opinion with the railroad's Kendal Abernathy and his hired muscle.

"Jamie," he addressed the child gravely as he unbridled Daumier, taking care not to let the bit strike the gelding's teeth. "I don't think those men pose a problem for anyone here on the Double Lightning C." He knew he'd hit the nail on the head with his remark when the boy relaxed visibly. Now if he could just keep everybody on the ranch safely out of it. "I think those men are just trying to get me alone to see if they can get me to reconsider selling them some railroad ties." He slipped Daumier's bridle onto a hook over the saddle rack. "Don't worry about it."

"But what if they hurt you?"

Kyle's smile was wintry. He'd no doubt that was exactly what they had in mind, but it wouldn't do to let the boy know it.

He clapped a hand on the boy's shoulder as they left the hay-scented barn. With a lightness he was far from feeling, he told him, "Well, now, son, for that they'd have to catch me first, wouldn't they?"

Wide-eyed, Jamie didn't answer. He was quiet the rest of the way to the house.

Sunday dinner was as excellent as always, and everyone settled down to enjoy the meal. "I shall miss this next Sunday," Julia announced as dessert was being served.

French looked up, surprised.

"Oh, yeah." Charlie put his fork on the rim of his plate, his elbows on the table, and turned to Kyle. "You're going to the Millers' barbecue, aren't you, Kyle?"

Kyle grinned. "If you all are going, I wouldn't miss it." The look he gave French brought quick color to her cheeks.

"Good," Charlie announced, taking up his fork again. "I'd hate to have to ask Miss Mary to pack you a lunch."

"Charles!" Julia was scandalized at her husband's inference that Kyle expected them to feed him every Sunday, whether they were home or not.

Charlie just grinned at her. "My turn to have an unforgivable lack of manners?"

"So it would seem." Julia's expression was stern, but her eyes danced.

"Kyle don't mind."

"No," Kyle said musingly, "I don't mind in the least." His mind wasn't on the words he was speaking, however, his mind was turning over the phrase Charlie had just borrowed from Jamie. His gaze moved to the boy sitting quietly across the table and rested there speculatively.

Jamie squirmed under his regard.

Strange that the child had used that particular phrase. Kyle had thought himself the only person to have been forced to say he'd been guilty of an unforgivable *lack* of manners. The standard phrase was "breach of manners," for a breach can always be healed. A lack of manners humiliated the person guilty of having it.

The boy's words, innocently repeated by his best friend, brought unwelcome memories of Kyle's childhood flooding back. He was silent for the rest of the meal.

Chapter Fourteen

KYLE LINGERED UNTIL it was almost dark. It was easy to linger, too damned easy. Julia was so enthused to have four people to enjoy an afternoon of the new card game, bridge, that she failed to notice he was unusually somber.

For his part, Kyle, Jamie's warning heavy in his spirit, used the time to fix in his memory the face of each person at the table with him, French's in particular. He loved the soft look about her as she concentrated on the game, the smiles when she won a hand by book and bid. If he didn't make it safely back to town, he'd at least have this pleasant memory of her as one of his last.

They all walked him to the door. Julia asked, "We'll see you at the barbecue next Sunday, won't we?" She was standing in the circle of Charlie's arm, her head leaning against his shoulder.

Kyle smiled a noncommittal smile and picked up his hat. He reached far back into his past for a phrase he'd heard his mother's coachman use. "God willing and the creek don't rise." He knew that whether or not he saw Julia again would depend on what Abernathy had in mind . . . and how successful he was at getting away from it.

He turned his attention to French. She was smiling gently with the aftermath of pleasure from the easy afternoon of games and talk. He extended his hand, and held his breath, suddenly afraid she wouldn't take it, that he might be denied her touch for what might be the last time.

She put her hand in his, and he held it far too long, reluctant to give up the contact. It brought back with startling clarity how fragile her hands had seemed to him yesterday when he'd washed them in the stream beside the ranch road.

Other memories rushed in. The softness of her as she'd leaned against his chest as they rode down the mountain. The trusting way she'd let him bring her back to the ranch, knowing he'd keep her safe. Her bravery with the wolf. Her tears. Each memory was as sharp as if he relived them at the touch of her hand. And, because he knew there was a chance he'd never add another to those cherished memories, they cut like a knife, each one an exquisite pain, each one tearing at him . . . at his heart, if he'd let himself admit it.

"Hey, Kyle. You gonna take French's hand with you?"

He turned to smile lopsidedly at Charlie. "No. I might like to, but I guess I won't." His smile became more intimate than he intended as he looked back at French. "Good night, Miss Richards." The moment lengthened. He was lost in her smile, she in his tender regard.

He tore his gaze from her with an effort and said briskly, "Good night, Julia, Charles. Thank you for a most pleasant afternoon."

Ignoring Charlie's knowing chuckle, he swung away from them and started for the barn with long, determined strides. As he went, he shut them each and all firmly from his mind. If he was ever going to see them again, he'd better get his wits focused on making it past Abernathy and his thugs.

The moon was rising. He weighed the difference that would make, and frowned. While it would make it simpler to race Daumier home, it would also make it a helluva lot easier for his adversaries to see him.

His back suddenly felt sensitive, as if it anticipated a bullet or two. He shrugged off the feeling. No need to borrow trouble. Unless he missed his guess, this first ambush was just to beat the hell out of him to try to soften him up for negotiations.

The barn was dark, but he knew from long experience where to find Daumier and his tack. He grabbed the saddle and bridle and went into the stall. He had the big gelding tacked up in no time. "Come on, boy." He took a deep steadying breath. The smell of warm animals and fresh hay filled his nostrils. Funny, he'd not noticed how good a barn smelled since he was a kid.

Daumier nickered and shoved at him with his head. Kyle smoothed the satiny neck for what might be the last time, and led the horse out of the stall.

That was when he heard the noise! Whirling to face it, he slapped his right hand to the spot on his thigh where he was accustomed to wear his gun. He cursed when he didn't find it.

"It's me!" Jamie Waring's panicky voice was loud in the quiet barn. "It's only me, Mr. Devereaux."

"Jamie." Kyle uncoiled from his crouch. "What are you doing out here?"

"Waiting for you, sir."

Kyle was silent. He waited for the boy to go on.

"I snuck up to the woods a while back, and those men are still out there. I think they mean to make trouble for you, Mr. Devereaux."

Kyle smiled.

In the moonlight that was just stealing into the barn, Jamie saw the smile. It wasn't reassuring.

"So you think they're waiting for me, do you?"

"Yes, sir."

Kyle relented. It wasn't the boy's fault he was in a tight spot. He reached out and tousled the boy's hair. "Go on up to the house and forget about it, Jamie. There's nothing you can do."

He refused to insult the boy by scolding him for risking himself on an adult's behalf. The boy was here, back from the woods safely, it was enough.

"We could ask Mr. Chambers to give you some men to escort you safely back to town."

Kyle's smile became genuine to hear the boy include himself in his problem. He had to admire his spunk. He also had to straighten him out. "Thanks, lad. On first consideration, that sounds like a great idea." He softened his voice to take any sting from his next words. "Don't you think, though, that if we involved any of the men from the ranch in this that those men up there in the woods might take it as a signal to make trouble for the Chamberses?"

"Oh, golly." Jamie was crestfallen. "That would be awful. I hadn't thought of that."

Kyle let him think about it as he swung up into the saddle. "Thanks for your concern, Jamie." He looked at the boy levelly. Weighting each word so the boy wouldn't think he was just politely dismissing him, he said, "I appreciate it." He started to ride out of the barn.

Jamie caught Daumier's reins just below the bit and hauled the horse to a halt. "Wait! Wait. I got an idea." Daumier snorted his disapproval of the boy's pull on his sensitive mouth and snatched his head away.

Kyle frowned down at Jamie. He didn't want to hurt

him, but right now, with his nerves stretched tight as fiddle strings, he didn't have the patience to play games with a half-grown boy, no matter how much he admired his grit.

Jamie saw his expression and read it right. Desperately he blurted, "No, really. I have an idea that may help."

Kyle sighed and leaned an arm on his saddle horn. "All right, lad." Dammit, he was probably about to get himself half-killed, courtesy of the railroad, and here he was taking time to be careful of this child's feelings. What the hell ailed him? If he survived the night, tomorrow he'd turn himself in to some lunatic asylum.

Jamie's earnest eyes shone. "Really, sir. I have a plan."

"There's no way I'm going to let you take any risks out there tonight, Jamie. Forget it." He lifted his bridle hand and Daumier moved forward a step.

Jamie's face fell. Then a guarded expression replaced the disappointment. "Please. Listen."

Kyle drew rein and sat waiting.

"I know a way to short cut through the woods. There's a gate at the end of the big pasture that'll let you out near a trail. It leads back to the road in about a half a mile."

Kyle was all attention.

"All you do is let yourself out the gate down there in the far corner of the pasture, and enter the woods by that huge boulder that has the pine tree growing out of it."

Kyle looked at him a long minute, aware that he'd actually hoped the boy could help him. It wouldn't do to put the boy down, so he just told him, "That's a long way in the open in this moonlight, Jamie, but thanks."

"No." The boy's voice shook with urgency. "I have a plan."

Kyle started Daumier toward the yawning doorway of the barn. He didn't have any more time to spare the boy.

"Wait!" Jamie sounded desperate. "Look, I'll let the horses out into the pasture to night graze like they do when it's been a scorcher of a day. You can hang off the side of your horse and get to that gate without anybody seeing you."

Kyle drew rein, turned in his saddle, and looked at him. Jamie's eyes burned with the conviction that he could get Kyle away safely. "Please. Let me set the horses free. Try it. Just try it, Unc . . . Mr. Devereaux. Please."

Kyle grinned at him. Then he laughed out loud. "You bet I will, Button. You may just have come up with a way to save my hide."

Jamie gave a breathless, whispered whoop of relief and ran back through the barn opening stall doors and shooing horses out. All but one. One horse neighed and stomped at being left behind in his stall.

Those the boy freed swirled past Kyle and a hard-held, dancing Daumier who was eager to join them as they trotted out into the pasture. When there was a big enough group headed away from the barn, Kyle slipped off the right side of his horse. He clung there and sent his big gelding into the middle of the bunch headed for the far end of the pasture. The herd was galloping now, snorting and shoving as they went.

When the horses, bucking and kicking with the joy of unexpected freedom, circled back toward the barn again, Kyle opened the gate and led Daumier through it. Nothing moved at the edge of the woods where Jamie had indicated the men were hiding. He'd made it. Thanks to Jamie Waring, he'd made it to the woods.

Now all he had to do was to get through them to the point where the faint trail he was following intercepted the road to town. With Daumier's gift for covering ground, he should be home free.

Suddenly he heard a stir in the woods off to his left, then noisy movement. "There he is!" The cry came to him clearly, but who the hell was it about? The moon was behind a heavy rack of clouds. It was as near to pitch-black where he and Daumier were as he'd like it to get. There was no way anybody could have spotted him here in the darkness of the deep woods.

Suddenly his heart jolted with fear. Jamie! Pulling Daumier off the trail, he crashed through the woods toward the cry. Jamie! What had the boy done to draw Abernathy and his men away from him? Was the child out of his mind? These men weren't the kind of men you played games with!

In the heavy darkness of the forest, Daumier stumbled and almost went down. Still Kyle pushed him onward at a pace no sane man would dare. "Damn you, Jamie," he heard himself shout, "if you get yourself hurt, I'll kill you."

He arrived at the place the men had been lying in wait to ambush him. Reining up, he let his sense of caution take over. He had to see what was going on before he dashed out into the open, or he'd be no use to anybody.

There on the road near the ranch house, a big horse walked. The moon came out from behind the clouds. The horse on the ranch road was a big chestnut with markings very like Daumier's. Jamie sat, straight as an arrow, on its back.

Kyle remembered then that Jamie had released all the horses but one. This one. The little fool had planned all along to act as a decoy to facilitate his escape. Blast! What if they got to the boy and took out their frustration at finding he was not Kyle Devereaux on the child? There was no way he was going to let that happen.

"Hey!" His shout reverberated off the surrounding hills. "Abernathy! You looking for somebody?"

The railroad men took an instant to understand what was happening. They milled around, unable to decide whether to go punish the decoy or pursue their quarry.

Jamie decided the matter for them. He spun the big horse he was riding on its haunches and lit out for the bunkhouse.

The railroad men turned then as a single force and charged back down the ranch road toward Kyle, spurring and whipping their mounts mercilessly in an effort to eliminate the head start the brave boy had risked himself to give their prey.

"Not very likely, you skunks," Kyle muttered through clenched teeth. Pausing only long enough to make sure the boy was safely away, he sent Daumier flying, willing him to show a clean pair of heels to the men after his blood.

Daumier flung himself down the trail out of the woods to the road. Great gouts of soft earth flew from his hooves until he was on the firmer surface of the road. There he increased his speed, his hoofbeats thundering a tattoo as he lengthened the lead he had on the men in cursing pursuit.

As he rode, flattened close to his horse's neck, Kyle tried to decide what he'd do to Jamie Waring the next time he got his hands on the boy. Would he thank him like a gentleman for possibly saving his life? Shake the brat until his hair fell out for taking such a harebrained chance? Or would he wring the intrepid child's neck for the jagged hole he'd just torn in the defensive fabric of

Kyle Devereaux's hard-won calm by putting himself at risk?

By the time he reached the safety of town, he still hadn't made up his mind.

Chapter Fifteen

KYLE OPENED THE telegram from Rafferty with an impatient slash of the antique dirk he used to open letters. Maybe the mystery of what had happened to his misplaced nephew was about to be solved. God knew he'd like at least one problem solved, and as this one concerned a boy who must be lost and alone somewhere, it was first on his list.

> *Mr. Devereaux,*
> *Have appointment to see your mother tomorrow. She will only see me if I bring her five hundred dollars. Please wire your instructions.*
>
> *Rafferty*

He crumpled the telegram in a savage fist. Blast her! She knew damn well what information he'd sent Rafferty to get. That it was information she hadn't immediately sent him herself was bad enough. That she was extorting money from Rafferty before she gave it went beyond even his remembrance of her callous greed. The lost boy was her own grandson!

He stood there a minute, letting the waves of anger and outrage . . . and pain . . . flow over him. Then he

138

stormed from the office to go arrange to get the money to Rafferty.

French locked the door to the schoolhouse and told Jamie, "I'd like to stop by the sawmill to see if they have a map of this area." She looked up at the sky. "I think we'll be able to do that and still get home before dark, don't you?"

Jamie followed her example and scrutinized the sky. "I guess so." He grinned at her. "But even if we don't, we'll get far enough down the road so Midnight will be able to take us the rest of the way with her eyes closed." He took a deep breath, then another. "I don't smell any rain."

French suppressed a smile. She wondered if Jamie really could smell rain on the way.

"I'll bring the gig around." He bounded down the steps, her books and papers clutched tightly under his arm, and headed off to the shelter for the mare. By the time French had checked the schoolyard for forgotten sweaters or toys, tossed an abandoned ball into the box that she kept on the porch for just such things, and made her leisurely way to the schoolyard gate, he was drawing the mare to a halt with a flourish.

A few minutes later they were at the sawmill. French left Jamie with the mare and hurried up the slight incline to the office. She was eager to have a map on which to plot the areas she intended to search. If she went about it systematically, she was sure she'd be able to find some clue as to what had happened to her Uncle Jacob. She just had to!

Knocking firmly, she opened the door and walked in. Kyle Devereaux sat at a large table with an equally large rolltop desk behind it. His dark head was bent over his work, his face quiet, his expression intent.

French leaned back against the door as her knees went a little weak. He didn't have his coat on. In his shirtsleeves with his throat exposed, he presented a very different picture from that of the man who was so properly dressed when he came to her Aunt Julia's.

His bare forearms were well muscled, and the muscles were clearly defined. His arms were not smooth as her brothers' were. Looking at them caused her to feel as if she were invading his privacy.

She wondered why she didn't look away, and realized it was because she didn't want to. The realization startled her a little, but she smiled and told herself that it was all right for a modern woman to enjoy the sight of a man. Heaven knew enough men stared at women in obvious enjoyment.

Her thoughts made her feel rather naughty, and suddenly, just watching him perform the simple everyday act of writing on an invoice became, somehow, too intimate for her comfort. It must be because she'd never seen the bare arms of a man with whom she'd socialized before, only those of workmen.

He scowled without looking up, annoyed that one of his men would stand there dumb. "Well, what is it?"

French drew a quivering breath and announced, "It is I, Mr. Devereaux."

His head snapped up. "French." He looked as if he were seeing a vision. Then he caught himself. "I mean, Miss Richards." He rose and stood staring at her.

Kyle felt as if he'd conjured her up by the way he'd held her at the edge of his mind ever since he'd returned from his bank, a talisman to save him from the bitter thoughts his mother's behavior had engendered. Finally he managed a smile. She was here and real, not the product of his imagination.

He moved around the desk. By the time he had reached her he was himself again. "To what do I owe the honor of this visit?"

French sank gratefully into the chair he offered. She watched as he rolled his sleeves down and closed the collar of his shirt.

She was careful to keep her voice casual. "I've come to see if you have a map of the area that I might borrow for a few days, Mr. Devereaux."

He went to the rolltop desk, opened it, and pulled out a paper rolled into a long tube. She was acutely aware of the lithe grace of his movements. Maybe it would have been a good idea to have had Jamie come in with her. Why couldn't she ever breathe properly when she was near this man?

In her mind she chided, *Honestly, Henry French Richards, you are just being ridiculous!* Aloud she said, "I'm so glad to find that there is a map. Aunt Julia wasn't sure there'd be one. Are you certain you won't mind me borrowing it for a few days?"

He came close and bent down to give the map into her hand, but he didn't let it go. One hand held out the map, but his other hand caught and cradled hers when she took hold of it as if he wanted to be sure she had it before he let go. Still he didn't let go. He kept her hand in his and studied her features as intently as might an artist planning her portrait.

When he spoke his voice was deep and oddly caressing. "Please, keep it, Miss Richards. I have no further use for it."

French closed her eyes and wondered if she were about to make a fool of herself. Fortunately Kyle Devereaux let go of her hand and moved back around the table that served him as a desk.

Immediately breathing became easier for her.

"Tell me, what are you going to do with it?"

She realized that she wasn't exactly sure she wanted to explain her purpose for the map to him. She vividly remembered his earlier objection to her looking for her uncle.

He had, however, given her the map, and she felt as if she owned him an answer to his question. "I want the map so that I may sensibly mark off areas to search." She left it at that, hoping he would, knowing he wouldn't.

"Search?" He looked puzzled. "For wha . . . Oh, no. Don't tell me you still intend to go looking for old Jake Price!"

"Mr. Devereaux, my Uncle Jacob is very dear to me." Out of courtesy, she tried not to look disapproving of his calling her uncle "old Jake." "I feel that he is somewhere out there." She swept her arm in a wide gesture that included most of Colorado. "If he is injured or lost, then there is very little time left to find him before winter sets in."

Kyle looked into her wide gray eyes. They were full of serious concern for her uncle and reproach for the man across from her for not understanding her urgency. It took only the one look. He was lost. In his mind he called himself all kinds of a fool, but he said, "Miss Richards, I'll be happy to aid you in your search anytime you ask it of me."

"Oh." She was really surprised. He was so obviously a very busy man. How kind his offer was! "Thank you. Thank you very much." The reproach faded from her lovely gray eyes.

His own blue ones became somber. "But you have to understand," he warned her, "that no one has any idea where your uncle's mine is located. Jake, er, Jacob Price came to town from what seemed to all of us a new direction each time he appeared. No one will be able to give you the vaguest notion of where to begin your search."

She sat quietly awhile, as if she were coming to grips with that. Then she lifted her chin at him as she had last Saturday when he'd been bringing her home. He almost groaned. Didn't the woman have any idea what she did to him? Obviously not.

"Mr. Devereaux. If there were somebody you loved who was missing, wouldn't you use every resource at your disposal?"

"Well, yes, of course." Evidently Julia and Charlie hadn't told her he was doing just that, looking for his nephew. He appreciated their keeping silent about his family business. "But I'm a man, Miss Richards."

French hardly needed reminding, no woman with eyes in her head would. Exasperated, she looked at him hard. She looked at his face that said as plainly as words could have, "Of course *I* would undertake the task, I'm the male of the species, and as such am equipped to accomplish things. *You*," his smug expression as good as said, "are only a woman."

She could feel anger rising in her. It wasn't just because of Kyle; it was all the anger she had suppressed on countless previous occasions when encountering just this sort of superior male attitude in the past. With heat she announced, "Jacob Price is *my* uncle, Mr. Devereaux." She rose from the chair as she spoke, never looking away from him, her eyes blazing. "I shall search for him at my every opportunity. If you would like to help me, you are welcome to do so"—she raised and pointed a finger right at his face—"but let me assure you"—she began shaking it at him in time with her words—"Mr. Kyle Devereaux, neither your nor anyone else is going to deter me from my purpose."

Clutching the map, she ran out of his office. The door slammed behind her.

Kyle raked the fingers of his right hand through his hair and stared at the door through which the impetuous Henry French Richards had just disappeared. "Now what in the devil brought that on?" He stared, bewildered, at the inoffensive surface of the door. "What the blazes got into her?

"And what the devil's got into you, Kyle Devereaux? Damned if you really want to try to tie up with French Richards and have her tell you she wishes you at the other end of the earth."

That was certainly the truth. Marry her he might want to, but ask her he didn't dare. He'd endured enough rejection from his mother to last him a lifetime. He didn't feel the need to collect any more bruises on his spirit.

So why did she have to attract him so? Why in blazes couldn't he get her out of his mind? Did he have to be haunted by visions of wide gray eyes and soft lips, and the memory of how wonderful and right she had felt in his arms? Did that memory have to taunt him every night while he tossed and turned seeking sleep?

Blast it all! Didn't he have enough on his mind fighting off the railroad and trying to find out what happened to his nephew without her invading his mind during all hours of the night or day? He slammed his fists down on the desk and groaned aloud. Finally he snarled in savage frustration, "And what in tarnation kind of name is Henry for a girl?"

He sank his head into his hands. There was nothing he could do to help himself. Just being near her made him want to lay down his life for her. It cut him to shreds that he couldn't claim all her time, that he couldn't keep her safe by his side where he could guard her every minute.

It was impossible. The whole damned thing was impossible.

Even if he was fool enough to want to try to marry her, and if by some miracle she accepted him, he wouldn't be able to go through with it. He was afraid. He cringed to admit it. Cowardice had always been in short supply for him. Yet here he was a coward, deathly afraid of what kind of husband he'd make. He had a bad feeling that, with his distrust of women, he might become some sort of jealous monster. He'd seen enough of such men to want to avoid the risk of being one himself.

Hell, even now, the mere thought of somebody else paying attention to French Richards nearly sent him up a tree. He could hardly pry his hands off her once he'd found an excuse to touch her, and he knew he'd want to kill anyone else who let his hands linger on hers.

After a long moment, he took a deep breath and let out a sigh that ruffled the edges of the papers he'd been working on. Then he shook his head and went back to them.

Outside, French flounced up into the gig and seated herself with a plop. Midnight snorted and moved restlessly between the shafts in protest.

Jamie looked at her, startled. "What's the matter, Miss Richards?"

"Nothing. Nothing at all," she said in a choked voice. "Just take me home."

Jamie watched her sideways out of the corner of his eye. She was certainly riled about something. His protective instincts rose in him. Had Kyle Devereaux done something to upset her? There was no way he could ask her, of course, but he'd be sure to keep a better eye on her when old Devil-Oh was around, uncle or no uncle.

One thing was for sure, he had no intention of letting his wonderful Miss Richards be upset. Not by any man. Even one as brave as Kyle Devereaux.

Chapter Sixteen

IT WAS SATURDAY at last! French had spent every spare minute she could find all week dividing the map Kyle had given her into sections that represented as much territory as she felt she could cover in a day. She knew it was all subject to change after she got out there and saw what the terrain was actually like, but at least she had lightly penciled in enough to give her a start.

She dressed quietly and tiptoed down the stairs, her boots in her hand. It was still well before dawn, and she hoped to raid the kitchen before Miss Mary got up.

"Drat." At the end of the long hall that kept the kitchen a safe distance from the main part of the house, she saw the light under the kitchen door and stopped dead in her tracks. She was too late to slip away unnoticed with a lunch.

She pulled on her boots and pushed open the door. "Good morning, Miss Mary."

Miss Mary turned and regarded her with surprise. "What in the world are you doing up so early, child?"

French smiled and said meekly, "I came to sneak a picnic, but now that I smell your cooking, if it isn't too much trouble, I should love one of your wonderful breakfasts . . . and some of that delicious coffee." She took a deep breath and sighed. "You make wonderful coffee, Miss Mary."

"I'm so glad you like it. I'm always afraid it's too strong for ladies, brewed as it is for the cowhands. You take it with cream and sugar like your aunt, though, so I suppose that saves you." She lifted the huge pot, swung it to the table, and looked up at French. "Do you mind one of these heavy, ugly cups?"

"Not at all."

Miss Mary put the crockery mug full of steaming coffee into French's hands and held on for an instant, as if she were making sure the girl's dainty hand could hold the man-sized cup. The gesture brought to French's mind the way Kyle Devereaux had been reluctant to let go of her hand when he'd given her the map earlier in the week. Somehow, as she stood there burying her smile in her cup, she didn't think Kyle had done it because he was afraid she'd drop it, though. Miss Mary was reputed to be fanatical about her clean kitchen floor.

As French waited, the large, handsome woman slammed plates around the table almost as though she were dealing them out like cards, then checked in the cavernous oven of the big black iron wood stove to see if her biscuits were done. In another minute she put a plate full of scrambled eggs, crisp curls of bacon, and two fluffy butter-drenched biscuits on the long table. "Miss French, come eat." She gestured to the chair she was holding out for French.

"Thank you." French knew that she should feel guilty for interrupting the cook at what must be the most hectic time of her day, but she was too hungry to let manners influence her appetite. Picking up her fork, she dug in.

Miss Mary paused to smile at her with satisfaction. After a moment, curiosity replaced the appreciation and her eyes narrowed in speculation. "Why *are* you up so early, Miss Richards?"

French swallowed her mouthful of biscuit. "I'm going out to look for my uncle, Miss Mary. Winter is coming and no one knows where he is or whether he's all right. And please call me French."

Mary Wells nodded absently to signify she would be glad to, but her mind was elsewhere. She blinked rapidly for a moment, seemed to consider her next words, and then spoke them very carefully. "Mr. Chambers, you know, sent all the hands looking for your uncle when he didn't show up for their regular poker game last month."

The housekeeper was watching her intently, and French wondered if she were sorry to tell her what she thought was bad news, or if there were something more to her words, something more she wanted to tell her. "How long ago was that?" French wished her voice hadn't choked up, she didn't want to give the impression that she was too emotional to institute a proper search.

Miss Mary's face softened. "Last month." Her own voice was a little husky. "About the middle of last month."

"Oh." It was all French could manage. She felt so foolish. Of course Uncle Charles would have searched. He'd no more have left it to the sheriff than she was willing to. She knew intuitively that he'd just never told her because it was such a painful subject for them all.

Now she had to face facts, though. What chance did she have if all the men of the Lightning Double C hadn't found her uncle? They were used to the area, and she was certainly what they called a tenderfoot, ignorant of the first thing about the mountains of Colorado. Her spirits plummeted.

Miss Mary raised a hand as if he would hold back

French's disappointment. "I know your Uncle Jacob, French." She sighed. "I know him quite well."

Hope blossomed in French. Miss Mary had used the present tense. Everyone else kept speaking of her Uncle Jacob as if he were dead. Mary Wells had given her the gift of her belief, and with it fresh hope, and she was overcome with gratitude.

Gruffly the housekeeper told her, "He's a tough, persistent, tenacious old man, Jake is. Maybe you'll be able to find him." Mary Wells didn't say any more, she couldn't. She just packed French a lunch that would have fed four hungry farmhands and saw her out the back door to the barn.

Tears welled up in French's eyes. Someone else believed there was a chance her uncle was alive. Someone who obviously cared for him, too. Someday, she'd want to know more about her uncle and Mrs. Mary Wells, but every minute of daylight was precious, and she had to begin her search. Besides, she could hear one of the men down in the bunkhouse calling to another to "stir his stumps" and someone else swearing he was going to eat all the biscuits before the rest of them got up to the kitchen. She knew that now wasn't the time.

Instead of the questions she longed to ask, she said, "Thank you, Mrs. Wells," with an intensity that spoke volumes more than a mere thank you for her lunch. Her gaze locked with that of the older woman, she pledged quietly, "I'll try my best to find him."

When she was a safe distance down the path to the barn, French stopped and stood. Dawn was breaking, and she stood on the path trying to cope with the heavy responsibility with which she had willingly burdened herself. She watched the first ribbons of rosy golden light stream over the horizon and watched the sky until the first rim of the sun appeared. Then, clinging to the thread of hope the housekeeper had given her, she hurried on to saddle her mare.

Behind her she heard the cowhands spilling out of the bunkhouse and charging up to the kitchen to Miss Mary's breakfast. She was glad she'd be gone before they came rushing down to the corral for their horses. In spite of the fact that she was finally getting her quest under way, somehow she just didn't feel much like seeing anyone just now.

Abernathy led his wrecking crew, as he thought of his hired thugs, to the area that Devereaux's men had most recently logged. In a small, natural clearing, the loggers had stacked the day's harvest of the long pine trunks. The railroader knew that Devereaux's men would begin snaking them down to the mill with mule teams in the next day or so. If they were going to cause mischief, they had to get at it. He dismounted and walked toward the first pyramid of logs, peering at the ground.

"Whatcha doing, boss?"

"Looking for the wedges," he told the man.

"What the hell's a wedge?" another man sitting uneasily on a rawboned gelding asked.

Abernathy didn't bother to answer.

A burly man on a scruffy bay answered instead, "A wedge is what holds them logs from rolling away when you stack 'em, Haley."

"Here's one." Abernathy pointed to a sharpened branch that had been pounded deep into the ground. "There'll be another at the other end of this pile." He looked the stacked logs over. "Check for one in the middle before you chop the end ones out. After you let this bunch go"—he yanked his head back over his left shoulder to indicate the pile of logs he wanted sabotaged—"get the one next to the rim of the gorge." He smiled a tight smile of satisfaction. "From up there, the tumble into the gorge should at least make them hard to retrieve." He laughed shortly. "If it doesn't make them toothpicks." Looking sharply at his men he commanded, "Do the one up on the ridge last."

He cleared his throat and fixed them each in turn with a hard look. "Be sure you wait one hour before you kick out the first wedge." He let them feel the weight of his regard. "Is that absolutely understood?"

"Yes, boss." The answer came in ragged unison. The reply from the three men satisfied him. He knew the kind of men these were. Devoid of decency, all they cared about was the money they made and spending it on women and whiskey. Fortunately, they knew where the pay that made that possible came from.

Abernathy mounted, turned without further comment, and left the three thugs sitting on their horses. The men watched the place he'd disappeared until his horse's hoofbeats had faded into the distance. Then one of them said, "I don't know about you galoots, but I'm getting down off this hayburner."

The other two dismounted, too. The taller one complained, "What are we supposed to do for an hour?"

The burliest asked, "Anybody bring a deck of cards?" When the others answered in the negative, he cursed them both and walked over to a place he could watch the trail. He hunkered down, snatched a piece of grass, and stuck it into his mouth, prepared to suffer boredom.

The faint sound of hoofbeats came to them. "What the hell? Is that Abernathy coming back? Don't he think we can knock down a pile a' logs without him telling us how?"

The man watching the trail signaled them to hurry to him. As they approached he gestured them down and hissed, "Shut your trap, Morris. This looks a lot better than Abernathy to me."

The other two crept to where they could see. On the trail below, they could see a single rider. It wasn't Abernathy.

One of the men whistled softly under his breath. Below them and coming their way was a woman on a black mare.

They slithered as far forward as they dared, eager gazes locked on her.

Haley began to breathe heavily.

Morris punched him in the ribs with an elbow. "Ease off, there, man. Remember Lartel saw her first."

Lartel grinned from ear to ear, but his eyes never left the girl. "Yeah, remember that. Both of you."

"But you'll share, won't you, old buddy?"

"Sure. Looks to me like there's plenty to go around."

Laughing almost silently, Lartel moved stealthily back from the spot where he'd watched. The others scuttled back after him. Standing straight, Lartel eased the belt he wore open a notch.

"Looks like we done found us something to do for that hour, boys."

French rode up the trail. She was trying to see through the trees and underbrush to the rocky side of the mountain, when Midnight threw up her head and whickered abruptly. "It's all right, girl," French soothed her mare not understanding her warning.

The mare kept her head up, ears straining forward, and began to dance along the trail. French nearly dropped the map she'd opened to check. "Stop that, Middy. How can I . . . Oh!"

Three men sprang out from behind a boulder next to the trail. Two of them seized her and dragged her from the saddle. The third made a grab for Midnight's reins. The mare screamed and reared, striking him with an iron-shod forefoot.

Haley dropped the reins. The mare whirled and galloped wildly down the trail.

French screamed, "Let me go!" She let her map fall and screamed, "Help!" at the top of her lungs.

They let her scream.

Her heart sank as she realized that they didn't care if she screamed her head off. There was no one around to hear her. Kyle Devereaux had been right, she thought frantically, she *was* ignorant of the dangers to be found in these mountains. But surely, she thought inanely, he'd been talking about cougars and bears. These were men. Ugly, awful men.

Her mind was working so quickly it dizzied her. These couldn't be loggers. She knew none of Kyle's men would frighten her like this. Somehow she sensed that his loggers would all be afraid of what he'd do if one of them harmed her. So who had attacked her? Where did they come from?

Even as she tried to figure it out, the men were dragging her off the trail and into a small clearing. She knew screaming wasn't going to help her. She tried to push fear out of her mind so that she could think clearly. There was no one to help her, no one at all. She must find a way to help herself.

Even as the two men who'd pulled her from Middy's back dragged her toward the third and meanest-looking of them she composed herself and asked, "Who are you?"

He stood holding his arm where Middy had struck him and leered at her. Pain showed in his voice. "Just three admirers, little missy." He grinned at the men holding her. "How 'bout we find the little lady a comfortable place to lie down, boys."

French began to fight them again then. Kicking and twisting, yanking her imprisoned arms in an attempt to free herself, she used every ounce of strength in her body. All reason fled as the greatest fear she'd ever known coursed through her. "No!" she shrieked at the top of her lungs.

Despair turned the day black as she went faint with it. Her mind filled with horror. She knew what they intended!

Chapter Seventeen

"THIS IS GETTING to be a habit, Midnight. Where the blazes did you leave her this time?" He blocked the trail as he had once before to stop French Richards's galloping mare.

Midnight buried her tail and slid to a halt on her haunches in the slippery pine needles that covered the winding mountain trail. Kyle caught up her reins and turned the lathered mare carefully in the narrow path until she was in a position to follow along behind his gelding. He urged them both to the trot. He wanted to find French as quickly as possible, but the trail was steep. He didn't want to kill the horses. Knowing French, he decided she'd probably just lost the nervous little mare when she stopped for a picnic lunch . . . again. He wasn't particularly worried about her safety. His men had been logging in this area just yesterday, so any animals big enough to cause her harm would still be miles away. So were his loggers and the railroad thugs harassing them.

He might not be worried about French, but he was sure as hell going to talk to Charlie about a steadier mount for her. This one was too damn quick to run off and leave her rider afoot to suit him. Especially when that rider was the delectable Miss Richards.

The mare kept dancing and carrying on at the end of her reins. Kyle turned in the saddle to look back at her. "What the devil ails you, mare?"

Midnight pushed into Daumier's flank so hard the gelding grunted. "Back off, mare." A frown creased Devereaux's forehead. Midnight slammed into his horse again, pushing and whickering as if she were frightened.

Instantly Kyle was infected with her sense of urgency. She might just want to be free to run home to her comfortable stall, but then again, she might have some serious reason to be in such a state.

Dear God! Suppose the mare hadn't just run off and left French? Suppose the girl was in some sort of trouble?

Suddenly he didn't care if he killed both horses. Spurring Daumier as he'd never spurred him before, he sent them rocketing up the trail.

Suppose there was something wrong? Suppose French were hurt? His stomach knotted.

How would he find her? There was no way to be sure he could backtrack the mare. He was a lumberman, not a scout, dammit! He couldn't read anything in the loose cover of pine needles on the trail!

Kyle Devereaux was as close to frantic as he'd ever be, and the horses were beginning to labor. Scrambling up the steep incline was tiring them at a rapid rate. Daumier was playing out and the little mare was still with him only because he was dragging her, stumbling with fatigue, along behind him.

Around a bend he saw something white lying in the path. He slowed the horses. Looking down he saw the map he'd given French, and his blood ran cold.

Just at that moment, the air was rent by a despairing cry. It was French! He knew it!

Slamming his spurs into Daumier's ribs he drove the exhausted gelding toward the scream. Midnight stood with her head down where he'd dropped her, her sides heaving. Daumier stumbled on. Right now, nothing mattered to Kyle but getting to French.

He flung himself off his lumbering mount. Just ahead, he caught a glimpse of French being thrown to the ground by two men.

Snarling like an enraged animal he sprang toward them. He was savagely intent upon killing the man who stood loosening his belt as he loomed over her.

At the sound of his shout, all three men turned to face him. Reading the purpose in Kyle's face, Lartel left his belt ends flapping and yelled, "You hold her, Haley. Morris! Let's get him."

They met Kyle's charge head on.

French murmured, "Kyle. Thank God!" She would have sagged against her captor she was so weak with relief, but she couldn't. He was too loathsome to touch, and she was too intent on the fight.

Kyle had driven both men back in his initial rush and pounded them savagely. Now that initial rush was over, and the other two men were having their turn at pounding Kyle.

French wanted to call to him to tell him to shoot them, or at least hold them at bay with the six-gun that lay along his right thigh, but she dared not. One of the thugs had a gun high on his hip, and she had no intention of having him remember it because she'd reminded Kyle of *his* weapon.

She watched the men struggle in awe. There was something so primitive about the fight that she could hardly bear to look their way. Kyle fought with his teeth bared, as if he intended to fight until his two opponents

were reduced to dust. The others fought like dogs
protecting a bone.

The savagery of Kyle's attack was taking its toll.
Slowly it became apparent that he was winning his battle.

French knew that the man holding her by the arms was
impatient to join in to turn the tide against Kyle. His
fingers kept clutching tighter and tighter around her
upper arms as he watched, holding her in front of him.

Frantically she looked around for some weapon to use
if he should let go of her. She saw it just as he did let go.
There was a thick branch, half-sharpened to a point,
lying just at the edge of a stack of logs not ten feet from
her. The instant her captor released her to hurl himself
onto Kyle's back, she ran over and snatched it up.

As Kyle fell to his knees under the sudden weight of
the man who'd been holding her, French swung the
branch with all her might. The one called Lartel dropped
like a stone.

She wasn't certain whether she'd chosen him because
he was the burliest, or because he'd intended to be the
first to rape her, but the satisfaction that soared through
her shocked her to the core.

The third man was circling Kyle and the man who'd
jumped him. While Kyle grappled on the ground with the
man he'd clawed off his back, the other looked for an
opportunity. Seeing a chance, he delivered a murderous
kick to Kyle's ribs.

French saw the strength drain momentarily from her
champion as pain swamped him. The man he was
fighting seized his advantage. Straddling Kyle, he clamped
his hands around his throat.

French kept her eyes glued to the man circling them
looking for another chance to slog his pointed boot toe
into Kyle's ribs. She hit him as hard as she could with her

branch. The resulting crack of wood against skull put him out like a light.

French heard herself give an exultant little laugh. How thin the veneer of civilization was! Eagerly she turned to Kyle and his assailant, her branch raised and ready.

She was faintly disappointed to see the man lying prostrate, already unconscious. The heat of battle had felt wonderful after the cold, bone-chilling certainty she'd felt when she'd thought she was about to be raped.

She turned toward Kyle where he stood, half-crouched and still panting. He was wiping the blood from the corner of his mouth with the back of his hand. "Are you all right?"

His answer was a short bark of laughter. "Shouldn't I be asking you that?" He straightened and came to her. "Are you all right?"

"Yes. Thanks to you, I'm fine!" Sparks of whatever had flared in her when she'd joined in the fight made her voice bold. Then the last of the excitement at having helped vanquish two of her foes melted away, and she was left with a sudden shyness as she registered afresh the nature of the attack from which he'd just so bravely rescued her.

Kyle saw the fine sparkle die in her eyes with regret. Then he saw the sudden maidenly confusion hit her. Gently he pulled her into his arms.

It was the last straw for French. She couldn't help it. Even as she despised herself for it, she burst into tears.

"There, there." He stroked her back as he had the day she'd saved the dog from the trap. Again he buried his face in her hair and drew in the marvelous scent of roses and jasmine that lingered there. "It's all right, French, you're safe now."

Unless, of course, she realized how very hard it was

for him right now, with his blood still screaming victory through him, not to claim the age-old reward of the knight who rescued his lady from such a peril. If she were aware of the feelings he battled, then she wouldn't be safe at all. The only thing that kept in check his raging desire to carry her off to a clean, fresh place in the woods was her innocence.

A single knowing glance from under those luxurious lashes of hers, and he'd savage her with kisses. He drew a deep shuddering breath and put her away from him. It wouldn't do to have her aware of his body's reaction to her nearness.

French understood. She really did. He'd fought hard, and he was hurt. He didn't want to have to stand there while she cuddled like a frightened child against his lean, hard body and cried all over him. He was a Westerner. Westerners expected their women to be courageous. Western women, she'd found, were strong. How he must despise her weakness.

She stood free of his embrace, sniffling and rubbing tears from her eyes like a frightened child. She must pull herself together. She didn't want to make him disgusted with her.

Kyle gritted his teeth against the effort it cost him not to snatch her back against him, to mold her body to his own fiercely. Everything in him cried out to crush her to him and cover her beautiful face with kisses.

It was all he could do not to tell her how he longed to make her his own. He needed every ounce of the self-control he'd carefully cultivated all his life not to tell her how . . . he stumbled over the words in his own mind . . . how he . . . *Dammit!* He could at least admit it to himself . . . how he loved her.

He feared his control might crack if he touched her.

Now wasn't the time to tell her how he dreamed of her and then tossed and twisted, sleepless, the rest of the night. That it was all he could do right now, with the blood boiling through his veins after the fight, not to claim her as his own and put a stop to the deep longing he constantly felt for her.

His conscience lashed him with scorn. All she needed right now was to find out her rescuer was very little better than the men he'd just saved her from.

The effort not to touch her as she stood there so vulnerable and sad brought a sound like a growl from his throat. *Ah, French, my French.* He spoke to her in his mind, too cowardly to speak aloud. *Someday I won't be able to hold back. Then where will we be, my darling?*

French saw the expression on his face and was all sympathy. He must be in pain. Then she saw the way he held himself away from her. He was ashamed of her. She knew it. She'd heard the sound he couldn't help making, and knew she'd disgraced herself with him beyond repair. Only the fact that she couldn't bear to add to his disgust of her kept her from bursting into tears again.

With a mighty effort she lifted her chin and turned away from him.

It nearly killed him.

The silence between them was broken only by the sighing of the wind in the pines. When French could bear it no longer she asked, "I suppose you came because Midnight ran over you again? Did you bring her?"

When he merely stood there, his eyes devouring her, she couldn't help herself. Her voice broke in spite of her best efforts. "I . . . I want to go home."

She saw his face tighten as if he felt some deep agony.

"Your ribs. They're hurting you, aren't they? That was a murderous kick."

Kyle put a hand to his ribs where the kick had landed as if he were unaware that he had ribs. He'd never given them a thought. French had sounded so lost and forlorn, hearing her had been far worse for him than any kick in the ribs. "Yes, I suppose so."

French's eyes flashed. "You suppose so? Of course they must pain you, and you have a dozen other wounds we ought to be seeing to and here I stand like some simpering fountain not doing anything to help you after all you've done for me." The shaky dam of her control was giving way. The harder she fought to keep it from bursting, the more fragile it became. Hysteria bubbled up just under the surface of her words.

Kyle stepped forward to calm her. She moved toward him as if impelled by a force stronger than either of them.

Suddenly, her eyes flew wide open and French leapt forward, her arms spread to cover as much of Kyle as possible, her back pressed close to him. "Look out, Kyle!"

In horror he watched as one of the fallen men lifted his gun waveringly at them.

"My God! French!" Kyle thrust her behind him in an agony of fear that he was too late.

A gray blur streaked from the nearest rock ledge. It crashed into the man, pinning him beneath it to the ground. Snarling, it clamped gleaming fangs into his gun arm.

Kyle left French in a little heap and ran to wrest the weapon from the thug's bloodied hand.

"Get him off me! Get him off!"

French gave a glad cry. "Rover!"

The huge gray animal turned and started toward her.

Kyle slammed his boot into the side of the man's head

to drop him. There was no time for niceties. He had to get to French!

French sat where he'd thrown her. She had her arms stretched wide, welcoming her old friend.

"French! For God's sake!" Kyle's shout filled the clearing.

In a gray blur the animal whirled away from the girl and disappeared into the woods.

Kyle dropped to his knees in front of French. Seeing the animal heading for her had drained him of the last of his strength. When he reached out to pull her into his arms, his hands shook.

In shock, he felt her shove him away.

"Why did you do that, Kyle Devereaux?" She was angry.

"Why did I do what?" He shook his head to clear it. He knew he'd been knocked around pretty good, but surely he hadn't missed anything important enough to make her this mad.

"Why did you frighten poor Rover away like that? I could have made sure his foot was properly healed." She looked at him sternly, gray eyes accusing.

He sat back on his heels, flabbergasted. He couldn't believe his own ears. After all that had happened . . . after all that she'd been through . . . hell! . . . after all that *he'd* been through!

His frustration exploded at her. "Henry French Richards! Of all the stupid women I have ever met you are the absolute stupidest!"

"Most stupid, Mr. Devereaux. And I am not."

He plowed on right over her. "You would have been raped if I hadn't happened to be on my way up here to check these damned logs." He swept an arm to indicate them.

"Please watch your language."

He thought he was going to froth at the mouth. Before he hit her he got up and started tying up the men he'd knocked out. Savagely he yanked off their own belts to bind them.

As he worked, he ranted. "Dammit to hell, woman. You don't ride around in the woods by yourself. I *told* you that!"

"There's no need to shout."

He ground his teeth, then erupted, "Blast you, French! You could have been shot . . ."

French interrupted him. "Rover saved us both."

Kyle thought his eyes were about to roll back in his head. His knee in the small of the back of the last man he was tying up, he turned to give her the full benefit of his snarl. "Your Rover, Miss Richards, is not a sled dog. Your little Rover is not a dog at all. Your Rover, Miss Richards, is a *wolf*!"

He could hear his own voice reverberating off the canyon walls. He didn't give a damn. "A wolf! A full-blooded wild animal wolf, dammit! Furthermore"— he pushed away from the man he'd finished securing with a force that whooshed the air out of the prostrate thug—"my beautiful little city-bred ninny . . ."

"You're shouting again." French made sure her voice was calm and gentle.

"Furthermore," he managed even louder, his throat aching with the effort, "your precious Rover is a she! A she, Miss Henry French Richards!"

French wondered what on earth had gotten into him! It was all over and they were safe. Besides, if anyone was going to lose control, surely it should be her. *She*, she automatically corrected her ungrammatical thought.

His behavior genuinely puzzled her. She would always

be grateful to Kyle Devereaux for saving her, but she didn't think she'd ever understand why he was behaving in this strange fashion.

Hoping to inject a note of propriety, she informed him coolly—in spite of the blush she could feel coming to her cheeks—"Mr. Devereaux. I am truly sorry to have misled you in the matter of the dog being a wolf." She held up a hand to forestall his comment. "However," she continued primly, "you have no justification for being surprised that I did not notice Rover's gender. Where I come from, ladies do not."

Kyle kept his mouth shut. He doubted very much that all the ladies in Boston were as ignorant as French, but he kept his mouth shut. He knew that if he opened it he'd say something he'd regret later.

Instead of speaking, he nodded curtly and stalked across the clearing to get the horses.

Daumier flicked his ears back and forth nervously but stood his ground. Midnight, who had finally come up to be with the gelding, sidled away, but let Kyle catch up her reins in the end.

Neither Kyle nor French spoke as he assisted her into her saddle and mounted. They rode out of the clearing in silence.

Once French turned to ask him what would happen to the three men they'd left trussed up like Christmas geese. One look at Kyle's stony profile stopped her.

Obviously, he wasn't the slightest bit interested in anything she might want to say to him. Absorbing that hurt, she told herself that if that was the way he wanted it to be, then that was the way she'd let it stand. She thrust her chin high and rode the rest of the way to the ranch without saying a word.

When they arrived at the ranch house, Kyle helped her

down and saw her to the door. Still without speaking, he tipped his hat to her and led her mare down to the barn.

Inside, French found a note on the hall mirror that told her Julia and Charles had taken Miss Mary over to the Millers' to help them get ready for the barbecue tomorrow, and that Jamie had tagged along. Reading it she understood why the house felt so empty. It was deserted.

She started for the stairs, her steps dragging. As her booted foot touched the lowest tread, she realized she couldn't stand the thought of being alone.

She must. Valiantly she strove to control the panicky feeling of need that assailed her. It was hopeless. She lost the brief battle to force herself to be brave. All her courage had been spent up there on the mountain. She couldn't be alone just now. She couldn't.

Outside she heard hoofbeats coming up from the barn. Whirling she ran desperately for the front door. Kyle! Kyle was out there. If she could only catch him in time, she wouldn't have to be alone.

Tearing open the front door, she ran across the front porch. With a sinking heart, she saw that she had missed him. He'd already passed the house and didn't see her running toward him. Panic filled her. "Kyle!"

Over the drumming of Daumier's hooves, he didn't hear her. "Kyle," she cried again, but the word was no more than a despairing whisper. She was alone.

Standing in the middle of the ranch road, she felt all the strength drain out of her. Every barrier that had held back the flood of her fears gave way. She dropped quietly into the dust of the road, covered her face with her hands, and wept.

As if her heart had called to his, Kyle heard her distress. Startled, he drew rein and looked back the way he'd come. French was sitting in the middle of the road, rocking back and forth like a child in pain.

Galloping back like a madman, he flung himself off his horse and scooped her up into his arms. Frantic, he crushed her to him and demanded, "French, my God, what is it?"

French just buried her face against the strong column of his throat and sobbed as if her heart would break. He swept her up in his arms and turned to carry her into the house. He stopped. If there had been anyone at home, they would have heard her come in and would even now be comforting her. Only a house empty of her loved ones would have driven his brave French out into the dusk like this, shattered and shaking, he knew.

He also knew he was incapable of trusting himself in an empty house with her. He was dizzy with the effort to play comforter instead of giving in to the driving need to love her into forgetting every wretched horror of the afternoon.

He walked with her cradled against his chest down to the lake in front of the house. There, he tried to put her down where she could lean back against the trunk of an old tree. He steeled himself for the slide of her body down his own, but she wouldn't let go of his neck.

So instead, he settled himself against the tree and his mind against the torture of holding her so close. When she snuggled deeper into his embrace, his eyes closed of their own volition.

Opening them with an effort, he asked her in an unsteady voice, "What is it, French?" Talking it out would be her only way to come to peace with it. "What's the matter?"

Her reply was a muffled sob.

That single sob broke all his own carefully erected

barriers of reserve. He kissed the top of her shining hair fiercely, gathering her even closer.

She murmured wordlessly, and her arms tightened up around his neck. When she raised her head, he lost the power to keep from telling her, "You're all right, French. I'll never let anything hurt you. I love you."

She looked at him as if she hadn't heard him correctly. Then she smiled radiantly. "Oh, Kyle. I love you, too."

He kissed her then. It wasn't with the fierce possessiveness he felt coursing through his veins. Right now, French didn't need the crushing embrace and demanding kisses his own inclination clamored to give her. She needed comfort. With a desperate effort, he kissed her gently.

She drew back when the kiss ended and looked at him in wonder. Her eyes were soft with love and misted with tears.

He smiled down at her and gently wiped from her lip the trace of blood left there by the cut on his own. Never had he felt such tenderness as this woman engendered in him. It made him her slave.

He dropped his head back against the trunk of the tree, attempting to come to grips with having admitted that he loved her. He couldn't. It was impossible. She filled his mind to the exclusion of everything else. His every thought was of her.

Not now, some small, sensible voice in the back of his mind groaned. *Not now.* How was he going to fight the railroaders and find his missing nephew when all he could think of was French Richards?

Frustration bubbled up in him like acid. Why the blazes couldn't love be convenient?

French lifted her chin and kissed the underside of Kyle's.

Then he groaned aloud.

French straightened in his lap so that she could reach his lips.

The movement nearly finished Kyle. He wondered if men ever swooned? When her soft lips pressed against his, he knew he'd have to do something or find out. Lunging to his feet, he lifted her with him.

He saw her eyes light with surprise at his strength. He laughed. He was damned surprised himself. Desire for her had left him feeling as weak as a kitten, only desperation had gotten him upright.

"French . . ." There was something he knew he had to say to her, but at just that moment she stretched up and brushed her lips lightly over his again. The little minx was reducing him to a quivering pile of rubble. And she was doing it with the most innocent of kisses.

From somewhere in the darker part of him a devilish urge surfaced. French should be taught not to go around kissing men like this.

It didn't matter that he intended to see to it that she never kissed any other man as long as she lived . . . except of course the sons he'd give her. He was still possessed by a purely masculine determination to turn the tables on her. She'd reduced him to less than the man he knew himself to be, and he was going to teach his precious French a very enjoyable lesson.

He felt the tenderness that had incapacitated him fade. Pulling her hard against him, he molded her softness along his hard frame and lowered his mouth to hers. Slanting kisses lightly across her mouth, he waited for the tension to leave her. When she relaxed trustingly against him, he feathered kisses across her eyelids and temples, down her cheek to her throat, and pressed one into the little hollow at its base.

Now that she was limp in his arms, he felt his own strength flowing back into him. Her eyes were closed. He lifted his head and waited for her to open them. He wanted to see her surrender there.

When she did, he saw the love glowing there instead, and was humbled. The kisses he'd planned, those that would have fueled in her a desire to match his own, were forgotten. Her innocence became his treasure.

He wanted to tell her again that he loved her, but the reserve engendered by the mother who had thrown him away was back in control. All he could do was stand there with her in his arms, trying to drink his fill of the love shining from her eyes.

With a sureness that shook him to the foundation of his being, he knew that should he stand there for all eternity it would not be long enough to exhaust her love . . . nor long enough for the lonely boy deep inside him to slake his thirst for it.

Humble gratitude washed over him. All his life he'd known with a searing certainty that he would never be loved for anything more than the pleasure his body could give or the fortune he'd amassed. Now there was French.

"French." His voice was husky with the strength of the emotions engulfing him. "I need to get you in the house, honey. It's getting chilly out here."

French wondered how he knew. She was aware of nothing but the comforting heat of his big body as he held her, and the wonderful warm glow that pervaded her now at the discovery that he loved her.

She turned her head and looked to where the cool evening air was forming a mist at the edges of the sun-warmed lake and smiled. "Yes, I suppose it is."

She let him lead her back toward the house. As they crossed the dusty surface of the road, she remembered how, just a little while ago, she had been huddling there in despair. Now she felt as if she floated over that very spot, borne on the love she and Kyle had for each other.

At the door Kyle stopped and turned her to face him. His fingers lifted her chin. "Will you be all right?" he asked softly. He searched her face. "I'll alert the men in the bunkhouse that you're up here by yourself if you'd like."

She smiled. "No, I'm fine. Don't bother anyone. I think I'll like being alone . . . now."

He leaned down to claim her mouth. With every ounce of willpower he possessed, he kept the kiss gentle. He wanted her to sleep. "Good night."

"Good night," she answered dreamily, full of wonder and delight. She felt as if she had been the recipient of a miracle. He loved her—someone for whom she'd longed more than anyone in the world loved her. It made her feel as if she had *value*. She felt as if she had wings. She drifted into the house.

Kyle stood watching through the glass beside the door as she mounted the stairs. When she was out of sight, he turned and went back to his horse. Mounting, he signaled the big gelding to move off.

He headed Daumier to town to pick up the sheriff. The scum he'd left up on the mountain still had to be dealt with.

He hoped French would be able to sleep tonight. He didn't believe he'd be able to close his eyes.

Chapter Eighteen

A BARBECUE. FRENCH had never been to a barbecue. She wasn't even sure she knew what one was. But Indian summer was still holding winter at bay, the day was sunshiny and fine, and her spirits were high because she knew she was about to see Kyle. Kyle, even his name could bring little shivers.

"You'll enjoy it. It's a great deal of fun." Julia turned to look back at her. "And you look so pretty that every man there will be falling all over himself to dance with you."

"Huh! Falling down drunk like as not." Charlie guided the team off the main road and through a tall arch that said "Bar M."

"Charles," Julia warned him. "You are not to spoil French's fun." To French she said, "There is drinking, dear, but sufficient of the men stay sober to see to it that no lady is ever offended."

French looked doubtful. "I've never been around men who overimbibed. Only that one on the train that Jamie chased off for me."

Jamie, bursting with pride, spoke right up. "Don't worry, Miss French. I'll keep an eye on you. I won't let anybody bother you, any more than I did that drunk on the train."

"Thank you, Jamie," she told the boy beside her. "I'm sure you'll keep me quite safe."

But she didn't want to feel completely safe. She wanted to feel just a little threatened. She planned to, in fact. When Julia had told her there'd be lots of dancing, she'd decided to do most of hers with Kyle. With the new confidence born in her by the knowledge that he returned her love, she let herself admit that she wanted to feel Kyle Devereaux's arms around her when he wasn't comforting her. She knew instinctively that whatever she might feel in his arms then, safe would not be it.

She sensed an intensity in Kyle Devereaux that thrilled her. She had no experience with men like him. In fact, she had no experience at all with men outside the circle of her family's friends, and they were a very staid group.

After the way Kyle had fought for her yesterday, she had the delicious feeling that in wanting more than comfort from his embrace, she might be playing with fire.

So far, the only passion she'd seen aroused in him was the savagery with which he'd fought the men on the mountain. That had told her he was a dangerous man. Now, without a qualm, she longed, and intended, to discover whether beneath the gentle kisses he'd given her last night there hid an equal passion . . . for her.

She blushed at the thought. Quickly she asked, "What kind of dancing will there be?"

"Some square dancing, and a lot of what will have to pass as dancing when the cowhands get up the courage to ask you."

"Hey, now, Julia. Don't discourage the girl. Some of us know a dance or two."

Julia smiled over her shoulder at French. "It's all good fun, dear. And Charles and Kyle and a few of the others do know how to dance"—she cut her eyes at her husband—"after a fashion."

Charles would have protested, but they'd arrived in the Millers' yard. He was busy for the next few minutes with greetings and introductions, and handing the team over to a wrangler to be looked after.

French was all but oblivious to the introductions, for she'd seen Kyle's big gelding, Daumier, among the many other horses at the hitching rail. She smiled and nodded pleasantly to the crowd of young men who pressed forward to meet her, and tried to give them her full attention. It was beyond her. More than half of her mind was busy wondering where Kyle was, and she was certain she'd never remember a single name, much less which face belonged to it.

Then she saw him. He was only a few yards away, leaning against a tree, watching her, a smile hovering at the corners of his mouth, his eyes full of his love for her. She had trouble with her knees again.

When their eyes met, she sensed that he was anything but as relaxed as he appeared to be. He was as tensely holding himself in check as she was.

She smiled. It would hardly do to run and fling herself into his arms as she so longed to, nor could he stride over to her to sweep her into his embrace. But the lightning that passed between them told it all. Neither was in any doubt as to the feelings of the other after that single glance. And the lightning lingered.

Finally, after she had promised dances to half the county, he was there beside her. She couldn't wait to touch him. She had to. She held out her hand. "Good afternoon, Mr. Devereaux."

He took her hand, and the electricity of his touch was all that she'd known it would be. She stifled her gasp only because she'd known there would be this lightning and had expected it to steal her very breath away. Blissfully she smiled.

"Good afternoon, Miss Richards. I trust I find you well?"

He spoke what was merely the conventional greeting in a deep calm voice, but his intent gaze let French know that he was seriously assessing the truth of her reply as she answered, "I'm fine, thank you, Mr. Devereaux." She let him see that she was indeed all right, reassuring him with a steady look. "Just fine."

With a sigh of relief, he drew her arm through his and turned away from the others, ignoring the protests of the young men. "Thank God." He bent his head near hers to tell her, "I was afraid you might have suffered nightmares."

Softly she murmured, "I dreamed only of you."

The rush of urgency prompting him to take her in his arms staggered Kyle. He stopped and looked deeply into her eyes. Love for this woman overwhelmed him. The world faded away, and with it every doubt that he could be husband to her.

"French." His voice was rough with emotion, his eyes full of that which he could no longer delay. "This isn't the place . . ." He looked around them at the crowd. "And God knows I'm not worthy . . . But you must know how I feel about you after last night. I . . . ."

"Hey! Devereaux! Where do you get off monopolizing the prettiest gal at this here party?" A big man with a good-humored face shouldered Kyle aside and bowed to French. "I'm Colt Miller, Miss Richards. And I intend to steal you from this here coyote for the first square dance."

Seeing French's expression, he guessed what she was

about to say. "It don't matter a bit if you don't know how to square dance, you being from back east. You just leave it all to me."

He grabbed her around the waist and whirled her off in the direction of the large square platform that had been built for the dancing. There was no way she could resist, and she went, laughing. Colt Miller was like a tornado in human form. He just swooped her up and carried her along. She threw a helpless glance back at Kyle.

He smiled and let her go, knowing that what he had to say would keep. Now that he knew he loved her, there would be a lifetime to tell her so, and no power on earth strong enough to stop him. He was certain that once he got it said, the declaration of his love for her would be enough to keep them together for the rest of their lives.

He found a place to lean against from which he could watch her dance. His shoulder against the trunk of an obliging tree, he reveled in her grace and humbly thanked his maker that he could see her in the arms of one of his friends without wanting to kill the man.

That was something he'd needed to know. Something that relieved his mind. Because French had been the first person to love him . . . really love him . . . he'd feared he might not be able to handle seeing her even dancing in another man's arms, that he might have been overcome with a savage jealousy. Relief that he was not rushed through him.

Now he could relax and watch French move gracefully through the square, guided by the others. She was laughing and obviously enjoying the dance, and he took pleasure in her enjoyment. With a broad smile, he watched as she found her way through the movements. He could give himself over to the pleasure of watching her, because he knew she was his, and that she knew that she was his. He trusted her. That was the key. His French was . . .

With a jolt he was snatched back to earth. There on the far side of the dance platform, he saw Abernathy. The man was chatting to Bertha Miller as if they were old friends. Kyle's jaw locked. What the devil was Abernathy doing here among decent people?

He straightened and watched through narrowed eyes. *How the blazes did that man get here?*

Bertha Miller called to someone among the dancers as the music stopped. To Kyle's consternation, it was her son Colt. French was on Colt's arm. He started for them. There was no way that skunk was going to be introduced to his French.

As he arrived beside them, French turned to him. She'd sensed his presence. The knowledge sent pleased masculine satisfaction through him even as he scowled at his enemy.

Abernathy looked at him and smiled. Derision was plain in his eyes. "Hello, Devereaux." His voice was lazy.

Kyle's stomach knotted with dislike. "What are you doing here, Abernathy?"

Bertha Miller looked a little startled. "Why, Miss Richards and Mr. Abernathy are old friends, Kyle. Didn't you know?"

No, he didn't know. He sure as hell didn't know. With burning eyes he looked to French to challenge the statement.

French said, "Mr. Abernathy is my brother's friend, actually." She saw Kyle's nostrils flare.

Troubled by the look on Kyle's face, she forced a smile and said to the tall stranger, "How nice it is to see you, Mr. Abernathy. Will you be in the area long?"

"As long as it takes"—he directed a level look at Kyle—"to finish my business."

Kyle picked up the gauntlet. "Then we shall look forward to having your company for a long time, Mr. Abernathy."

French became very still. She'd sensed rivalry between the two men, but here was something deeper. Something that gave her a chill despite the warm sunny day.

Abernathy was saying, "Perhaps not, Mr. Devereaux. I generally accomplish my assignments rather quickly."

Bertha Miller might be confused by the undercurrent she heard in the voices of the men, but she knew what was expected in the way of hospitality. "Let's hope not too quickly, this time, Mr. Abernathy. It will be so nice for our new schoolteacher to have a friend from home visit for a while."

Kyle reached for French.

Abernathy was quicker. He snaked an arm around her waist and headed for the platform, crooning, "May I have this dance, Miss Richards?"

French had no choice but to let herself be led off by Abernathy. She glanced back at Kyle wishing she could have resisted. Then she registered the look on Kyle's face. His expression reminded her of the way he'd looked during the fight on the mountain. She realized then that the slightest show of reluctance on her part might precipitate unpleasantness.

Abernathy threw a triumphant look back at Kyle. Chuckling at Kyle's thunderous expression, he turned the full battery of his charm on the girl in his arms. He knew he danced well, even though the music the fiddlers were scraping out seemed a slow travesty of anything he'd ever danced to before. No matter, it made it easier to talk.

He was determined to keep French Richards's attention centered on him. No woman was going to search for another man while he held her. Especially not if the man were Kyle Devereaux. Especially when he could see so plainly that it mattered so desperately to Devereaux.

Smiling, he told her, "I have messages from your family, Miss Richards." That should hold her attention.

French was startled. In her heart she'd been so sure that her family would have been so glad to be rid of her disturbing presence that it would be months yet before they'd think to send her messages. If then.

She couldn't hide the eager smile his words brought. They were thinking of her. How wonderful to know that they had spoken of her to this friend of her brother's, that they had even sent word to her. Messages proved that they thought of her . . . and maybe even missed her. Her heart filled with joy.

Abernathy looked down into her face and began, "Your brothers send their best. They hope you like it out here. Sorry there's not more, but you know how young men are. I can tell you, though, that they seem to be doing well at your father's bank, and that your middle brother is courting."

French smiled again at that. Clarence had always been the shy one, and she'd wondered if he'd ever get around to looking for a wife.

"Your father is very busy." He wondered what to add, and decided to play it safe. "He sends you his love and reminds you that he's thinking of you." He saw her frown a little at that and decided to infuse some warmth into his next "message."

"Your mother, of course, misses you dreadfully. She said to tell you that she prays for you always, hopes you are taking good care of yourself and that you are enjoying your visit here. She says she is concerned about the sad loss of your uncle, as she knows how much it affected you."

French's voice was strained, her gray eyes wide and strangely intent. "Yes, I'm quite desperate for word of my uncle."

Abernathy saw that she was sad, and brightened his voice. "And she sent word that she misses the chats the two of you used to have"—he could feel her stiffening in his arms, and threw in another safe, cheering bit of news—"and all the wonderful shopping trips you used to go on together."

That ought to do it. All the women he knew were wild about acquiring pretty little things. God knew his mistresses had quickly spent every penny they could pry out of him. He smiled down at the little beauty in his arms and waited for her response. She was a taking little thing. Pity she wasn't the sort he could have a brief affair with while he was here.

French looked at him gravely. When she spoke, her tone of voice was stiffly formal. "Thank you so much for the trouble you've gone to in bringing me these messages, Mr. Abernathy."

Her wide gray eyes held a strange expression. He was puzzled for an instant at the sadness he saw there. Obviously, he decided, he'd made the pretty little thing homesick.

Small wonder. She was Boston-bred, after all, and like himself no doubt yearned for the many attractions of the bustling city. He set himself to cheering her up. Detaining her from leaving the platform at the end of the dance, he claimed her again as the next one started. For the rest of their second dance, he applied himself to the task of bringing the smile back to her lovely little face.

Kyle cursed under his breath and made himself relax his jaw before he ground his back teeth apart. Maybe he'd decided too soon that he wasn't going to turn into a jealous monster. Certainly he wanted to jump onto the rough platform full of dancers and smash Abernathy flat.

Only the knowledge that any man would hate seeing the woman he loved in the arms of his sworn enemy kept him from condemning himself completely. God knew he'd like to wring Abernathy's neck for keeping French for a second dance, not to mention their other differences.

Kyle Devereaux wasn't a man to just let life happen around him. "Hey, Colt," he called to the Millers' oldest. "Why don't you tell the fiddlers to play another square dance? Looks like Miss Richards isn't exactly enjoying herself."

Colt Miller glanced from French to Kyle. "Looks like she ain't the only one."

Kyle snapped his head around to glare at Miller.

Colt shrugged innocently. "Lots of folks wanna square up."

Kyle scowled at him and set off for the platform. He was going to be there when French stepped off it.

Abernathy saw him coming and tried to change direction, but the press of youngsters forming squares for the next dance made it impossible. Forcing a friendly smile he asked, "Ah, Devereaux, do your talents stretch to square dancing?"

"No." Kyle didn't return the smile. "I've come for Miss Richards." So that he didn't sound like a dog coming to wrest away a bone, he added with some civility, "She promised to let me take her for her first barbecue."

"Ah, very well." Abernathy turned to French. "Thank you for the dances, Miss Richards."

"You're welcome, Mr. Abernathy."

"Please." His smile was unctuous. "In light of my friendship with your family, couldn't you call me Kendal?"

"Thank you for your . . . kindness . . . in bringing me messages from my family . . . Mr. Abernathy." French turned and put her hand out blindly to Kyle.

He caught it and drew it through his arm, clasping it close to his side as if he sensed she was in need of steadying. Glaring at Abernathy, he told him, "I'll see you later, *Kendal*."

Abernathy grinned at the implied threat. "Very well, *Kyle*." He spoke in the same tone, making as much an insult of Devereaux's Christian name. "I'll look forward to it."

French was so lost in her own misery that she didn't notice anything unusual in the exchange between the two men.

Why had the man lied to her about having messages from her family? Hope had soared in her, hope that they valued her after all. Then that hope had been dashed to death as she'd realized from its content that her mother would never have sent such a message. She could not have.

Her mother had never had time to chat with French, never taken her shopping, never had time for her at all. Why had this stranger deliberately lied to her? She couldn't accuse him, even in her mind, of intending to hurt her, for he'd merely told her innocuous things that any family might have sent to a daughter so far away from them. His "messages" had been the least that any normal family would have sent—any normal family to a daughter they loved who was alone so far from them. Even as tears choked in her throat, French hid her true feelings behind a brightly smiling face.

Colt Miller, standing nearby, was troubled, too. He *had* noticed the animosity that had flared so strongly between Kyle Devereaux and this Abernathy fellow. Quickly he made up his mind he'd keep a sharp eye out. The last thing in the whole wide world he wanted was to have his parents' annual barbecue end in a brawl.

Lordamighty, please. Not the very first time he'd been old enough to act as one of the hosts to the family's big, county-wide party. A brawl was the last thing they needed. Especially not one as dangerous as he knew it would get if Kyle Devereaux took it into his head to start it.

Chapter Nineteen

Kyle hadn't a chance to be the man nearest French while she sat attempting to eat her barbecue, not with every unmarried cowpoke and ranch owner for miles around vying for a place near her. Standing nearby he watched them.

Young face aglow with admiration, one of the Bar M hands offered, "Would you like some beer, Miss Richards?"

"Ladies don't drink beer, Hopkins." The eager cowhand who'd asked got hooted down, then shoved out of the group for his trouble. He scowled for a minute, then settled down to watch, like Kyle, from the edge of the little crowd, grinning sheepishly.

"Would you like some *lemonade*, Miss Richards?" The second youth learned fast, Kyle saw.

Devereaux stood quietly drinking in the sight of her. It was enough just now to watch her sitting there with her skirts spread around her on the rough wooden bench under the tree, her hands clasped in her lap as if she were holding tight to this moment. Suddenly he knew that his precious French hadn't had a lot of moments like this, moments when she had been the center of a ring of admirers.

Observing her so closely, he understood with a little

shock of wonder that his beautiful French was shyly grateful for all the attention she was receiving. He shook his head in disbelief. The men of Boston must be blind. If they'd ever really looked at her, French would never have been allowed to leave Massachusetts, he was sure. He chuckled and thanked Providence that the poor benighted Bostonians *had* been blind. Their loss was his gain.

He smiled and shifted his shoulders to a more comfortable position against the tree. Standing there, he reflected that life had never been better for him. Even his worry about his lost nephew was over, though he could wring Rafferty's neck for the brevity of the telegram that had ended it. *"After check Beckman, will return. Boy safe. R."* might have been designed to ease Rafferty's penny-pinching mind, but it didn't do a whole lot for his employer's. Would Rafferty be bringing the boy with him? He could only suppose so.

Perhaps the lad would make a good playmate for Jamie Waring. He knew that his nephew, or indeed any youngster, would benefit by association with the young man who had won such a solid place in Julia's and Charles's hearts. He hoped his nephew would be half as fine. He hoped that the boy wouldn't be . . . He cut off his speculations as useless.

Only time would solve it. The fly in the ointment was that he didn't have any idea how much time. Rafferty's notions of thrift were causing the foreman to solve two problems with one trip, but it was general knowledge that Kyle Devereaux had never been known for stringent economies . . . or patience. He wasn't happy that Rafferty wouldn't be back until he'd satisfied the doubts they'd had recently about one of the New Orleans ship captains that ferried Devil-Oh Lumber aboard. Not happy at all.

But he was happy to stand here on this lovely Indian summer day and look at Henry French Richards. So he cleared his mind of the impatience Rafferty's too-brief telegram had caused it, and watched her, the beautiful, gentle woman he knew to be the love of his life.

French's head was in a whirl from trying to answer all the questions and offers that were being hurled at her. "Yes, I do like it here in Colorado, thank you. No, thank you. I don't care for wine."

She turned to her other side, her dark hair swinging against her shoulders and making Kyle long to run his fingers through the silk of it. "Thank you, I'd love some more lemonade." To another, "Yes, it is a beautiful day, very pleasant."

"How do you like our barbecue, Miss Richards?"

French recognized Colt Miller as one of her hosts and knew she must give an answer. She sighed and told him apologetically, "I'm sorry, Mr. Miller." She caught her lower lip with her teeth and shook her head helplessly. "I haven't had a chance to taste it yet." Her eyes were full of mischief.

"That does it," Kyle pushed away from the tree trunk that he'd been leaning against. His voice was firm. "Back off, men. I promise you can talk to her again as soon as she's eaten her lunch."

None of them questioned his right to shoo them away from French. To a man they seemed to acknowledge he had one.

Kyle hoped it was because he was her employer, and not that the possessiveness he felt for French was showing. Neither he, nor, he was certain, French, was ready to have the whole community aware of and sharing in the glory that had rushed unchecked to the forefront of their relationship last night.

Not yet. Not so soon. The love they'd admitted there in the evening mist by the lake was too fresh, too fragile. Their love for each other was still too young to bear the delight and teasing of their friends. Kyle was relieved that no one seemed to have an inkling.

The men began to drift away with promises to return as soon as French had finished eating to "dance her feet off." One shot a resentful glance at the tall lumberman standing guard over her, and wondered aloud, "How come Devereaux thinks he can run the rest of us off?"

In the general laughter, one voice called out, "You be sure you're the one to ask him that, Travis. The rest of us like our noses the way they are." There was no hint that any one of them had guessed the truth, though. Relieved, Kyle kept his expression carefully neutral as he listened to their banter.

"Aw, he ain't so tough."

"Yeah. Just why don't you go find out?" But there was no malice in any of it. They were only giving one another a hard time.

From the edge of the group, Colt Miller watched and wondered if it was going to be tougher than he'd thought to keep things in hand. He ran his finger around the inside of his collar, uneasy. After all, he hadn't his pa's experience in judging the mood of barbecue guests, and to him, this had looked like a near one.

He knew that his parents' shindig had ended in a good fight a time or two over the years, but he sure didn't want that to happen this time. Not when they'd charged him with keeping things pleasant and on an even keel for the first time.

He looked around for inspiration. "Hey, fellows! Ain't that a new keg a' beer I see over there?"

There was a general rush in the direction he'd indicated. He grinned and let go a gusty sigh of relief. With a salute to Kyle, Colt Miller trailed after his friends.

Left alone with her, Kyle smiled down at her, nodded at her plate, and asked French, "Do you like it?"

French nibbled at a bit of her barbecue. "Yes. It's different. But it's quite nice."

Kyle knelt on one knee and rested his forearm on the other to look into her face. He could sense that she was upset. Surely, the young men who had been so pleased just to be near her couldn't have upset her. "What is it, French? What's the matter?"

All her life she'd longed for someone who'd be perceptive enough to know what she was feeling. Now here he was, kneeling on the grass in front of her to bring his dear face level with her own, and she didn't want him to be, didn't want him to guess. Not now.

"What's troubling you, French?" His voice went deep with concern.

French couldn't tell him. She simply couldn't. She'd seen his dislike of Abernathy. It had been obvious.

This was a pleasant gathering of all Kyle's friends. She wasn't going to ruin it by telling him of Abernathy's hurtful prevarications. There was no way she was going to add fuel to the fire of their mutual animosity.

She felt guilty enough just for bringing this look of concern to Kyle's face without adding more reason to feel guilty. With all her heart, she wanted to avoid making any more problems for Kyle. She was already worried half sick about him because of the three men he'd bested saving her up on the mountain. She sighed before she could stop herself. For someone who'd started the day so happily, she was certainly in a sorry state now.

Her eyes were full of the misery and she was fighting. Kyle saw it and his blood ran cold. What was she hiding from him? She'd been all right before Abernathy had shown up.

Silently he vowed he'd find out what Abernathy had said to her to dim the joy he'd seen in her before she'd danced with that snake. He'd find out what was causing his beloved French this distress if he had to beat it out of Abernathy. Something inside him stirred, and he realized he'd *like* to beat it out of Abernathy.

French saw Kyle stiffen and realized that the bleakness of her mood was affecting him. She made an effort to shrug off the deep, familiar sadness Kendal Abernathy's cruelty had caused to well up in her again.

What difference did it make that he'd given her fake messages he'd pretended were from her family? None really. She knew her parents and brothers didn't truly care for her. She'd always known it.

In time, she'd get over the hurt he'd inflicted by leading her to believe, even for an instant, that they'd cared. She'd gotten over it before.

In time, she hoped that she would get over the underlying cause . . . permanently. She recognized that she was behaving like a child crying for the moon. It was past time that she grew up enough not to mind so dreadfully.

Besides, hadn't her children hinted that Kyle Devereaux was in the middle of a fight to keep the sawmill going in spite of interference from the new railroad's people? Wasn't that enough? There was no need for him to have to fight her battles, too. No need at all.

Right now, the important thing was to keep Kyle from knowing that it was Abernathy who'd been instrumental in the hurt she was striving to overcome. Trouble on her behalf was the last thing Kyle needed just now. And she didn't want him to have it with her brother's friend, especially.

Lying to Kyle was difficult, almost impossible she found, even if she were only doing it with a smile. She must keep the truth from him, though. She couldn't be the cause of his having yet another enemy. She'd truly no idea how she'd be able to bear that.

"Nothing's the matter, Kyle." Her smile was brilliant. She popped up from the bench, brushing her skirts and saying brightly, "I'd like to go find some dessert now, may we?"

Kyle offered his arm, his expression grim. He was pierced through by the overbrightness of her smile. Kendal Abernathy moved to the top of his list of things that urgently needed his attention.

They made their way across the yard without speaking, Kyle's other hand reassuringly covering hers that rested on his arm. He could feel the tension in her. Unconsciously she clung to his arm like a small child seeking comfort.

Julia came up to them at the dessert table. "Are you enjoying the barbecue, French dear?"

"Oh, yes. The food is wonderful, and I'm truly enjoying meeting all your friends." Her niece smiled at her with a radiance to rival the sun.

Kyle stood, a stark contrast beside her. His puzzled, half-angry concern was clear to Julia.

She spent a minute or two longer with her niece. "Are you really having a good time, French? Meeting so many new people all at once can be tiring."

"Oh, yes, Aunt Julia. I can't remember when I've had

such a delightful time. Everyone is so nice, and the food is simply delicious."

When another couple drifted over to be introduced, French chattered at them with a false gaiety that was in stark contrast to the austere man beside her. Immediately, Julia decided to develop a splitting headache.

She left them with a meaningful look at the quiet, watchful lumberman and a vague smile for the others. Threading her way through the visiting throng, she found her husband in a crowd of his ranching cronies. "You don't mind if we go home, do you, Charles, dear? I have the most dreadful headache." She ran her fingers across her brow, then pressed them to her temples, closing her eyes.

Charlie looked at her sharply. His own eyes narrowed.

Expressions of concern came from all around her. Several of the men left the group and went ahead of them to see to getting the team hitched back up to the surrey.

Charlie helped Julia along, his arm protectively around her. Bending down solicitously, he demanded, "What's going on? What in tarnation's got into you, girl? You never have headaches."

"It's French. And I don't know what's wrong yet, but it looks like something dreadful."

"We'll get her home then." He looked around. "Where's our boy?"

Julia looked the tiniest bit startled before she smiled in spite of her worry and said, "Here he comes, Charles, he's driving your surrey." Charles was very careful of his surrey.

"Let him. The boy's good." His voice was full of warm affection. "We'll put French up front with him," he tried to lighten her mood, ". . . and you and I can spoon in the back."

Julia smiled at his attempt and reached up to touch Charlie's cheek. For a moment, lost in tenderness for her husband, her concern for French was almost forgotten.

Kyle stood watching until Jamie had driven the surrey out of sight down the ranch road. His heart was heavy with concern for his beloved French. Obviously, she was troubled about something.

He was glad they'd taken her home. Without the slightest doubt, he trusted Julia to find out and fix whatever was bothering the girl. Thank God for that.

For his part, he was going to see just what, if anything, Abernathy had had to do with French's dramatic change of mood. With that purpose in mind, he turned to go look for the man.

He hadn't far to go. Abernathy was leaning against the end of the hitching rail, watching him. "Looking for somebody, Devereaux?"

"Yeah. You."

"What's the matter? Your little sweetheart upset about something?"

Kyle flexed his fingers to keep them from curving rigidly into talons. With softly voiced menace he said, "Her aunt had a headache."

"Yeah. Sure."

Kyle assessed the man in front of him. Obviously Abernathy had something stuck in his craw. "Well?"

"Well what?" Abernathy lounged against the hitching rail. His posture was elaborately casual. His eyes were not.

"What did you say to her?"

"What did I . . ." He straightened, but his voice was still lazy, almost a drawl. "Oh, you mean what did I tell Miss Richards."

"Yes, you low-down snake." Kyle bit out the words. "What did you tell her?"

"How do you know I told her anything?" He unlooped his horse's reins from the hitching rail.

"Because she wasn't upset before she danced with you, damn you."

Abernathy swung up on his horse. "Oh, that." He grinned down at Devereaux, enjoying the advantage of height he'd gained by mounting—and the anger that was blurring Devereaux's judgment. "I only told her that she ought to ask you where her dear Uncle Jacob is."

He grinned mirthlessly to see Kyle's puzzled frown. "I told her that you'd be the best one to ask." He looked back over his shoulder as he turned his horse toward the ranch road.

Kyle locked his jaw. He refused to ask Abernathy why. He'd be eternally damned before he'd give the skunk the satisfaction. He was trying to figure it out for himself when Abernathy started to ride away.

As the railroad man pushed his mount into a brisk walk, he called back to Kyle, "I told her you'd know where he was . . ."

Kyle started forward, driven by an urge to pull the man off his horse and smash his face in for offering French the false hope that he could lead her to her uncle.

Abernathy spurred his horse into a lope and delivered his coup de grace, ". . . because you were the one who'd killed him for his silver mine."

Kyle was shocked to immobility. He stood there absorbing the enormity of Abernathy's lie. How the devil could he have come up with that one? Jacob Price had been his friend. Righteous rage surged through him.

He started for his own horse. He'd catch and beat the living hell out of that lying bas . . .

Then suddenly he saw French's face. The memory of it stopped him as if he'd walked into a brick wall. As clearly as if she stood before him, he saw her dear face and the distress he'd seen there.

French. Ah, God. Somehow she had become his whole life. How could he live if she . . . Agony shot through him like a red-hot lance.

His soul began to wither.

French had believed Abernathy.

His French had *believed* the lie.

Slowly the certainty penetrated his unwilling mind. It lay like cold steel in his heart, draining the life away.

Henry French Richards believed that he, Kyle Devereaux, could have killed her uncle.

Chapter Twenty

KYLE DIDN'T KNOW how he got back to town. He didn't even know whether or not he'd thanked the Millers, and he'd be willing to bet that he hadn't told anybody good-bye. He did know, however, that he couldn't leave things as they were. He had to see French. He had to know . . . All last night he'd tossed and turned, sleep eluding him.

He'd gotten up and paced into the dawn, alternately cursing Abernathy and his own frustrated condition. He ran an empire, dammit, an empire he'd built from nothing by the sheer power of his will. He'd fought the elements and avaricious men and never once had he flinched or turned from his purpose. Now he couldn't even get a good enough grip on himself to face the woman he loved.

All he'd have to do was walk across to the school-house before she'd left, and he hadn't even found the courage to do that. Was this what love did to a man? Leave him afraid to face one small and gentle woman? Did love make him too gutless to face up to, like a man, what could . . . probably would . . . be the greatest sorrow of his life?

Slamming shut the ledger he'd been pretending to work on, he snarled, "Well, I'm through hiding from it.

I'll have the truth of it from French Richards." He grabbed his hat as he flung himself out of the office.

He'd have the truth. Whether he truly wanted to hear what he got or not, he'd have it. Hell, he wouldn't even have to hear it. He'd know it the moment he saw her eyes. *Did* she believe Abernathy's lie? *Would* she condemn him out of hand, or would she listen to his denial?

His *denial*. Hell. Love for her had even reduced him to that.

First he neglected all he should be doing, now he was going, hat in hand, to beg from her . . . To beg what? Reassurances that she believed in him? Forgiveness if she didn't?

His stomach was so tied in knots it was affecting his brain. He'd never attempted to justify himself or his actions to a living soul. Never. Not once. What the devil was ailing him?

What was the hellish nature of this thing he was certain was love that it did this to a man? It had stripped away everything but the driving desire to be with French Richards, the agonizing need to know she still loved him . . . no matter what she believed.

That was what he wanted from her, wasn't it? Wasn't he suffering the tortures of the damned, burning to know that she loved him whether or not she believed him innocent of harm to her uncle?

"Damn you to hell, Devereaux," he snarled aloud. "You're not asking much, are you?" But it was what he must have, for he, God help him, would love French Richards if she turned into Medusa before his very eyes. Every self-protective instinct that had guarded him from his mother's cruelty since his birth was howling at him to pull back, to turn away, to preserve his soul.

It was too late for him. Far too late. He was bound to

Henry French Richards for all eternity . . . even if she no longer loved him in return. Unflinchingly, he admitted it.

He hated himself for neglecting his responsibilities to run off to look into French Richards's gray eyes. He scorned himself for his weakness.

But he went.

Wondering was something he had no stomach for, he never had. This time it was tearing him into painful little fragments. He was no good to the mill, no good to himself. No good at all.

He cursed the whole time he saddled Daumier. "Dammit, boy. I have to see her. God help me, even if she hates the sight of me, I have to see her."

He shoved boot into stirrup, remembering that he was going to Julia's, and stepped back down again. Impatiently, he untied the rawhide thong that snugged the bottom of his holster to his thigh, yanked the gunbelt tight enough across his flat midsection to free it of its buckle, and hung it and his six-shooter on a peg in the barn wall.

Julia didn't like guns.

Swinging up on Daumier, he rode out of the barn into weather that threatened rain. So he'd get wet. It wouldn't be the first time. He had to get to French.

He guided Daumier down the long slope of the hill through the town to the main road that ran through the valley. As he rode, he turned up his coat collar. Even though he told himself it might have been a good idea to have broken out a slicker, he didn't stop. He wouldn't take the time to do it.

The wind rose as he headed down the valley for the Lightning Double C. There was a bite in it that hadn't been there before. Low clouds scudded across the wide expanse of sky as the day became threatening.

Kyle decided that yesterday's pleasant weather for the Millers' barbecue had been the last of the mild Indian summer days. The few crisp mornings lately hadn't lied. The frost they'd left on the meadow grasses hadn't lied either. Winter was finally on the way.

Trotting Daumier on out of town, he scanned the sky. Now, heavy gray clouds, their bellies swollen with rain, were coming up from the south to hang low over the valley. Kyle sent Daumier into a ground-eating lope and headed for the Chamberses' ranch. No sense in asking to be caught in the rain.

Some of the knots were loosening in his stomach now that he was on his way to find French. The demons that had tortured him through the night gibbered away into the far corners of his mind, and he began to feel more like himself again.

He almost regretted not having eaten breakfast.

Abernathy and his men pushed their horses harder. "We want to get up to the clearing and let those logs go into the gorge. Then I want you to . . ." He lifted his hand to signal his men to stop. "Damn." He sat his horse, a nasty smile on his face. "Now here's a piece of luck."

He spun his horse and spurred him into a gallop, his startled men strung out behind him and trying hard to catch up. "Com'on, boys! If we get to the next trail down the mountain, we can cut him off."

"Cut who off, boss?" Morris asked, instinctively keeping his voice low.

"Devil-Oh, boys, our good friend, Devil-Oh." He grinned back over his shoulder at them. "I aim to teach Mr. Devereaux an interesting little lesson about bucking the railroad, and this looks like a mighty good time to do it."

The others, still smarting from the days they'd spent in jail after the sheriff and Devereaux had hauled them down the mountain trussed up like turkeys for Thanksgiving, grinned back at Abernathy. To a man they liked the thought of the four of them getting hold of Kyle Devereaux.

They lashed and spurred their tiring horses. They were more than eager to teach the mighty Mister Devereaux a lesson. A lesson he'd never forget.

Kyle's mind was on French. Daumier flicked his ears forward and lifted his head abruptly, but Kyle registered the warning too late.

"Get him, men!"

Kyle went down cursing under the weight of the two men who'd jumped him. The fall, with the weight of two men on him, knocked the breath out of him.

Before he could struggle to his feet, he was pummeled and kicked by the other two until he was groggy.

"Let's lay off a minute, boys." Abernathy was panting from his efforts.

A disheveled Kyle glared up at him from where he was forced to and held on his knees in the dust of the road. "Abernathy. I was . . . coming looking . . . for you later."

"Glad I could save you the trouble, Devereaux." Abernathy regained his breath and spoke as if he and Devereaux were two men talking in a business office. "We've been hoping to get you someplace private. Someplace where we wouldn't be disturbed. Where we could explain a few things to you, you know." He drew back his fist. "Here's a little message for you from the railroad."

As Abernathy's fist shot forward, Kyle whipped his head to the right. In the split second it took for the blow to land, Kyle decided that he'd rather take the heavy signet ring the railroader wore across a cheek than full in the face. He had an aversion to having his nose broken again, and he sure as hell liked having all his teeth.

Blood had hardly had time to run from the gash in his cheek before Abernathy's second blow caught him under the chin. Then the others, excited by first blood, piled on.

The momentary elation Kyle felt when they let go his arms to hit him was short-lived. He was too dizzied from Abernathy's second blow to put up a stiff resistance, and the three thugs he'd bested and jailed for their attack on French were systematically beating him into the ground. Consciousness began slipping from his grasp.

Emboldened by the sight of their enemy barely able to focus his eyes to see them, the railroad men increased their vicious attack. Morris aimed a kick that caught Kyle under the edge of his rib cage and left him fighting for breath. While the lumberman sent a fist to Morris's midsection, Haley slammed both fists into the small of his back and catapulted him forward into Lartel's flying fists.

Kyle lost count of the blows as the men he'd fought to a standstill up on the mountain got their licks in. He was bloodied and half-conscious when Abernathy called a halt.

Panting from pain and the effort to give as good as he got, Kyle attempted to stand. He got as far up as one knee.

Abernathy, rubbing his sore knuckles, told him, "Let this be food for thought, Devereaux. The next time the railroad asks you for something, come across. Or you'll get more of the same."

"When pigs . . . fly, Abernathy." Kyle shoved a shoulder against the boulder behind him and struggled to rise.

It wasn't in Abernathy's plans. "Stubborn fool. Guess you need a little more persuasion." With that, he drew back his booted foot and kicked Devereaux under the chin.

Kyle's head snapped back against the unyielding granite of the boulder. Bright lights exploded behind his eyes. Stygian darkness crashed down on him and he sprawled bonelessly into the dirt.

In the sudden silence, one of the thugs stepped close to the fallen man. He bent over Kyle's prostrate body. When he spoke, his voice was hushed. "Boss. I think you may have killed him."

Abernathy merely looked at the man, his face expressionless. Then he shrugged. "Mount up. Let's get back into town."

"Whadaya want us to do with Devereaux?"

"Leave him. Just bring his horse. We'll take it into the woods and shoot it."

The man he'd spoken to reached out for Daumier's reins. With a snort, the big horse whirled away from him and ran for all he was worth. Frightened by the smell of blood and the sight of his master lying motionless on the ground, he pounded down the road. He was running for the safety of the snug stall that had always been his reward for bringing his rider out this way.

One of Abernathy's men started to go after him.

"Leave it!" Abernathy ordered sharply. "Let's get the hell out of here. If Devereaux's a goner, I don't want us to be seen anywhere near this place."

The men ran for their horses. A minute later the dust settled and there was only the sound of the wind sighing through the tops of the pines. There was nothing left to indicate they'd been there.

Nothing except the battered body of Kyle Devereaux.

Chapter Twenty-one

KYLE'S HORSE, DAUMIER, tore past the Chamberses' ranch house and hurtled down the lane to the barn, stirrups flapping and reins flying. A ranch hand used his cow pony as a barrier to stop the panicked gelding. Talking softly, he caught up the quivering animal's reins.

Alarmed by the frantic tempo of Daumier's hoofbeats, Charlie came running out of the house. "What in tarnation's going on out here?"

"It's Mr. Devereaux's gelding, sir."

"Bloody hell! Where the devil's Kyle?"

"He must have fallen off, Mr. Chambers."

Charlie let loose a string of curses. "Kyle Devereaux never fell off a horse in his life."

Julia appeared in the doorway behind him. Her voice was high with tension. "What is it, Charles? What's wrong?"

Charlie ordered, "Get back in the house and keep French inside."

Julia stepped back into the house immediately. Charles had never spoken to her in that tone before. That he had now must mean that something awful had happened. Fear gnawed at the edges of her mind.

Julia lost no time obeying her husband. Turning back toward the stairs, she hurried to find French. Whatever was going on, it was obvious Charles thought French was going to be distressed by it.

Outside, Charlie ran down to the barn. "Get some more of the boys together while I saddle my horse. We're going to find Devereaux."

"Yessir!" The cowhand was off like a shot, yelling to the few men still left in the vicinity of the ranch building, "Come on, men. Mount up. Mr. Chambers wants us!"

They jumped to it. Some got a foot in a stirrup before they sent their mounts galloping toward the boss; some just grabbed the saddle horn and made flying mounts. There were five eager cowpokes on milling horses surrounding Charlie before he'd finished tightening his horse's cinch.

"Good men," he said with grim satisfaction. Mounting up, he spurred his horse into a gallop, the others following. They charged past the house, a mass of yelping cowboys, flying manes, and pounding hooves. They were out of sight before the echo of their passing had died.

Inside the sprawling ranch house, Julia's mouth tightened to a firm line. Such incautious haste confirmed her suspicion that something was terribly wrong. Irritably she wondered how she was expected to keep French inside when the men made so much commotion that a deaf octogenarian would fight her for an explanation of what was happening. She put her hand to her stomach where flights of butterflies were careening around, and composed herself to face her niece.

French rushed out of her bedroom, her eyes wide. "What is it? What's all the noise outside, Aunt Julia?"

Jamie tore out of his room and rushed to one of the front windows in the upstairs hall. When he caught a glimpse of the ranch's youngest cowhand walking Kyle

Devereaux's Daumier to cool the big horse out, he muttered, "I have a bad feeling about this."

The horse was steaming. Jamie figured it had to be a good case of fright as well as a hard run that had put him in that condition. Kyle saw to it that Daumier stayed in fine shape. He wouldn't be that hot even if Kyle had galloped him every bit of the way out here from town. The big liver chestnut was quivering all over, too. Something pretty bad must have happened to put him in such a state. Jamie's fists clenched.

Thinking that something must have happened to Devereaux flooded him with guilt and fear. Fear for his uncle's safety overcame the guilt, but it still troubled him. He'd meant to tell his uncle who he was, he really had. Time had just seemed to get away from him. Before he knew it he was so much a *part* of things, and he'd never belonged before. Not in his whole life.

Now, French needed him to drive her to school. And Charlie Chambers was teaching him everything about cattle ranching . . . And Julia and Charlie Chambers were so like parents to him, parents he'd never had . . . And he was so darned happy here!

Miserably, he admitted that all of that was no excuse. He *had* no excuse.

Suppose something really terrible had happened to his uncle? Suppose he never got to square things? He stood there hating himself for his selfishness in not telling Kyle Devereaux that he was his nephew.

Suddenly he wasn't sure that all the contented happiness he'd found here on Lightning Double C was worth the price he was paying at this moment. Pressing his hot forehead against the cool glass of the window, he stared with unblinking eyes down the road where the men had gone.

Behind him, Julia, love and concern for the boy in her eyes, watched him and longed to comfort him. She knew her heart would break if Jamie ever left them. So, she guessed, would Charles's. Perhaps that was why he'd never asked the child where he'd been heading when he'd come to brighten their lives. Surely, if God were kind, Jamie would never leave them.

But Jamie's shoulders were squared and tense. He was managing his anxiety manfully. He wouldn't welcome her interference, she knew, this boy-man who had become such a vital part of their lives. And there was someone else so very dear to her heart who needed her even more, her precious French.

French was watching her aunt's face with wide, beseeching eyes. "Please tell me why the men galloped off like that, Aunt Julia." Her voice was frightened, as if she'd already guessed that something had happened to Kyle and was frantically denying the knowledge.

Julia reached for French's hands. She put all the reassurance she could into her clasp on them. Leading French to the love seat just behind Jamie, she urged the girl to sit. As she did, flashes of memory came to Julia. She remembered all the times she and Charlie had sat here, overlooking the road and the lake it curved around, and spoken gentle, secret things to each other.

Now what would come to this haven? What would they see when Charles and his men came back into view? Her heart was heavy. A riderless horse meant trouble in the West.

And this riderless horse was Kyle's.

Knowing that Kyle was in danger from the railroaders, Julia's nerves were screaming. Why couldn't they hurry? Why couldn't she know what it was that she had to protect Henry French from? Or indeed, if she had to protect her at all.

Her own anxiety was high, and if hers was, what would French's be? Was Kyle injured? Could she hope that he'd just been spilled from his horse?

The absurdity of that chided her. *But oh, dearest Lord, don't let him be . . .* Her mind skittered away from that thought like a frightened colt. She forced herself to finish the prayer. *Dear God, don't let him be dead!*

French read the fear in Julia's eyes. Always close, in spite of miles separating them and infrequent visits, French read her aunt rightly. "It's Kyle, isn't it?" Her voice choked.

Julia took refuge in the only fact she had. "Only Kyle's horse, darling. Daumier has come in . . ." She knew she had to be frank with her beloved niece. It would prepare her for whatever was to come. Lies and platitudes never served to do more than cloud issues in times of real trouble. ". . . all lathered and frightened. The men have gone to find out what happened . . ." Her voice failed her, she couldn't go on.

"To Kyle," French finished for her. She rose like someone in a trance and went to stand beside Jamie at the large windows looking out over the ranch road.

Jamie's voice was loud in the quiet of their waiting. "They're coming! I see 'em."

Julia jumped up and joined them at the windows. Her far sight was exceptionally good and she saw . . . pressing her hand to her mouth, she stilled the telltale quiver of her lips. Soon enough—in another instant— the others would see the limp form Charlie carried in front of him.

French saw it, too. She touched the window frame as

if seeking support, then half turned and reached blindly for her aunt.

Julia gathered her into her arms and held her, but neither of them looked away from the window and the terrible sight that met their gazes.

Kyle was limp and still, his head back over Charlie's arm. Blood covered his face. Under the blood, his face was white as death.

With an inarticulate cry, Jamie thrust himself away from the window and pelted down the stairs. Julia looked at French.

French stood as if she'd been turned to stone, her breath coming in shallow little gasps. Kyle. Kyle! Her mind refused to do more than to call his name. Again and again, Kyle, in a frantic litany of fear.

It was as if her mind simply refused to consider anything about his condition. It had locked up her faculties somehow, denying her the use of them. She could only stand there, stunned.

Kyle. Was he . . . injured? Dead? As she thought the question, they were not words, not concepts. They were phantoms haunting the edges of her mind, threatening to become real any moment so they could attack her sanity. Right now, she could understand only his name, cried from the depths of her heart, her very soul.

Julia shook her shoulder gently. "French?"

It was a reminder to rejoin the living, but French couldn't manage it, not yet. She could only look down to where her uncle was handing Kyle's long body carefully down to the strongest of his men.

He was handing him down so he could dismount, her mind registered dully. He would come tell them, she had only to wait. Uncle Charles would come tell them.

Some part of her mind stirred and began to rage at her

to go find out for herself. It told her waiting was impossible, but still she couldn't move.

The cowhand who received Kyle's lithe form cradled him in his arms like a small child, and stood waiting. Her Uncle Charles gave an order and two of the men spun their horses back toward town and galloped off, and French's heart lifted. Surely there would be no need for haste if not for the doctor.

Suddenly she could move again. She'd already turned eagerly to her aunt before the thought hit her, *Or the sheriff.* Her heart began to hammer fiercely, painfully, but she was alive again, and no power on earth was going to stop her from seeing for herself what had happened to Kyle.

Whatever it was, if he still breathed the breath of life, she was going to make him well and whole again. She left the comfort of her aunt's arms and ran down the hall to the top of the stairs.

"French! Be careful!" Julia couldn't bear it if something happened to French, too.

She needn't have worried. French rose on her toes, poised like a bird ready to fly down the wide oak stairway, and stood there. She had no need to go down. Led by a grim-faced Charles, the man carrying Kyle was coming up the stairs.

Julia, leaning over the side of the grand stairwell, saw them coming up and ran to open the door to one of the bedrooms. Rushing in, she turned down the sheets and waited, wringing her hands.

The men brought Kyle in and put him on the bed. He groaned faintly as they settled him.

French darted around them like the bird she'd resembled as she'd stood poised at the top of the stairs. The instant they laid Kyle on the bed, she brushed his hair back from his forehead and peered anxiously into his face.

Kyle groaned again as the men began pulling his boots off, and French's heart felt as if it would leap out of her chest with relief. He was alive! He was hurt, perhaps even grievously, but he was alive! *Praise God!*

Her tremulous smile dissolved in tears of gratitude and relief. She turned away from the bed looking for her aunt and comfort while the men took care of getting Kyle's clothing off him.

Julia took her into her arms and held her. Her own tears spilled over.

Jamie came into the room, followed by Miss Mary with a tray full of clean rags and a big bowl of warm water. Soft sounds of sympathy issued from the housekeeper almost against her will. She'd meant to be quiet as befit a sickroom, but seeing poor Kyle's battered face made it impossible.

"Good," Charlie gave them his approval for the tray. "I'll clean him up a bit."

"No!" French whipped out of her aunt's embrace. "I'll do it."

They all looked a little startled, but, after an exchange of glances, they let her have her way. Charlie went to Julia and took her in his arms. Whispering softly to her, he calmed Julia's motherly anxiety for French. "She can do it, Julie. She needs to be busy. Come away. There's nothing we can do until the sawbones gets here."

Julia let herself be led from the room, melting into her husband's arms for the comfort for which she herself had such a need. Miss Mary and the big cowhand went by them on their way downstairs.

Charlie took Julia around the railed stairwell, back to where she had waited so fearfully with French, back to their favorite love seat. From there, they watched the road for the return of Charlie's men with the doctor, their arms entwined about each other.

In the room with the injured man, Jamie asked French, "Can I help? Is there anything else that you need?"

Smiling at him gently through her tears, French said, "No, Jamie dear. You were wonderful to think of having Miss Mary bring up the water." Her lips trembled, but she managed to make her voice firm. "Cleaning the b-blood off his face is all we can do to help until the doctor arrives." She settled in the chair beside the bed, turning it to give her the best access to Kyle.

"*You're* gonna wash off all that blood?"

French felt herself flinch a little at that, but hoped Jamie hadn't noticed. "Yes. I'll try to clean his face for the doctor."

"Okay. I guess I'll go check to see if Daumier's all right. Mr. Devereaux sets a powerful store by that horse."

"That's a fine idea, Jamie. That will probably be the first thing he'll want to know when he awakens."

Jamie's smile thanked her. He truly needed something at which he could keep busy. Quietly he left the room.

Left alone, French whispered, "And I will clean your face, my darling." Her voice shook uncontrollably now that there was no one to hear. Her tears fell unchecked, but it didn't matter. She was alone with him, and he was unconscious, there was no one to see.

Gently she began to wash away the blood. She started with a cut under his chin surrounded by an angry red bruise. He frowned as she laved the blood away, but neither spoke nor moved.

Next she dampened a fresh piece of linen and began to clean the gash along his cheekbone. It was going to need stitches. Numbly, she hoped Dr. Burton could do a neat job of stitching.

Concentrating on cleaning the cut, she wondered what had torn it so deeply, for it didn't look clean-edged as a knife wound would be. She was trying so hard to be analytical about it all. She knew she wouldn't be able to function if she thought in other than clinical terms. She daren't let herself think that this was Kyle's cheek she was inspecting. It had to be an impersonal wound, that was the only way she could keep up her courage. Inside she could feel herself shaking, she was so terribly frightened for him. He was so pale and still!

She cleansed the gash in his cheek as thoroughly as she could, using a little of the soap Miss Mary had put on the tray. She knew that unless she got all the dirt out, he would have a nasty scar. As it was, she hoped the doctor was clever with his stitches, because it was going to take quite a few to close the gash.

Satisfied at last that it was as clean as anyone could make it, she turned her attention to his split lip. The same held true here, she was determined he'd have no scar if she could help it.

Her hands were surer now, her breath easier. Being of some use to him was steadying her.

She listened to his breathing, then she put her hand against his heart. Feeling the steady rhythm under her hand, hearing his deep, regular breaths, was reassuring to her. "Oh, Kyle. You must be all right. You *must*!"

The urgency in her voice reached him. "French," he murmured. "I didn't. I swear to you I didn't." He rolled his head from side to side on his pillow, agitated, desperate to tell her. "I didn't."

"Shhh. Hush now, darling, hush. Lie still."

He was still for a long minute, then, "Oh, French," he said without opening his eyes, "I hurt."

He sounded just like an injured child, and she felt as if her heart would break. Her tears fell again. She dashed them away with the back of her hand so that she could see to finish cleaning his face.

When she had, she sat quietly beside him, holding the hand nearest her in both of hers. Where was the doctor? It seemed to her as if he were taking forever to come.

She smoothed her hand across Kyle's forehead, rose from her chair, and kissed him there, her lips lingering on his smooth, warm brow. Kyle Devereaux had to be all right. She'd waited all her life, and had even come to think there was no one for her in the whole wide world, then she'd met Kyle. He had to be all right. He had become her world.

French sat down again to wait for the doctor.

Chapter Twenty-two

THE DOCTOR STOOD in the hall just outside Kyle's door and told the Chamberses, "He'll be all right. He just took a hell of a beating. He's lucky those ribs aren't broken." He patted Julia on the shoulder and smiled tightly at Charlie. "Just keep him still for a while. He has a mild concussion, so I don't want him ranting around. He'll probably have trouble seeing straight for the first day, maybe two. Couple of days after his vision clears up should do it. He's a very fit man. You shouldn't coddle him too long. Might turn him mean."

Julia offered a wan smile in appreciation of the doctor's mild joke. "We'll be careful of him."

"Want me to tell the sheriff what happened?" Doc Burton peered at Charlie, standing on Julia's other side with an arm around her. "It was the railroaders, wasn't it, Charlie?"

"Who the hell else?" Charlie remembered Julia. "Forgive me, my dear."

"Well, what about the sheriff?"

"We'll take care of the matter." Charlie's voice was almost as grim as his face.

The doctor was an old friend. "Watch you don't do anything you'll be sorry for when you cool off, Charlie, because I don't have the impression you meant you'd take care of notifying the sheriff."

"Thanks for the concern, Burton, but I reckon I can handle this."

"Yeah, I guess you can." The doctor started for the stairs. "Just remember Kyle Devereaux might not thank you for taking care of something he might think came under the heading of his own personal business."

Charlie looked thoughtful. "Maybe you got a point there, Burton. How long before he wakes up?"

"Not so long you wouldn't do well to wait."

Charlie pursed his lips thoughtfully and narrowed his eyes. "Much obliged, Doc." He gave Julia a quick hug and walked away with the doctor. "I'll see you out." Charlie thought it might be a plenty good idea to see if the sawbones had anything more to say about the shape Kyle was in, any little something he might not want to say in front of Julia.

When he came bounding back up the steps, Julia was waiting at the top of them. "Well?" Her voice was breathless with concern.

"He's fine, Julie, just kicked and pounded to hell an' gone . . . 'scuse the language. Doc Burton says he'll be up in a few days with no lasting effects except a dandy collection of bruises." He frowned a little, but he had to tell Julia the truth. "And a scar on his cheek. Doc says there's no way around that."

Julia sagged gratefully into his arms. "Oh, I'm so relieved that it's no worse. Oh, Charles. When I saw all that blood, I was so afraid." She snuggled into his embrace.

"Hell, honey . . . I beg your pardon . . . I've seen half our hands look at least that bad after a Saturday night brawl and be no worse for wear a few days later. Kyle'll be fine, you'll see."

Julia just sniffled once and let him lead her away.

Beside Kyle's bed, French tried to smile. "Did you hear that? Uncle Charles says you're no worse off than a brawling cowhand." She held her smile for an instant, then burst into tears and sat there crying as if her heart would break.

"Hey." Kyle cleared his throat and tried for a stronger voice. "You sorry I'm not hurt worse than a Saturday night cowboy?"

French's head snapped up, her face radiant with relief. "Kyle, you're awake!"

He grinned lopsidedly, carefully favoring the torn side of his mouth. "So it would seem." He lay there quietly, drinking in the beauty of her tear-drenched face. She was so lovely, so obviously caring. He'd never seen a woman's face show such tender concern.

Then fear hit him like ice water off the glacier, knotting his maltreated stomach. She was all sympathy for him now, while he was hurt, but what about when he was back on his feet? How would she feel about him then? His heart turned over in his chest. He couldn't bear the thought of losing her and the gentle love he saw in her right now. If, when he was well, she despised him, how would he bear it? Now that he'd come to know and love her, how could he live without this woman?

"Oh, Kyle, does it hurt horribly?" Her eyes were brimful of fresh tears.

He laughed, then winced as pain from his abused ribs shot through him. "Ah!" The exclamation held a wealth of pain. "I'm fine, French, honey. Just some bruises and a cut or two. Don't get yourself all upset."

Anger replaced the pity in her eyes. "How can you say

that? How can you lie there and say you're fine when you flinch with pain when you try to laugh, and your poor, beautiful face is . . . is . . . is a *mess*!"

"Was my face beautiful to you, French?" he asked in wonder.

She blushed fiercely. Priming her lips, she took a deep breath and told him the truth. "Yes," she said defiantly, ready to argue the point. "Yes, you *are* beautiful." Her expression dared him to make fun of her for her honesty.

It was the last thought in his mind. He was overwhelmed by the fact that she might think him beautiful. Plenty of women—women who shouldn't even be remembered in the same thought as his French—had told him that his body was beautiful, but none of them had ever mentioned his face. He was fascinated by this further proof that his French was the most special woman alive. He realized with a sense of wonder that he thought she was even more special than Charlie's Julia . . . and she was, because she was his, Kyle's. The realization washed over him like a benediction.

His. He savored the word, savored the warmth that transfused him. French was *his*.

At least he hoped she was.

Then the glacier fell on him.

Suppose she wasn't? Suppose the goodness in her that was one of the things he so loved about her was all that was causing her to look at and after him so tenderly?

Frustration bigger than he could contain welled up and exploded in his brain. He wanted to howl! Damn this idiotic vacillation he was experiencing! Never in his life had he been swayed and swung from one side of an issue to the other like a weathercock in a high wind, and it was driving him out of his mind! He swore it had to stop.

Then he was doing it again, for God's sake!

Suppose when he was back on his feet, French looked at him with the loathing he'd deserve if Abernathy's foul lie were true? What would he do then? How would he stand it if she looked at him like the worm he'd be if he'd killed a good man like Jake Price for nothing more than his silver mine . . . for greed? The very thought was enough to gag him, and the way he was letting it dominate his mind was driving him wild.

He shook his head to clear his mind, then again in an attempt to clear his vision. Both shakes forced a groan from him. Worse, there was no improvement in his vision. He'd been seeing double since he woke up. So he had a concussion. He decided he'd just have to live with it.

There was something he could not live with, however. He blurted to the clearest of the two Frenches he saw, "French, I didn't kill your uncle." Kyle rolled his head back and forth restlessly, grimacing with the pain the movement caused him. "Abernathy lied. I didn't." He gasped the words between spasms of pain. "I swear to you I didn't kill Jake."

She recoiled from him in astonishment. "What . . . ?" Her mind reeled under the assault of his blunt statement. "Why are you telling me this?" The shocked horror she felt filled her voice. Of all the things that he might have said to her, this was surely the most unexpected. She tried to make sense of it. Why would Kyle say such a thing to her? It was almost as if he thought she might believe something so terrible of him. Surely he knew there was no possibility of that?

Kyle was watching her face as carefully as he could. His eyes seemed impossible to focus. Anxiety crucified him. French sat looking at him as if she couldn't get her mind to function. She must have thought that Abernathy had told her the truth. She must have believed the lie.

No doubt she'd hoped to nurse him back to health before she had to face what was, for her, the awful fact that the man she'd thought she'd loved had killed her uncle. How agonizing this must be for her. Like a fall of bright ice shards the thought sliced through him. *How can she stand the sight of me?*

French's head was awhirl as she strove to comprehend, then suddenly she understood. Abernathy must have told Kyle that he'd accused him to her of murdering her uncle! Her heart sank. How could he think for even an instant that she might believe this? Surely Kyle knew she was better than that? Surely he understood her well enough, *valued* her enough, to know she could never believe that he could harm an innocent man? He had to know that she was perceptive enough, a good enough judge of character, not to throw away her love on a man who could take the life of another for no more reason than common greed.

Her spirits plummeted as she looked into his face and knew that he'd judged her and found her wanting. He was asking her to believe him innocent of something that she knew with all the instincts of an honest woman he could never have done. Tears welled in her eyes. She blinked to clear them, to keep him from knowing how deeply his distrust of her had wounded her.

Her heart wept.

Kyle Devereaux valued her no more than did those she loved at home. Just like her parents, he needed to ask her to prove herself to him.

Kyle saw her battle to hold back her tears, to keep him from seeing them, and his heart stilled, frozen, in his chest. She'd weighed the evidence and found him guilty.

With a single, foul lie, Abernathy had sealed his fate. French Richards, his soul's only hope, believed him capable of killing her uncle.

Heaviness like a mountain crushed his spirit. It didn't even matter to him whether or not she believed that he had killed Jacob Price for his mine. That she merely considered the possibility that he might have was enough to destroy something deep in his very core.

"French?" The single word, her beloved name, was wrenched from the depths of his soul.

She reached for him then, and put a gentle hand on his arm as if she reached out to him from a very long way away. Speech was denied her. There was nothing she could say to him, so lost in misery was she at the certainty that he had never known her, never believed in her, never valued her as she had him. If he had, he would never have had to tell her such a thing, for he'd have known that she could never have believed it of him.

If he'd believed in her, he'd never have felt the need to utter the words that had catapulted her back into icy loneliness.

She couldn't even begin yet to wonder what had triggered his strange statement. Her mind was as numb and useless as if it had received a mighty physical blow. She could only sit there beside Kyle and hold tight to his arm until the pain and confusion she was suffering eased. When it did . . . if it did . . . perhaps she would be better able to deal with the awful thing he'd said. Perhaps later she would find the strength to help with whatever was burdening her dearest lost love, Kyle.

Perhaps.

Chapter Twenty-three

Winter had come in earnest. They'd had their first snowfall. Soft and white it had blanketed the country around them and turned it into fairyland. Now it lay waiting patiently for reinforcements that would turn the fairyland into an environment to be reckoned with.

The pace had slowed on the ranch, on the mountain logging had speeded up, and the schoolchildren were getting excited about Thanksgiving. Still things were no better between French and Kyle.

Julia went to Charles for comfort. "Oh, Charles. I'm so miserable."

"Don't be, Julia honey." Charles pulled her into his embrace and held her. "There're enough people miserable around here without you tryin' to join 'em. Even the boy mopes around these days."

Julia snuggled closer as she always did when things threatened to overwhelm her. She couldn't worry about Jamie now, much as she loved him, she had more important things on her mind. All her plans for French and Kyle had gone awry. "I'm upset about French and Kyle. Why do they have to be so stubborn?"

"Because they are," Charlie told her calmly. "That's the way of people, Julia. The weak ones get whiny and the strong ones get stubborn. Give 'em time. They love each other. That'll bring 'em around in the end."

Julia pulled away and began to pace. Charlie looked faintly surprised. She'd never done that before. Finally she stopped and faced him. Her lovely face was drawn. "Perhaps I should speak with French."

"Aw, Julie." Charlie smiled at her. He knew his Julia so well. "If anyone can get 'em together, you can."

"I hope so. I'll talk to her the minute she gets home."

As good as her word, Julia was waiting for French when Jamie dropped her off at the front door. "Come in, dear. You must be frozen." She watched as French pulled off her scarf and gloves, then helped her shed her winter coat. "I have hot tea in the parlor. It'll warm you up."

French trailed her aunt listlessly. She knew Julia was more worried about her emotional condition that her physical comfort. Hot tea might warm her chilled body, but she felt so wintry inside she knew there was nothing that could ever make her feel warm again, and she really wished her aunt wouldn't bother. She also wished she could avoid the chat she knew was coming.

Her aunt was pretending to be worried only about her chilled person, though, and hot tea might help that. Nothing could help the cold wilderness inside . . . the awful longing.

The silver tea service waited for them on the table in the best parlor. Her aunt poured and fixed two cups with cheerful efficiency. She offered one to French. French took it with a sigh.

Julia didn't waste any time. To her way of thinking, too much time had already passed since Kyle, silent and grim and as stiff in body as a cigar-store Indian, had demanded his horse and ridden back to town—in spite of all her and Charles's protests—with two of the ranch hands close behind him to see that he made it there safely.

None of them had heard a word from him since . . . not even on Sundays when he had always used to come to dinner, and Julia had frankly had enough of it. She got right to the point. "What happened between you and Kyle, French?"

French went white, then hectic color returned to her cheeks. She dropped her long lashes to conceal the pain in her eyes. Lifting her cup to her lips, she inhaled the warm, fragrant steam gently rising from it before she answered. "I . . . I'd really rather not talk about it, Aunt Julia."

"Fine, dear," Julia forced herself to sound nonchalant, "I'll just ride into town tomorrow and ask Kyle."

French's gaze flashed to her aunt's face. She bit back her protest. She knew Julia would do just as she'd threatened—and French clearly recognized her aunt's proposal to ride into town as just that, a threat. The only way to prevent her from making that threat good was to answer her question.

Tears trembled on her lashes as she capitulated. "Oh, Aunt Julia." She put her cup down as her control began to go. She didn't want her shaking hands to spill tea over the beautiful pastel colors of her aunt's fine Oriental rug. The cup safely in its saucer, she clasped her hands tightly and admitted, "I love him so."

Julia frowned. "Of course you do," she said soothingly. "And Kyle loves you, too. So what, then, is the problem, dearest?" She reiterated, "I know that Kyle loves you, too."

French looked away toward the window, her face forlorn in the wan afternoon light, tears shimmering on her lashes. After a little while she spoke. "He doesn't *value* me," she said in a tiny voice.

Julia fought down her impatience, striving to understand. "What do you mean, dear?"

"I mean he doesn't . . . value me."

Julia was quiet for a long moment, then she asked very, very gently, "Doesn't value you, French?" She drew a cautious breath, then ventured out on thin ice. "Don't you think it might be that you are accusing Kyle of something that your parents have been guilty of, not he?"

French's tears were sliding down her cheeks in a steady stream now. She tried hard to be fair. "Perhaps that's true. Perhaps I do have them all tangled up. But it doesn't matter. He can't truly know me for what I am . . . for all that I am . . . if he doesn't know that I could never believe he could kill Uncle Jacob."

"Kill Jacob!" Shock derailed Julia. "What on earth do you mean?" Her voice was no longer gentle. "Why in the world would you think Kyle had killed Jacob?"

"That's just it. Kendal Abernathy lied to Kyle and told him he, Abernathy, had told *me* that Kyle had killed Uncle Jacob for his silver mine."

"Preposterous!"

"Of course it is," French said in a tired little voice. "Kyle couldn't have killed my uncle. He could never do such a thing! And that's the point, don't you see? Kyle should never have thought, not even for a minute, that I would believe such a thing of him. Not if he knew my"—French sought desperately through the riot of her emotions for the right words. When they came, it was as if they were torn from her—"my true *worth* as a person."

"And that's the problem, isn't it?" Julia understood. She had seen enough of French's young life to know how

the girl had always worked so hard to please her parents and always fallen short. She'd seen how the young French had longed for the acceptance her brothers had been freely granted whether they'd merited it or not . . . and how she had been denied it.

Now French wanted it from Kyle. She'd grown up, but her childhood had left its mark on her. Evidently she was powerless not to impose this condition on any truly meaningful relationships she might have for all the rest of her life.

Perhaps being here with Charles and her had shown French that she *was* valued for herself. Julia hoped it had. Certainly the adoration her pupils had for her and the grateful approval of their parents must give French the sense of self-worth she'd long sought.

Julia was glad for all that, but why, oh, why, must the foolish child let this childhood hunger stand in the way of the glorious happiness that Julia knew she would find as an adult with Kyle? Julia felt as if she couldn't bear this. She tried one more time. "Kyle loves you, French."

"No," French insisted forlornly, her lovely face implacable. "Not if he thinks that I could ever believe him capable of murdering Uncle Jacob for the sake of greed."

Julia sat there. She could find nothing to say. Instead, she offered French her lace-trimmed handkerchief and simply sat there, her own heart breaking for her beloved niece.

The next morning Julia rose with determination to set things right filling her every thought. As soon as she knew that French would be safely occupied in teaching her pupils, Julia came downstairs in her handsome split-skirt riding costume.

Charles was safely out on the range with the majority

of the hands, so she could go to the sawmill without his being any the wiser . . . and without his interference. Charles had a way of turning into a mother hen the moment he saw a truly serious expression on her face, and Julia didn't want him hovering over her. Not today.

She stopped by the kitchen. Mary looked up from the pan of rolls she was getting ready for a second rising. The heady smell of yeast filled the warm kitchen. "Mary, I'm riding into town to talk to Kyle. I'll only be a little while, I hope, but I thought you'd want to know where I was off to."

"Does Mr. Chambers know you're going to town all by yourself?"

"Mary! I'm perfectly capable of riding into town by myself."

"I just don't like it. Not with all those railroad people around making mischief."

"I suspect that Kendal Abernathy is very carefully orchestrating the trouble Kyle's been having, and I'm sure that he is far too intelligent to cause, or even to permit, anything to happen to me. Charles is, after all, quite a force to be reckoned with."

Mary seemed reassured by that. "All right, Julia. Just be careful, dear. I couldn't bear to have anything happen to another friend."

Julia knew she referred to Jacob. "Don't worry, Mary. I shall be very careful." She smiled impishly. "You don't think I'm going to risk missing dinner when you're making rolls, do you?"

"Just don't you be late." Mary shooed her friend out of her kitchen and got back to work.

Julia went down to the barn, wrestled her saddle off the rack, and swung it up onto her mare. In another minute she'd bridled her. She smiled in satisfaction. She liked knowing she could, if allowed, still do for herself.

She mounted and headed for town, her thoughts churning. She hadn't the faintest idea what she intended to say to Kyle Devereaux, but after her fruitless conversation with her niece, she was determined to say something. She worried it around in her mind the whole ride in from the ranch.

She found Kyle at the mill proper. He was out in the big building that housed the huge circular saw, and she had to touch his sleeve to make him aware of her.

Startled, he asked her something that she thought might have been "What are you doing here?" but the noise of the saw slicing its way through a log made it impossible to hear. She put her hands over her ears; how did the men who worked the saw stand it?

Kyle took her elbow and guided her firmly back to his office. As soon as she felt she could make him hear her, she asked, "How in the world do you keep your hearing, Kyle?"

Kyle smiled and removed the bullets he'd put in his ears to block most of the screeching from the mill and showed them to her. "An old trick I learned from the man who taught me all the rest of what I know." When he saw she was truly interested, he added, "I make the man wear 'em, too." He grinned, but only faintly, and Julia saw that he was as miserable as French. "That way they can't claim they're too deaf to hear and follow my orders."

His face became serious. "What are you doing here, Julia? You never come into town without Charlie."

"That's hardly a cordial greeting, Kyle." The rebuke was mild, but it served its purpose. Kyle was momentarily off balance. Julia pressed her advantage. "I came to see what was the matter between you and French."

"You needn't have bothered." His face closed and became grim.

Julia looked steadily at him. This was proving harder than she'd thought it would be. She drew her riding gauntlets through her hand and told him, "Kyle, I know that you love my niece." Giving him a brief moment to absorb the fact that she had every intention of forcing him to discuss this subject, whether or not it pleased him, she went on. "Won't you please tell me what has gone wrong between you?"

He stared at her, not answering.

She said very softly, "This means a great deal to me, Kyle."

Her honesty defeated him. He'd always known he could deny Julia nothing she might ask of him . . . even something this difficult. Finally he spoke. "Yes, I love her."

Julia heard the words, given to her as if they were pulled out of him with hot tongs. It grieved her. Love shouldn't be so painful to express.

Kyle stood watching her from across the room, warning her with his eyes to be careful. Warning her that there were boundaries he would not permit even her to cross.

Julia had to cross them, though. If she didn't, something very precious was in danger of becoming lost. "Kyle. French loves you."

With a grimace, he threw up a hand as if he intended to prevent her from attacking him bodily. "No," he grated out. "No, Julia." He went on in a more normal voice. "She believes I killed . . . *murdered* her uncle."

"How can you say that?"

"Easily!" The word exploded from him. Hot-eyed, accusing, he glared at her. His anger, driven by weeks of pain and frustration, was a tangible force. It flared out at her. "Just look at her reticence. Look at the sad, wide-eyed looks she gives me. Suddenly her love . . . if she feels any . . . doesn't *glow* anymore. It's listless . . ." His voice broke. With an effort he strengthened it and said firmly, "It's gone, Julia. Gone. It's dead. And I . . ." He bit off the rest of the sentence, and Julia knew that wild horses would never drag the words he guarded out of him.

Aching for him, aching for them both, Julia repeated, *"Henry French loves you, Kyle Devereaux!"*

The agony on his face stopped her, numbing her. She could only sit where she'd perched on the edge of his desk and wish she could bear in her own heart some of the pain she felt emanating like a tangible force from her dear friend.

Before she could find words to say, comfort to offer him, the door slammed behind him. Kyle was gone. Julia knew that his departure should have signaled her own, but she could only sit there and struggle not to weep over the misunderstanding that was keeping her two dearest young friends apart.

Chapter Twenty-four

FRENCH'S CHILDREN WERE as excited as she had ever seen them. Today was the big day. Teddy, who'd acted as class monitor—French preferred to think—the first week of school, had found out from his father that Kyle Devereaux planned to spend the entire day out on the mountain supervising the logging there. So, the children and French were going to spend this day at the mill.

French stood in front of the room, watching the children bringing their coats, mittens, and mufflers from the cloakroom. "I'm so proud of you." She smiled at them, trying to let them see that she was, indeed, proud of her students. When she'd asked them to think up a class project or expedition that would culminate in a big pre-Christmas essay contest, several of them had gotten their heads together and come up with this one.

The contest was going to be won by the pupil whose essay best explained the lumber operation to someone who had no idea how it all worked. Other prizes were planned to go to the writers in each grade of the best essays on what the author had learned about the lumber mill. The majority of the children, those whose parents weren't involved in lumber operations, were further placated by the promise that the next contest would be about the town, its beginnings and legends and the jobs their parents did. While this seemed a big sacrifice on the part of the town and ranch children, French believed their insatiable curiosity about the inside of the mill had a lot to do with their acquiescence.

The little town of Sunrise had been started to cater to the needs of the cattlemen scattered through the broad valley at its foot. Having Kyle Devereaux and his Devil-Oh Lumber move in had not only caused the town to grow, to accommodate him and his men, but had brought excitement to its inhabitants.

The whole town had long been bursting with curiosity about the lumbermen, from the mill's owner, who'd come and built the biggest house in town while he built his sawmill, right down to the cook and his helpers who lived in the large building they called a shanty with the other unmarried men. As a result, the town and ranch children were happy to wait for the Spring Essay Contest to compete on their own terms.

Danny Conners, whose father owned the feed store, waved frantically. "Miss Richards! Miss Richards!"

"Yes, Danny?" She made no effort to correct his speaking out before being recognized. There was too much excitement in the classroom to stand on formalities today.

"Miss Richards, can I write my essay about how the town was before the lumberman came and how we felt about Mr. Devereaux coming? How he promised the sawmill would stay here and be part of the town and how that shut up a lot of grumpy people?"

French smiled at that. "As long as you remember to be *tactful*, Danny. Remember, words committed to paper cannot be recalled, and they endure forever."

"Yeah"—one of the boys prodded Danny in the side—"you don't want to make old man Kitteridge mad all over again. It took him long enough to settle down as it was."

"Aw, that was just because he was the one who . . ."

"Children," French curtailed the discussion before it took hold, "we must be going. We have a lot to see, and before we can go, we must review our safety precautions."

She waited for them to begin. Danny said, "Never let go of the hand of your partner."

A girl with long blond braids spoke from her position closer to the front of the double line the children had formed after they'd gotten their coats on. Glancing shyly at Teddy, she said, "We must all listen to Teddy, because he knows the dangers of the mill."

Teddy grew an inch and blushed. With a mighty effort, he stopped himself from grinning at his favorite schoolmate. He'd die if the other boys found out that he was sweet on Hildy Swenson.

French drew the attention of the other students back to herself. She must work to keep her own mind on the trip to the mill. Just seeing this evidence of calf love between two of her pupils had caused the ever-present ache in her to flare up again. *When was she going to be able to put Kyle Devereaux completely out of her mind and find peace? When was this terrible longing for Kyle Devereaux going to ease?* As she shepherded the children, staunchly linked in pairs, to the door, she demanded an answer. No answer came.

Sighing, she opened the door and stood to one side. Jamie hung back so that he could be the one to walk with her. The children filed out and marched up the hill to where the mill stood separated from the town by a short road. Soon they were standing expectantly at the edge of the mill yard where Teddy had stopped them with an uplifted hand. "From here on," he said self-importantly, "you gotta do just like I say so nobody gets hurt."

All up and down the line, nods promised obedience. Teddy turned and led the way into the cavernous mill. Even though the mill was not working today, the huge interior was not quiet. The sound of the river flowing under it filled the big structure.

Teddy spoke loudly, to be sure they all heard. "Here is where we cut the lumber up into the planks you see stacked up out in the yard. That little devil standing in the 'O' that's stamped on wood here is the mark of Devil-Oh Lumber. It's Mr. Devereaux's own mark. Some of you have probably seen it on the ends of the logs. It's put there by a man who stamps it in with a hammer after the tree is cut down."

"Be a little hard to put it on the end of a log before the tree was cut down, wouldn't it, Ted?" one of the boys at the back of the line called out tauntingly.

Teddy's face flamed, but he ignored the jab and went on. "The planks will be shipped all over the world . . ."

"The world?" The question was a chorus from the startled children.

Teddy ignored that, too. ". . . to be used for building things. Boats, houses, carts and carriages, furniture. This is where it all begins." Almost swaggering, he led them to a long row of windows along one side and pointed. "That there's the millpond out there. That's where all the logs stay until it's time to cut 'em into planks." He shot a glance at Hildy, saw her attention was firmly on him, and went on in a stronger voice. "The logs come to the saw on the ramp you see coming up here. Those chains on the ramp have hooks that catch the bark and drag 'em up from the pond, see?" There were murmurs and nods. "There aren't many logs left there in the pond, because we log in the winter, and we ain't got good and started yet. Right now, Kyle . . ." He allowed himself the use of his father's employer's first name to add to his self-importance, then was instantly ashamed of having done so. He added hastily, ". . . Devereaux, of Devil-Oh Lumber, is logging pines for ship masts and floors for houses back east and in Europe."

"Europe!" The word was another startled·chorus.

"Yeah, Europe. Didn't you know that the forests over there are about played out?"

The children looked at each other in amazement. Never on their longest day had they thought that Sunrise, Colorado, had anything people on the other side of the world wanted. Even French had never thought of it. She frowned slightly. Kyle's holdings must be vast, and so must be his responsibilities. And yet . . . and yet he had found time for her. Not much time, but more than he could spare, she was certain.

Her father had had only one bank, but he'd never found time for her . . . unless she'd done something of which he disapproved, of course.

Teddy's voice pulled her back from her thoughts. "Look outside again. See that dam up there over the mill-pond? And the other wooden trough coming down this way from there? That's the millrace. It powers the saw."

"Aw, come on, Ted," one of the boys scoffed, "the waterwheel turning is what powers the saw."

"Yeah?" Teddy thrust out his jaw, not liking to be diminished a second time in front of a certain young lady.

French was swamped by a memory. She remembered how Kyle had bristled and glared when he'd found out Abernathy had a right to talk to and to dance with her because he was a friend of one of her brothers. Smiling faintly, she began to wonder if all males were cast from the same mold.

Teddy was saying, "Well, what do you think turns the waterwheel?"

The boy reddened and looked away.

Teddy explained. "The dam gives the water lots more pressure, so when we open the end of the trough up there, it rushes down and turns the waterwheel and powers the saw. Later on, when it's deep winter, the waterwheel freezes, and we won't be able to cut lumber."

"Good," the girl holding Hildy's hand called out. "Then maybe it'll be quiet around here again."

She jumped when Hildy pinched her and told her, "Hush."

"Well, as to that, my Uncle Rafferty says that next year, when there's gonna be a lot less logging done, they'll only run the saw a day or two a week. That should make it better. Wouldn't run it at all, but for the fact that Mr. Devereaux promised to keep the mill open to take care of what Sunrise needs in the way of lumber and firewood. That ought to make you happier, Grace."

The girl holding Hildy Swenson's hand blushed, and Teddy led them over to the big saw. "This is a circular saw. Circular saws are the thing. The old muley saws that went up and down only cut on the down stroke. They take a lot longer to do the job. Some of Mr. Dev's mills have three saws, three *circular* saws, my Uncle Rafferty says."

One of the boys shot a hand up, remembered Teddy wasn't Miss Richards, and flushed. His curiosity overcame his embarrassment, however. "What happens out in the woods? What do all those men do?"

French could see Teddy swell with pride. She glanced at little Hildy Swenson and saw the look of adoration on

the girl's face. Unbidden, Kyle's face rose before her, and
the pain of loss rose with it. She'd no doubt that people
could have read her adoration for him on her own face
once. Her heartbeat hurt her. Would things ever be right
again between Kyle and her?

"Well," Teddy was saying, "as to the men, Mr.
Devereaux is at the top, o' course. He owns all the
Devil-Oh lumber mills in this country, and he's the
boss."

French was reminded again of Kyle's vast enterprises.
It was strange, she'd never thought that Kyle had other
lumber mills. Somehow she'd never thought of his
holdings at all, only about him . . . only about Kyle.

"Then comes Rafferty. He's *my* uncle"—Teddy placed
his hand on his chest, just in case some of the boys had
missed it when he'd called Rafferty uncle twice before—
"and he's the bull of the woods."

"What's a 'bull of the woods'?" That was from
Frankie Daniels, whose father's sprawling Rocking D
Ranch had given him experience with bulls, and that
experience said that bulls didn't much like woods.

"That means he can do everything any man in the
woods can do, only better. He even fixes up cuts and
things. Just like a doctor."

Cuts and things. The words brought back to French's
mind the cuts on Kyle's face that she had cleaned so
carefully. She hoped they were healing well and that her
care had minimized the scarring. With all her heart she
wished there were some way she could see those cuts,
some way to reassure herself that they were fine. But it
was hopeless. She could hardly invade his home and
peruse his sleeping face, and she hadn't the courage to
see him any other way. She had only so much courage

left when it came to Kyle. The reproach she'd seen in his eyes as he left her had stolen most of it away.

Teddy was still teaching about the mill. "My uncle has an assistant foreman, Evan Haislip, to take over for him when Mr. Dev needs my Uncle Rafferty for something else." His voice dropped, but a few of them heard him as he muttered, "Like guarding his back from these railroad toughs."

The children who had heard exchanged uneasy glances among themselves. Everybody knew about Mr. Devereaux being bushwhacked by the railroad men and beaten half to death, and their parents had issued solemn warnings to steer clear of all of it.

"Then there's cruisers to go find the best trees . . ." He interrupted himself to tell them, "Mr. Dev started out as a cruiser in Vermont when he was barely fourteen years old, he was so good at spotting trees. He did his own cruising here around Sunrise." Teddy smiled around at the startled murmurs. "Yep. Did it himself 'fore he decided to build the mill here."

He wiped the smile off his face and went on. "Then comes toppers, and choppers, fellers, stackers, then the teamsters who snake the logs to the skidway and down to the river or the millpond with the horses and mules . . . some places use oxen . . . and you got . . ."

The children were fascinated as a swaggering Teddy opened a new world for them, but French wasn't listening anymore. She was thinking of Kyle *barely* fourteen and all alone in the woods, looking for trees to be felled for whomever he'd worked for in Vermont. Vermont. That was a world away from New Orleans, and she knew from Julia that Kyle was from New Orleans. How on earth, when he was so young, did he get all the way to Vermont, so far away from his family? And *why* so

young? Her own brothers were still mere schoolboys
when they were fourteen . . . and still with their family.

A sense of the loneliness Kyle must have felt washed
over her. She tried to concentrate again on what Teddy
was saying because she'd caught Kyle's name.

". . . does a lot of his own cruising still. Mr. Dev
likes to keep the woods in good shape when he cuts
them, not just leave 'em bare hills with everything cut
down to stumps and the rain left free to tear the land to
pieces. He talks a lot with his fellers to be sure they can
take out the trees he wants without knocking everything
else down. If they can't, he mos' generally just leaves the
tree." Teddy waited for approval for his idol's methods.

It was duly given, especially for the two Foster
children who told their classmates, "We saw some of
those places. The hillsides with no more trees! We saw
them while we were on a trip east. They look awful!"

Teddy nodded sagely. The others looked at the Fosters
with round eyes a minute, then turned back to Teddy.
French was pleased to see he held their attention. He
went on to talk about log jams and log drivers and how
many of them got crushed and drowned, and the little
girls quailed nicely.

French, though, was lost again in thoughts of Kyle.
Being here among one of his accomplishments—evidently one of his many accomplishments—was bringing
him strongly to her mind, and causing her more pain than
she'd thought possible. Her stomach tightened to the
point of discomfort as she tried to banish memories of his
embrace, his kisses. She thought she would be unable to
endure it.

When Teddy finished their tour with a severe admonition not to climb the sawdust pile unless they fancied

suffocation in the clinging sawdust, French set about dismissing her pupils. "Now go home immediately, children. Go straight home and get to work on your essays as soon as you can. If you have chores, try to find time to make a few notes on all you have learned today so that you won't forget before you go out to do them. You've all been very good, and I know you've enjoyed this, haven't you?"

"Yes, Miss Richards."

She smiled at the happy chorus. "Then what do you say?"

"Thank you, Teddy," and "Thanks, Ted," and "Thanks a lot" rang out over the sound of the river flowing under them. The children looked to their teacher again, then, smiling and eager, ran for the big doors and home as she waved them off.

"Thank you, Teddy. You did a fine job."

"It was really great fun, Miss Richards. Thank you for letting me do it. Good-bye." Turning to her self-styled escort, he said, "See you tomorrow, Jamie," and was gone.

French stood looking after him as he ran out through the big double doors and headed for home, and an unbearable sadness filled her. She'd miss him. She'd miss them all, especially her beloved Aunt Julia and her Uncle Charles . . . and Jamie, dear solemn Jamie . . . and Miss Mary with her wonderful picnic lunches and gentle encouragement . . . and Teddy's Hildy and all the rest of her children. Tears filled her eyes as she remembered them all, as she silently said an early farewell to them all.

She hated the thought of leaving them, but she knew now that she had to go. There was no way she could stand to be here after she finished this school year. She didn't even know how she was going to be able to finish the year, but she knew beyond a shadow of a doubt that she would have to, and then she'd have to go away.

She knew she could never endure even one additional day of the sorrow and pain she'd been experiencing since Kyle had ridden away from the Lightning Double C.

Jamie watched her with deep concern. It was obvious she was grieving about his Uncle Dev. His teeth clenched. He wished there was some way he could make his uncle come chase the sadness out of Miss French's eyes. He'd beat him until he promised to if only he were bigger, he told himself.

Then he remembered that four railroad thugs had taken his Uncle Dev by surprise and beaten him unconscious without being able to change his mind about anything. He heaved a great sigh. He guessed he wouldn't be able to change his mind, either, even if he grew to be ten feet tall. Reluctantly, he turned to more practical matters. "Want me to go get the mare harnessed up, Miss French?"

"Yes, Jamie. That would be lovely. I'll walk down to the road to meet you in a minute."

He saw she was battling tears, and decided the best thing was to leave her alone to cry it out. He went out the door with steps that dragged. Having his own problem, that of explaining to his Uncle Devereaux how come he'd not reported to him right off, was bad enough. Adding his cherished Miss French to his burden was beginning to sink him.

Jamie kicked a rock or two on his way down the road. When he reached the crossroad, he looked both ways. It was a habit that hung on from his days of dodging carriages in the crowded streets of New Orleans, and he always felt a little foolish when he caught himself doing it here in peaceful Sunrise. This time, though, there was traffic coming. Shocked, he saw a band of railroaders heading purposefully his way. And there wasn't anything up this way but the Devil-Oh sawmill!

He threw a frantic glance over his shoulder. If Miss French came out now, they'd see her for sure. If she ran for it, they might just decide to try to catch her. The chances of his getting up there to get her out were nil, also. The open doors were in full view.

Frantic, he chanced one word, shouted at the top of his lungs, "Hide!" With all his heart, he prayed that French would hear, recognize his voice, and hide, while the railroaders ignored his child's cry as part of a harmless game. Then Jamie took off running to the lean-to and the mare faster than he'd ever run in his life. The sheriff, every schoolchild knew, was on his way to the capital and wouldn't be back until day after tomorrow. There was nothing for it! He'd have to ride for Devereaux and his men!

As he flung himself on the startled mare's bare back and galloped out of town, he prayed, *Please, God, let Miss French stay hidden!*

Chapter Twenty-five

INSIDE THE MILL, French thought she heard Jamie's voice yelling, "Hide!" She couldn't be certain over the babble of the river that filled and echoed through the mill, but her body reacted to his cry before her mind could decided whether or not he was speaking to her.

She began to shiver as if she were afraid. An instant later the feeling that she might be in some danger hit her. Uncannily, she knew then that Jamie had been speaking to her . . . been trying to warn her! She knew that she had to hide! But where? The mill was empty, just a huge bare expanse of swept floor except for the giant saw and its attendant structures!

Fear such as she had known on the mountain fell on her like an icy pall. Frantically, she looked around for a place to conceal herself. A tall stack of lumber against one of the walls offered the only place she might hide, and she ran over to it, all thoughts of Kyle flying from her mind.

What could Jamie have seen? Surely he must be warning her about something? All his schoolmates were out of reach of the sound of his voice by now. They had all gone home to do their homework and chores. Besides, Jamie wasn't playing hide-and-seek, Jamie was going to get the gig.

Foolish as one part of her mind told her she was being, she was powerless to behave any differently. The encounter with the three men on the mountain must have made a coward of her, for she was quick to go and conceal herself.

Prudence told her that she wasn't being cowardly, only careful. It would be a simple enough thing to emerge from where she cowered if this awful fright she was feeling were groundless.

She almost smiled as she squeezed farther in between the boards and the wall. At least there was no one to see her behave so peculiarly.

She'd wanted to be alone to think of Kyle, and now she was. She should be satisfied. The loved ones who were always interrupting her thoughts with little gestures of concern were far away, and she was alone at last. She could, common sense told her, think of Kyle Devereaux just as well standing behind one of his stacks of fresh-cut lumber as she could standing in the middle of the open floor of his mill.

Silly as she felt, she leaned back against the wall inhaling the clean scent of newly sawn wood and proceeded to let her mind return to Kyle and the tender way he had taken her in his arms that night and . . .

Suddenly every nerve tingled. She heard heavy footsteps, many of them, on the sturdy floor of the mill. That she could hear them so clearly above the water below told her they were men, large men, and she knew that no group of large men from the complement of those who ran the mill would turn up here just at suppertime.

A rough voice called out a man's name, and her blood ran cold. She recognized the name as belonging to one of the men who'd attacked her on the mountain. French began to shake uncontrollably.

Clenching her teeth to keep them chattering, she pressed her back hard against the wall. She earnestly thanked God that she'd heard the warning Jamie had given. And that she'd heeded it. She couldn't bear the thought of actually meeting those awful men another time. Ever!

"Get that big bucket of oil they keep for the saw, Morris. Haley, you get some boards to pile up. Help him, you two!" The man's voice was rougher than she'd heard it on the day of the barbecue, but French would have sworn she was listening to Kendal Abernathy. The knowledge sent waves of shock through her.

"Make a pile around the saw," Abernathy ordered. "Not that it matters, but it might be good if the sheriff thought the fire started there. Not much else in here that might start a blaze. Devereaux keeps a clean mill. Besides, the saw's the most important thing in here."

Arson! They were talking about arson. Kendal Abernathy and his men were going to set fire to Kyle's sawmill deliberately! French was outraged. She searched her mind for anything she might do to stop these men from burning Kyle's property.

No answer came. It seemed to be a day without answers for her.

What must she do? She could run out at them and tell them that she knew who they were and what they were up to! Decency demanded that she act. Though that thought was a brave one, French's common sense prevailed.

These men hadn't cared who she was on the mountain, she remembered with a shudder. Nor had anything they'd done then or since indicated that they had any respect for the rights or opinions of others. These men were barbarians. And if Abernathy, friend of her brother or not, was their leader, then he was no better. He just had a more polished facade, and realizing now what lay behind that social mask made her skin crawl.

What had made her think, even for an instant, that her presence would deter them? No, they'd probably use her as kindling.

She'd made the feeble joke to shore up her flagging courage. She knew that if they discovered her, they would probably carry out their original foul designs on her person. She was literally shaking with fear at the mere thought of such violation. With all her might, she prayed that wherever Jamie had gone, he'd gone to get help.

French's heart nearly stopped when two of the men came over to the stack of lumber behind which she was hiding and began to drag boards off the top. Cringing lower as the stack was quickly reduced, she prayed they weren't planning to take it all. She turned sideways to give herself the space to bend, she dropped to her knees so that her head would be even farther below the top of the stack, in case one of the men should peer over the boards.

"That's enough!" French heard the order with a rush of relief. She flinched as a board was pushed violently back on the stack and slammed into the wall just over her head. "We haven't got all day. Slop that oil on the lumber and set it afire. Shake a leg!"

The smell of oil came to French as she heard great splashes of it. Then she heard a whoosh and knew they'd ignited the oil-soaked pile they'd made around the circular saw. The light of the flames shot up the timbers around the big saw and lit the mill. Shadows danced against the walls.

Suddenly French was afraid she'd be trapped in the

burning mill, trapped behind her stack of boards that just a moment ago had been such a comforting shelter, and now, in her fear-filled mind, had become merely . . . flammable material.

Already the heat was palpable. Even behind her pile of lumber, French could feel the blast of the towering pillar of flame in the center of the sawmill.

Smoke from the fire was filling the top of the building, thickening, and roiling downward. Soon it would be impossible to breathe!

French held her breath as long as she could. When she could hold it no longer, she coughed in spite of all she could do.

From where they stood in the fresh air in the open doorway watching the results of their handiwork, one of the men called to the others, "Hey! Did you hear something?"

"It's just the fire, Haley. Relax." Abernathy's voice was almost bored.

"What if it was somebody coughing? What if we're leaving a witness?"

French, in spite of her desperation, was taken with a paroxysm of coughing. Her eyes were watering with the acrid sting of the smoke that now hung down around her in a choking cloud. Breath became more important than fear, and her straining lungs forced her to seek clearer air.

The smoke that made it impossible for her to breathe hid her from the arsonists at first. Then, as she was driven nearer the open doors, the men sighted her.

"There! A woman! Get her!" All six men charged toward her.

French would rather die than have such men touch her again. She whirled and ran back into the mill, heedless of the searing heat that was building there. Perhaps she could make it to the windows along the side of the mill overlooking the millpond. Maybe she could get one of those windows open. There was a chance that she could jump . . . and grab a log . . . to stay afloat in . . . spite of her . . . heavy . . . coat . . . But it was too late for French. Choking and gasping, she fell to her knees, unable to go on.

Startled cries came from behind her. There was a thunderous pounding of hooves on the thick floorboards of the mill. The panicked scream of a horse sounded off to her right. A huge body loomed out of the smoke.

Someone leaned over her from the saddle and she was grasped round the waist and swung up onto the plunging animal. The superhuman effort that had held the half-maddened horse near the crackling flames was relaxed, and the beast lunged around and flew for the open doors.

As French watched in horror, the doors began to close! Two men on each door were struggling to get them shut before the horse could reach them. She heard herself whimper.

Kyle—it was Kyle who held her, she knew it— shouted, "Daumier!" And the big gelding miraculously increased his speed. She felt Kyle move, then was deafened by the explosion as he shot at the men in the doorway. One of them dropped. She pressed her hands over her ears. The gun sounded again.

At the other door a man grabbed his shoulder and staggered away. The others took to their heels. They were running for cover as Daumier thundered out into the open.

Kyle turned the big horse away from the men. They were returning his fire now. He asked his mount to put more distance between them and the men whose shots whistled close in passing.

The smoke Daumier had inhaled had taken its toll, however, and the big horse stumbled to his knees as deep wracking coughs felled him.

Kyle couldn't keep his seat and hold French safe. Cursing, he twisted as they flew through the air. French crashed down on him as they hit the ground.

Daumier struggled up again. His eyes streaming from the acrid smoke, he misjudged his footing and tumbled over the edge of the trail to the wider lane several feet below. Picking himself up, he shook violently, then trotted off toward home, dazed.

The railroad men came streaming out of their hiding places. "Get 'em! Stop 'em before they make it to town!"

What a piece of luck! They thought he and French were still riding Daumier! Kyle drew back into the brush with French held high in his arms. He hesitated only an instant to see that Daumier was safely out of range of the pistols of the men pursuing him, then turned and ran farther back from the trail.

Unable to bear not knowing French's condition, he stopped and looked down at her. "French?" There was an agony of tension in his voice. "Are you all right?"

French brushed the smoke-engendered tears from her eyes and gulped another breath of the cold, sweet, pure, pine-scented air. One cough, and she could speak. "Oh, Kyle. I couldn't stop them. I was too afraid."

His arms closed convulsively around her, driving the breath back out of her. "My God! Surely you didn't consider for a moment confronting those animals?"

"No." She squirmed down out of his arms. She wanted to be on her own two feet. She had to be honest. "I merely wished that I could have found a way to save your sawmill. I was too cowardly to try, though, even if one had come to mind."

He looked at her, incredulous. Then he burst into something akin to laughter. "Ah, God, French. What's a sawmill when *you* are in the balance!"

She stood looking at him, stunned. *He did value her!* With a silly smile, she registered that she was more important to him than his sawmill. She stood looking up at him with a beatific smile on her face. Never had she known such contentment.

Kyle looked down at her. Had she lost her mind? Did she think they were safe here? Already the railroaders were charging back up the hill to look for them, and he couldn't risk shooting it out with them when he had French to keep safe. He snatched her hand and made a run for it.

After a few minutes, French gasped, "Please. Kyle." She was stumbling with every step and her breath refused to catch up to her desperate need for it.

Kyle looked back at her. She was so damned beautiful with her hair all down and her color high with exertion. "Not now," he growled at himself. This was no time to admire his beloved French. There was no time for anything but getting her to safety.

"Yes, now!" French dug in her heels and stood panting. "I . . . have to . . . stop . . . *now!*"

Kyle couldn't help it. He grinned down at her recklessly and kissed her crushingly, catching the breath she'd fought for in his own mouth. The kiss was lightning fast, and he laughed at the expression of outrage it brought to her face. Then he was dragging her on, seeking a place to hide her from his enemies.

He knew his men would come soon. They'd be about ten minutes behind him. They were on foot, but they hadn't been far away when Jamie had come charging into their midst. He knew, too, however, that they might stop and be occupied trying to save the sawmill. It was up to him to save his precious French.

They were on the mountain now. At least now he might find a cave or a crevice in which he could hide French. He had his gun—damned lucky for them both that he hadn't been heading for Julia's!—and his gunbelt was full of ammunition. If he could find a defensible cave, they should be able to hold out until the sound of gunfire brought help.

"Kyle! I . . . must . . . stop!" French fell to her knees.

Sorry that it would make catching her breath more difficult for her, he swung her over his shoulder and plowed on. He could hear the shouts of the railroaders clearly now. They were catching up. There was no time to worry about French's comfort.

There! It was no more than a thin shadow against the face of the rock, one he'd never seen before and would probably not have noticed now if it hadn't been for the fierce light of his burning sawmill, but Kyle saw it. A crevice! If it were only deep enough for him to put French safely behind him! He ran for it with renewed determination.

Reaching it, he put a gasping French down and shoved her against the wall. She choked and fought for breath and glared at him from behind the veil of her disheveled hair. He grinned at her. God, she was beautiful . . . and game. Most of the beautiful women he knew would be fainting and crying, and here his French was shooting him a look that wished it could kill because he'd refused to let her catch her breath. She wanted to be able to be more his equal. He breathed a heartfelt "thank you" that she was his . . . that she was safe.

And she was safe. Even if the railroaders filled him

full of lead, he'd hold them off until help arrived. He knew he could, because just looking at her made him invincible.

He grinned again and stood calmly drinking in the wonder that was Henry French Richards.

If it turned out that he had to spend his life as the price for this sight of her, Kyle Devereaux would consider it well worth it.

Chapter Twenty-six

FRENCH DECIDED KYLE Devereaux had *lost his mind!* There were at least four men with murder on *their* minds coming up the mountain working through the underbrush toward them, and he stood looking at her with a sappy grin on his face! She stamped her foot and turned her back on him.

With a reckless laugh, Kyle spun her around and yanked her hard up against him. "Oh, no, you don't." He spoke with his lips almost touching hers. "If I'm gonna die here, it isn't gonna be looking at your back!"

He claimed her mouth hungrily. His hands smoothed down her back from her waist, but they weren't touching her in the soothing way to which French had become accustomed. And they weren't staying politely on her upper back! With a faint sense of shock, French felt his hands smooth down her over her hips, and for a split second, as they molded her lower body to his, the proper Bostonian in her thought she ought to protest. Then she heard Kyle groan deep in his throat, and the proper Bostonian disappeared forever.

French wrapped her arms around Kyle's neck and pulled herself even closer to him, taking comfort and a heady delight in feeling the hard contours of his body against her own softness. She opened her mouth to him when he insisted, and the small, faraway part of her that could still think thought that if she was, indeed, going to die, this was a delicious way to do it.

Die!

Suddenly the word penetrated. Die was not a word she was willing to accept. Especially not now! She had no intention of letting Kyle *die*! She snatched herself out of his embrace and stood, breathing quickly, her lips bruised from his kisses, staring up at him.

Everything about him registered on her mind with unusual clarity, as if she were imprinting it on her memory forever. She saw the fresh scar on his cheek left by the gash that she'd so carefully tended, and thought inanely that it was extremely becoming. She saw his eyes, smoky blue with passion at first, then bright with the light of battle as he reluctantly transferred his attention from her to his present problem, the men outside.

Impulsively, to be completely certain that he didn't misunderstand why she'd taken herself out of his embrace, French threw herself back into his arms and kissed him for all she was worth. Before the startled Kyle could hold her there, she tore away again, leaving him muttering, "Well, I'll be . . ."

French didn't hear what he'd be, though she had a pretty good idea what it was he'd said. All her attention was focused on what she considered the immediate problem now. And it was the grimmest problem she'd ever addressed. She had to find a way to keep Kyle alive. Standing, as he was, near the mouth of the crevice, there was no cover for him. Anyone shooting into the opening would have an excellent chance of hitting him. She *had* to find some way to keep him safe. Even a curve in the rock wall, an outcropping . . . something to give Kyle half a chance.

She turned away from Kyle again, and started walking back into the darkness. When she did, she noticed what she thought was a movement in the depths of the crevice in which they sheltered.

What had moved? She felt a little frisson of worry . . . not fear. Her fear was gone because she was with Kyle. And, she told herself practically, Kyle had a gun.

But what if they were disturbing a hibernating bear? She'd heard that you could empty your gun into a bear, and it could still keep coming and maul you to death before it died.

She backed up to be just a little closer to Kyle.

The movement came again, and she saw two yellow eyes glowing at her from a spot about three feet off the rocky floor of the crevice. A wolf! It was a wolf. Kyle had made very sure that she could recognize wolves, now . . . even by no more than their yellow eyes.

Suppose they'd inadvertently invaded a den of wolves? Kyle had told her that wolves never attacked humans . . . unless they were cornered. Did Kyle and her standing in the entrance—*and exit*—of their den count as cornering them? She was very much afraid that it might. "K-K-Kyle?"

"Shhh."

She wanted to rail at him not to shush her when she had something of major importance to tell him, but her good sense stopped her. The wolf wasn't doing anything.

The men outside definitely *would* do something. And if they heard her voice and found the crevice, they would still have a straight shot at Kyle. There was still no cover for him.

That would never do! Wolves or no wolves, she must at least find a bend in the naturally formed rock tunnel in which they hid that might offer Kyle a chance. With that purpose firmly in mind, she moved boldly toward the wolf.

It moved just as boldly to meet her. Her heart in her mouth, she hesitated. She'd hoped it would retreat. Then she saw in the dim light that filtered back here into the tunnel that the wolf was wagging its tail. It was Rover!

Relief sang through her. She ran forward to meet Rover, ignoring Kyle's startled gasp. She dropped a hand to the springy fur of Rover's ruff to show Kyle it was all right and heard the breath explode from him in relief.

Perversely, she was glad she'd given him a bad moment.

Rover turned and began leading French deeper into the crevice. It widened as they went, bending and twisting as it meandered deeper into the mountain. Here was cover for Kyle.

"Kyle!" She made it a long soft whisper. A whisper with force, however, and she heard his footsteps as he came after her.

Up ahead French saw light. Perhaps there was another way out! She ran back to meet Kyle. "Kyle!" Still she kept her voice to a whisper. She evaded his arms as they reached for her so surely, so possessively, even while her heart thrilled to the gesture.

He loved her. She had no doubt of that now, and her heart nearly undid her purpose with its response to him. She took a firm hold on her fast-beating heart and tried to stick to her subject. She told him, "Kyle, there's light up ahead. Do you suppose there's another way out?"

He followed her and Rover to the place from which she'd seen the soft glow of light ahead of her. The light was gone.

"That's funny." She was sure she'd seen light up there

just beyond the next bend in the tunnel. "I saw a glimmer of light up ahead just a moment ago."

"It doesn't matter. Unless they find the opening and come in, we're probably safe back here. I have a good chance of dropping them as they enter." He gave her a hard, quick kiss, and pride filled his voice. "By coming back here, you've saved me taking lead for you. I gotta tell you I appreciate that."

French was appalled. His voice held more than a hint of laughter. She led him back to a place where there was enough light for her to peer at his face. She wanted to see what he thought was so amusing.

He stood quietly and let her look at him, grinning. Obviously this was something men did in times of stress, French decided. No doubt this was, as her Aunt Julia had said there would be, one of those times when a woman was completely at a loss to understand a man.

She absorbed the wisdom quietly. Finally she put it down to some warrior side of her man, and let it be. The knowledge seeped through her that there would be many times she would have to just let something be if she was to spend her life with a man like Kyle . . . a real man.

Certainty and exultation shot through her. She *was* going to spend the rest of her life with this man, this Kyle Devereaux, she knew it. Then, like a drenching of ice water, the thought assailed her, *However short that might be!*

Immediately, her teeth clenched and she made up her mind that that was going to be a very long time. Turning on her heel, she headed back into the darkness, back to where she'd been certain she'd seen a light. She was going to get them out of here!

Kyle grabbed her arm and swung her back to face him

again. Abandoning her mission temporarily, French leaned comfortably against his lean frame and waited for whatever it was he wanted.

He looked down at her, his face a study in perplexity. How could she lean so trustingly against him if she believed he had killed her uncle? How could she look at him as she had done ever since he'd snatched her out of his burning sawmill, with such love and liveliness in her face, if she thought he'd murdered Jake?

He was split two ways on this, and he didn't like it. He was grateful as all get out that she loved him, but he couldn't fathom how she could be so blasted changeable. She'd been so listless and depressed just yesterday, and now she was all vital and aglow . . . like his old French. What the bloody hell had happened?

A thought struck him. "You don't believe I killed your Uncle Jake, do you?"

She rested her head against his chest, liking the way his voice rumbled under her cheek. "No, of course not."

"You never did believe it, did you?"

"No."

Kyle felt as if he'd been given a double-edged sword, one that cut through to his happiness on one side while the other edge cut the ground out from under his feet. "French." His voice was severe as he pried her off him so that he could see her face. "Tell me why you didn't believe Abernathy."

French looked impatient. "I couldn't think that you killed my Uncle Jacob. I couldn't think that anyone had, Kyle." She smiled up at him reassuringly. "Uncle Jacob and I are very close, you see, and I simply have never felt that Uncle Jacob was dead."

"But I thought . . . I mean . . ." He took a breath and tried again. "After Abernathy told you . . ."

French took pity on him. "I could never have believed such a thing of you, Kyle, but Abernathy never told me anything but a pack of lies that were supposed to be messages from my family." She stood very still. "That was why I was sad, because, for just a minute, before he carried it too far, I thought that they had sent the messages, that they cared."

She waited for the sadness to claim her again, but it didn't. Even as Kyle reached for her, she realized that she didn't need coddling when it came to her family any longer. Somewhere here in Sunrise, Colorado, Henry French Richards had grown up. Like a child that outgrows and packs away her dolls, she'd put her need for her family's love and approval firmly behind her.

She had more than she could ever use up right here.

She accepted his comforting embrace for a moment, cherishing it, then placed her hands on the nicely muscled wall of his chest and pushed herself away. "Right now, I have to get you out of here safely," she told him briskly.

Kyle laughed. "I think that's supposed to be my line."

Uneasy because the light she sought was still not there even though she'd led him back past the place she'd first seen it, French snapped at him, "Kyle Devereaux! This isn't a play and I haven't got time for your nonsense."

His soft laughter echoed in the small bend of the tunnel. "Henry French Richards, you're a warlike little goddess, and I adore you."

"Well, hell!" A man's voice spoke from up ahead of them. "If that's who you are, then come the blazes on in here." Light glared out, blinding them, as the owner of the voice unhooded his lantern.

Chapter Twenty-seven

"JAKE PIERCE! YOU old . . ."

French heard a string of odd words and mild curses that would have amazed her father and brothers. Even as her head spun with the knowledge that she'd found her dear Uncle Jacob—safely alive as she had known he would be—even as she pretended not to hear Kyle's words, she had to admire his impressive fluency. The proper Bostonian in her had indeed given place to a woman of the West.

Far from being offended by the names Kyle was calling him, Jacob Bently Price III sat on a filthy heap of blankets smiling up at the two of them. "Sure as hell took you long enough to find me, Devereaux," he growled finally. Then to French, "Come over here and let me see how you've grown yourself up, French honey." He laughed. "Just don't come too close, I must smell like a polecat."

French ran across the cave and hugged her uncle fiercely. "Oh, Uncle Jacob! I knew you were alive, I just knew it! How glad I am to have found you at last." With that, she burst into tears.

Behind her back, Jake gestured a query to Kyle. What in tarnation was the matter with his niece?

"She's had a rough day, Jake. She'll come around in a

minute." He smiled with pride and affection in French's direction. "She's a tough one."

French was flattered. She was aware she was being praised, she just wasn't sure that she liked being described in precisely that way. Nevertheless, she sat back on her heels smiling through her tears of happiness as she wiped them from her eyes with unsteady fingers. In spite of the threat posed by the men just outside on the mountain, French had never been happier. Even Rover was here, sitting quietly on the other side of Jake with her tongue lolling out of her mouth, content.

Jake pushed up into a position higher against the rough wall of the cave and threw off the blanket that had covered him to the waist.

French saw her uncle's leg. "Oh, your poor leg. You've broken it!"

Jake had splinted his leg between the handles of two of his shovels, but the effort hadn't been completely successful. He grimaced as he looked down at it. "Yes, dear, I'm afraid I have. I couldn't get it set right, or I'd have hobbled out of here somehow."

French made a comforting little noise and patted his arm. "I'm here now. You'll be fine."

"Yeah," Kyle said laconically. "You'll be fine. We'll get a bunch of men to drag you out of here and break that leg again so that we can set it right for you."

Jake cursed him softly, his gentlemanly speech patterns momentarily forgotten. "Thanks a lot."

Unrepentant, Kyle grinned at him. "I better go see what's happening outside."

"Kyle Devereaux, you be careful!" French spun away from her uncle, her eyes wide with apprehension.

"I'll be fine, French. I'll be just fine." He was ten feet tall, just from the way she was looking at him. Who could hurt him when he was that much larger than life? Confidently he left them and strode back toward the entrance to what was obviously old Jake Price's fabled silver mine.

Jake's mine. No wonder none of them had ever found it. Not claim jumpers nor the friends searching for Jake. The mine was practically in the town of Sunrise. Nobody'd thought of searching so close to home.

When he got to the end of the tunnel, he heard a familiar voice out on the mountain. He pushed his way out of the narrow mouth of the crevice to find his long-lost bull of the woods calling urgently, "Dev! Devereaux. Are you here? Are you all right?" Then, impatiently, "Dammit, boss, where the hell are ya?"

As soon as he was a safe distance from the hidden mine, Kyle eased Rafferty's mind with a few mild oaths of greeting. Rafferty whirled around and catapulted himself onto his employer and friend. They pounded each other on the back for a few seconds, grinning at each other. Finally Kyle demanded, "What the hell took you so long?"

"What's the matter, boss? Miss me?"

Kyle blistered his foreman's ears again.

Rafferty relented with a grin, then sobered as he saw the fresh scar on Kyle's cheek. "You look like they played a little rough. From the looks of what's left of the mill, they were playing a pretty nasty game, too."

"Looks like," Kyle agreed impatiently. "Out with it, Raf. What about my nephew? Where is he?"

There was a small uncertain sound from the other side of the massive Rafferty, and Jamie stepped forward from where he'd been hiding behind the big Irishman. Very softly he said, "Here I am, Uncle Kyle."

Kyle was struck dumb. It was Jamie. Emotions that

boded ill for the boy's continued ability to sit down tore through him. "Jamie Waring!" He stared at the boy with fresh insight. "What the hell did you think you were doing? Didn't you know that I'd be looking for you? Didn't you know I'd be worried?" He shouted the last words at the boy, his fingers itching to shake Jamie good.

Jamie gulped hard and said faintly, "No, sir." His expression was one of genuine surprise. "Nobody's ever worried about me before."

That took the wind out of Kyle like a blow to the stomach. He stood there a full minute as he wrestled with the feelings assailing him now. Obviously the boy had been given the same loving care and guidance Kyle himself had received at the hands of the Devereaux females. No doubt the child had the same feelings Kyle had had at his age.

A kinship of spirit blossomed and drew him closer to the boy than any kinship of blood could have done. He knew those feelings too well. He'd had them all his life. Hell, he'd had them right up until he'd found French.

Jamie had no more need to worry about being able to sit down. Not because of Kyle Devereaux, anyhow, Kyle vowed. Gently he shook the boy's shoulder. His voice deepened as he said, "Well, button, you have a whole raft of us to worry about you now."

Jamie looked up at Kyle as if he couldn't believe what he was being told. Then he threw his arms around his tall uncle's waist and sobbed his relief.

Kyle held him tight and let him cry it out. He could feel the tension ebbing out of the straight young body, and remembered how brave the boy had been the night he'd saved him from Abernathy's thugs out at the ranch. He felt like a damned lucky man to have such a nephew.

For the first time in his life, Kyle let himself wonder if

the austere man he'd been shipped off to had felt glad to have him at any time. It was a question he'd never permitted to enter his mind before. He guessed he'd feared the answer. Somehow, he'd felt that if he didn't look too closely at the things that really mattered in life, he'd get through it with less . . . pain. Now, he'd never know.

Suddenly, there were many things he was beginning to wonder about. His friendship with Julia and Charles had let a little water flow over the top of the dam behind which he'd locked all his hopes and dreams and emotions. French's faith in him had opened the floodgates.

He grinned down at the top of his nephew's head. Tousling his hair he made a solemn promise. For the first time in his young life, this boy was going to be half-drowned.

A long minute passed as he let the boy compose himself, then Kyle said, "Raf, go get half a dozen men and meet me back here in fifteen minutes."

Rafferty nodded and charged off. One bellow would have brought a lot more than a dozen men, but Rafferty was smart enough to know his boss wanted him gone for a quarter of an hour.

To Jamie, Kyle said, "Come on, Jamie. This seems to be a day for uncles. Come and meet French's Uncle Jake."

When the two of them reached the cave in which Kyle had left French and her uncle, they found a mild argument in progress. Introducing Jamie and waiting for French to give the boy a hug and her heartfelt thanks for warning her to hide in the mill broke it up momentarily. Jake continued it as soon as Jamie had been introduced to Jake's wolf, whose name, Jake was quick to make known, was Fang *not* Rover. While Jamie settled down beside the wolf to cement this new friendship, Jake pressed on. "I'm not sure I like the idea of having my leg rebroken just yet."

French looked startled for a moment, decided her uncle believed Kyle was going to have his lumberjacks rebreak his poor leg, and hastened to reassure him, "We'll have Dr. Burton reset your leg, dear. He has chloroform. You won't feel a thing, I promise. Don't let Kyle frighten you."

Jake looked over his niece's head at Kyle. The men shared an amused glance. Kyle knew Jake meant he had unfinished business to clear up before he went to invalid status, not that he was afraid of a little discomfort.

"Well, whatever happens next," Jake said, deciding evasion of the whole subject was his best defense, "I'm sure as hell glad you got here. I've about run out of supplies."

French took his too thin hand and held it to her cheek. It looked to her as if he had run out of supplies some time ago. In fact, she wondered if he would have still been alive for them to find if it hadn't been for the tiny trickle of water that seeped down one rock wall. Her voice went all husky as she told him, "We'll get you to Aunt Julia's right away."

"Julia's?" Something akin to panic showed in his eyes. "Wouldn't it be simpler to put me at Kyle's? Closer to the doctor and all."

French ignored Kyle's jeering chuckle as she said, "Oh, but then Julia would have to drive into town to visit you. It wouldn't be the same as her having you right at home to nurse and watch over."

"Yes," her uncle said dryly, "I know."

French misread his attitude. "Oh, you're worried about being a burden. You wouldn't be any trouble, honestly.

Julia could nurse you all day, and I could take over the minute I got home from teaching so that she could rest."

Her uncle rolled his eyes at Kyle like a frightened horse. He certainly didn't look best pleased at her suggested arrangement. Perhaps he was too used to being solitary. She smiled at him brightly. "Miss Mary does all the work at our house, and all the cooking, too, so there's nothing to keep Julia and me from taking care of you."

"Mary who?" Jake asked sharply.

"Why, Miss Mary, of course." She saw disappointment touch his face. "Mary Wells."

Jake brightened right up and grinned broadly. "So Mary Wells is still out there at the ranch." Jake's grin turned to a tender smile. "Don't know why you said 'Miss' Mary. Mary's a widow. Husband used to mine on the other side of this very mountain until a cave-in got him. I was afraid some lucky man might have courted her away from these parts by now."

French remembered Mary's face when she'd spoken of Jacob Price. "I think she's . . ." She closed her lips firmly. It wasn't up to her to tell her uncle she thought Miss Mary was sweet on him. Mary's secrets were her own to tell. French wasn't going to even hint to her uncle that she thought Mary was waiting for him.

Interest flared in his eyes. "She's what?" Jake was quick with his question.

In a flash, French decided she wasn't above misleading her uncle if it meant that he'd go home with her and get the very best of care. "I think she's very close to making a momentous decision."

Jake glared up at Kyle. "Sorry not to accept your kind invitation, son, but I think I have an interest to protect out at the Lightning Double C."

Kyle didn't bother to point out that he hadn't issued

any invitation. Jake would be welcome in his home at any time . . . in any of his homes, in fact.

Jake's willingness to subject himself to the constant care of the women in his family—care that would probably drive the poor man round the bend—was one Kyle could easily understand. He'd stand chin deep in icy water for a week if that was what it took to get near his French.

"I need to get you out of here, Jake."

"Yep."

The way the two men looked at each other told French that they both knew that it was going to be a hurtful process. Understanding that neither wanted witnesses for it, especially not feminine ones, French told Jamie, "Bring Rov . . . Fang, Jamie. I'll carry Uncle Jacob's rifle." She picked up the fine old weapon from where her uncle had kept it close by his makeshift bed, and started for the mouth of the tunnel, Fang and Jamie on her heels.

There was a single gasp of pain behind her as Kyle lifted Jacob in his arms, then silence except for Kyle's firm footsteps following her out into the evening. Then she heard her uncle chuckle nastily and say, "Goddess, Kyle? Goddess?"

"Shut up, Jake," was Kyle's snarling reply.

French blinked back quick tears, and straightened her shoulders. When she came out into the dusky twilight, she was smiling. It had been quite a day.

Chapter Twenty-eight

IT WAS A good thing the next day was Saturday! French felt she really needed a day off. She was exhausted from all the excitement of the preceding day. So was everyone else.

Rest wasn't easy to achieve, however. The whole ranch was turned topsy-turvy, and had been since the minute they'd brought Jacob Price into the house. It had been quite late by the time Dr. Burton had gotten Jake's leg rebroken and reset. It had been a process Jake hadn't made any easier on anyone, including and especially himself, by refusing to be chloroformed.

He said he wanted to be sharp when he got to the Chamberses' ranch, and that he wasn't going to stay one night in town in order to be able to do it.

The minute French and Kyle saw the look on Miss Mary's face when Jacob had been carried in, they'd understood his stubborn determination. French had slipped her arms around Kyle's waist and buried her face against his shirt, while he'd rested his cheek on the top of her head and looked away to give the older couple their privacy.

Julia and Charles had seen how things were immediately, and had settled Julia's brother in the second-best guest bedroom and told Miss Mary to go along to see to it that he was comfortable.

"Huh," Charlie'd said as soon as they were out of earshot, "it'd take a whole tribe of Arapahos to stop her."

Julia had dug him in the ribs and called out to Mary, "You just take good care of my brother, Mary. I'll cook for the ranch tomorrow and Sunday."

"Lordamighty!" Charlie was thunderstruck. "We'll all *starve*!" He'd stood looking at Julia as if she'd taken leave of her senses.

Now that morning had come, French thought that Julia just might have, indeed, taken leave of her senses. She was trying her best to help her aunt. They were both in the kitchen, doing their best. Julia was attempting to cook breakfast for the hands as she'd offered to do while Miss Mary nursed her dear brother Jacob.

French really was earnestly *trying* to help, but she'd never been in a kitchen before except to beg food from a competent cook, and she felt more than just woefully inadequate. She *had*, she hoped, managed to set the table correctly for the gang of ranch hands that boiled into the kitchen hungry for their predawn breakfast, but right there she ran out of expertise. From then on she just bumbled along, and her aunt did little better.

Julia and she had both been reduced to limp heaps by the time the first cowhand asked hopefully, "Will Miss Mary be back soon?"

When the men left the big kitchen, Julia turned dazed eyes to French and asked, "Were all those men ours?"

French could only shrug, she had no idea.

Julia complained, "I'm *certain* Charles doesn't have *that* many men working for him."

Before they'd finished the dishes, with French to wash and Julia to dry and put away—on the vague notion that Julia might know where the dishes belonged since it was, after all, *her* house—the men were in the saddle and following a direly muttering Charles out to the north end of the ranch.

By the time the two of them finally got out of the kitchen, their frocks were a mess, and Julia had taken a sacred vow to give Miss Mary—or her replacement, as she strongly suspected it was going to be—a huge raise in pay.

French told her aunt gently, "I'll help you to write a notice advertising for a new housekeeper-cook, Aunt Julia." It wasn't much, and certainly Julia didn't need her help, but it was the best she could do to quiet the guilt she felt about being so inadequate in the kitchen. Sadly, it was obvious the two of them together weren't competent to do the job of just one good ranch cook.

Julia responded by throwing her hands up and running for the bedroom. French followed at a slower pace, wondering how the usually sedate Julia, who surely must be as tired as she, could outdistance her so easily.

French had barely changed and freshened up when Kyle arrived. Seeing him was like having the sun come up. Feeling very much more like herself, she stepped confidently into his arms and hugged him. It was like coming home.

Kyle grinned. "French Richards, you're the best thing that ever happened to me." He crushed her to him as if he wanted to imprint her very bones on his flesh. French, his French. He was still overcome by her and about her . . . by the miracle of her, with her caring and trust and the way they'd healed him . . . with gratitude that he'd been in time to rescue her from the fire . . . and mostly by the fact that she was his. Still his.

Emotions he'd never thought he'd be able to let himself feel inundated him. It was with the greatest effort that he kept his voice casual. "I'll be gone awhile, honey. Will you miss me?"

"Of course I'll miss you. Where are you going? And must you go?"

"To the capital. Sheriff says that my testimony will put Abernathy and his thugs away for some time. It might just do in this whole bunch of fly-by-night railroaders." He touched a strand of her hair. "I'd sure hate to miss out on an opportunity like that. If we can get rid of them, maybe Sunrise can build our own line, like the people of Denver did."

"Are you so very important, then?"

He laughed down at her, loving the adoring way she waited for an affirmative reply. "No," he disappointed her. "But my lumber sure is. At least to Denver." He grinned down at her and ran his finger along the curve of her jaw. "The new capital is growing faster than ever with this new boom in silver . . . and, of course, the railroad Denver put in to link 'em up to the Union Pacific. I've shipped them half the buildings up there in the form of Devil-Oh Lumber."

"Oh."

"Oh," he teased, lifting her chin to steal a kiss before someone came into the parlor. The kiss almost got out of hand.

French was breathless when she pulled away to ask, "So they'll listen to you better than to the sheriff?"

"The sheriff didn't get his sawmill burned down." Kyle had lost interest in anything but the lips that tantalized him. He bent his head, desire for her coursing through him, to claim them again.

French pushed away from him, her mind on the parting that loomed before them. "Oh, Kyle. I want you to go. It's the right thing to do. It's what I teach my pupils . . . civic responsibility." She put a hand up to his lapel and toyed with the edge of it. "It's just that"—shyly she glanced up at him—"I don't want you to leave me."

Leaving her was the last thing he wanted to do. He pulled her hard against him, and locked her there in the steel circle of his arms. "I don't want to leave you, French." His lips feathered across her own, then captured them in a long, demanding kiss.

"Oh, dear." French's knees began to feel very unreliable.

"Come with me, French."

She pushed lightly against his chest and leaned back to look up at his face.

The movement set him on fire. His nostrils flared as he fought for control. They were supposed to be having a conversation, he reminded himself.

French saw the muscle jump in his jaw. Under her hands she could feel his strong heart thundering. She loved him so. She belonged to him, to Kyle Devereaux. She belonged to herself, too, however, and she was learning for the first time that *she* valued *herself.* She knew she did, because even though she loved Kyle more than anything in life—perhaps more than life itself—she couldn't dishonor herself by becoming a scandal.

She couldn't just go to Denver with Kyle, no matter how much she wanted to. The knowledge ran through her like strong wine, dizzying her with the intensity of it. She reached out to touch his face. As she searched for words, he spoke and resolved it all.

"Marry me and come with me to Denver." He spoke huskily, his mouth just over her own. "It won't be much of a honeymoon, because Denver's not much of a city yet. But hell, French"—he lifted his head and looked at her like a naughty little boy—"I want you so bad my teeth ache, Henry French Richards. I'm not going to let you out of the room except to eat, anyway."

French thought she should be shocked, but she wasn't. She smiled at him radiantly. She was happy, just happy. Happier than she'd ever been. Kyle was hers and she was his and all was right with her world.

Belatedly, she remembered the proprieties. She straightened up and told him. "You must ask my aunt and uncle, you know. My parents are so far away, I'd die before we got an answer from them . . ." Her voice trailed away. She stood stock-still, and a puzzled look came over her face.

Concern for her shot through Kyle. Without even knowing them he disliked her parents. What memory of them was hurting his French now?

Suddenly she laughed, and the eyes she turned to him were glowing. "Kyle, I've just made the most wonderful discovery."

Kyle was looking hard at her, frowning slightly. "What discovery, French?"

"That, for the very first time in my life—my *entire* life—I don't really *care* what my parents think."

Kyle swept her back into his arms and smothered her with kisses. His heart lightened and soared. He wasn't the only one liberated from childhood hurts . . . for finding his nephew Jamie Waring, who had suffered as much as he ever had, had affected him profoundly. Deciding that he, Kyle Devereaux, was going to be the one to make things up to his heartless sister's child had enabled him to put aside the last of his own tortured feelings about his mother. That door was closed, the subject and his agonies about it dead and buried at last.

Now his precious French was free as well. He could see it in the clear brightness of her lovely gray eyes. The shadow that had always lain in their quiet depths was gone, now there was only the glow of her love for him and the shining happiness she held for their future together.

In humble gratitude, Kyle sent off a prayer of thanks for this gift to their love. Finally, they were both free to pursue to satisfaction the deep and wondrous longings they had for one another.

Things didn't work out as simply as Kyle had planned, however. Julia and Jake refused to "let French run off with" Kyle.

Charlie had told him, "You'll just have to ask the authorities in Denver to postpone Abernathy's trial for long enough for you to attend a wedding, boy." He grinned and slapped Kyle on the back. "Hell, boy . . . sorry, Julia . . . they'll be glad to do it when they hear that the wedding's your own!"

They had been, and Julia had feverishly thrown into action all the plans she had dreamed for French's wedding. The house was decorated to a fare-thee-well, and everybody within fifty miles was invited. To French and Kyle it looked as if they had all come!

"Isn't it wonderful?" French, radiant and glorious in her aunt's elaborate wedding gown, looked up at him. "Everyone seems to be having such a good time. They all seem so happy for us."

Kyle looked out over the large group of well-wishers crowding the parlors and dining room and foyer of Julia's big house, and smiled. "I guess it was a good idea to wait and do this right, after all."

Jake, leaning on a cane with Mary Wells hovering over him, said, "Julia would of skinned you alive if you'd tried it any other way, Kyle."

"I certainly would have," Julia said as she came up behind them. "I've been saving my wedding gown since

French was flower girl in my own ceremony, dreaming of this wedding. And"—she cocked her head at Kyle and sent him a satisfied smile—"I have been planning this wedding since the very day I met you, Kyle Devereaux."

"Well, I'll be . . ."

"Not on your wedding day you won't, my dear," Julia told him firmly. "Come along now, Henry French. It's time to change if you're to make it to your train on time." Julia took her niece's hand and pulled her toward the stairs.

When they came down again, French, clad in an elegant blue traveling suit with a matching, sable-lined cape, went to Kyle like an arrow from a drawn bow.

"You look lovely," he told her, his voice husky. He stood holding her hands close against his chest in both his own and gazed down into her eyes. "I have the most beautiful bride Colorado's ever seen."

Neither of them noticed being guided out to the waiting sleigh. Their gazes locked, they were lost in some magic place together.

Laughing and chattering, everybody else piled into various sledlike conveyances and escorted them down to the depot. There they found Phinehas Faraday proudly awaiting the newlyweds. His station was lavishly decorated with greenery and big white ribbons in their honor. Sunrise had outdone itself.

The train had already arrived and was sitting waiting, puffing softly, every roof of every one of its cars wearing a blanket of snow. From the windows of the passenger cars, curious faces were staring out at the decorated station and the crowd of celebrants crowding it.

"Good-bye, dears. See you back here in two weeks!" Julia put her handkerchief to her lips, her eyes filling with happy tears.

French flew back to her and hugged her. "I love you, Aunt Julia."

Jake stepped forward, Mary Wells on his arm. "Be happy, niece."

French hugged him, too. "I will, Uncle Jacob. How could I be anything else?" She smiled radiantly as Kyle swept her onto the train. They stood and waved good-bye to everyone from behind the little iron railing at the back of the last car as the conductor signaled the engineer to pull out of Sunrise.

Their friends cheered as Kyle Devereaux gathered Henry French Richards *Devereaux* into his arms and soundly kissed her. Then the engine stopped softly puffing and began to chug faster and faster, steel wheels slipping and gripping on steel rails. Leaving behind a great cloud of smoke and a whisper of steam from the engine, they were gone.

On the rough wooden platform of the depot, Julia stood weeping happily in the circle of her husband's arms. "This is where it all began, darling," she told him softly. "Right here."

"Yep." Charlie remembered. He remembered a whole lot about what happened that day. "Sure did."

"Yes." Julia sighed happily, leaning back against his chest a moment longer. Then she took a deep breath of the crisp fresh air and turned around so that she was facing him.

The dreamy expression was slowly fading from her face as she smoothed the lapels of his Sunday-best coat. Smiling up at her beloved husband, she asked with bright curiosity, "By the way, dearest, what was it you were going to tell me that Kyle said to you when he first saw our Henry French?"

Epilogue

THE BLIZZARD HOWLED down out of the mountains and tore through the streets of Sunrise. It slammed and sliced around the houses and sought cracks into which it might insinuate freezing fingers, but the whole of Sunrise was buttoned up tight, firewood stacked near doorways and animals safely locked in sheds and barns.

In the small park that surrounded the tall house that was the finest in town, trees bent before the force of it and against the outer walls of the mansion great drifts piled. Snow smoked in long streamers from their tops when the wind intensified, then swirled and settled again as it lessened. Inside the huge house, the roar of the wind was only a whisper through the heavy damask and velvet draperies the Chinese houseboy had drawn to shut out the tiniest of drafts.

As the wan, gray light of the storm's day faded, Henry French Richards Devereaux sat on the study floor, held comfortably in her new husband's arms, and stared into the fire, more content than she'd ever thought she could be.

"Penny for your thoughts."

She felt the words rumble in his chest where her head rested and smiled. No matter how often she *felt* his voice, the sensation never ceased to send delectable little shivers through her. Turning her face up to him, she said, "I was thinking that I've never been so content."

"Hmmm, me, too." He kissed the tip of her nose and settled more comfortably against the heavy wing chair that propped his back. Kyle pulled some of the huge quilt they'd thrown down on the hearth rug in front of the fireplace more closely around French.

French smiled and pulled a part of it over his long legs, making a cozy cocoon for them. Then she settled against his chest again, pressing an ear to it. "Do you suppose everyone is all right out at the ranch?"

"Hmm-hmmmm." His murmur of assent tickled her ear. She smiled again. She loved exploring everything about Kyle, but having his voice come to her this way had been one of her first discoveries, and it was still a thrill for her. It always would be, she knew. Finding him and having him return her love had been the answer to her every longing. She knew that the thrill of it would never fade, it would remain a cherished part of her existence for the rest of her days. She asked another question that she expected him to answer in the affirmative so she could feel the resonance of it in his chest again.

"I'm silly to worry, aren't I?"

"Hmm-hmmmm."

She laughed a little and sat up then, turning to face him, loving to watch the play of firelight across his strong features. "Why? Tell me. I need reassurance, you know. I've never been in a blizzard before."

Astonished at her prevarication, Kyle laughed at her. "You're from Boston!"

"Of course I am." She lifted her chin at him, daring him to disagree. "And the snowstorms we call blizzards back there are much more . . . *civilized*."

"Civilized?" He reached out to capture one of her curls. Her rebellious hair never failed to charm him.

"Yes. The buildings tame them a bit, I think. They don't come roaring into town with such . . . savagery."

"I'll give you that. You haven't the open space for the wind to get any kind of a good start back east."

"So?"

"So what?" He wound the curl around his forefinger and gave it a gentle tug.

Ignoring his gentle pull on her hair, she uncurled her legs and stretched them out beside his, lying back against his chest again. "So are they safe out on the ranch? Uncle Jacob is from Boston, you know."

"Honey, your Uncle Charlie was born out here. He knows all about blizzards and he'll keep your Aunt Julia and Jamie safe. Julia means more to him than life, and Jamie is on the way to being the child they never had." He grunted "Huh" and added, "If the little scamp isn't there already."

"Jamie's not a scamp, he's a wonderful boy, one of my best students. I look forward to teaching him. To teaching all of them again. You're just cross that he didn't report to you for duty the moment he arrived."

"He should have."

"No doubt he would have if you hadn't frightened him half to death, you were so angry when you met the train." She smiled to remember how magnificent she had thought him, how instantly she had fallen in love with him.

He chuckled, and her head bounced against his chest. French patted his hard-muscled chest as if he were a pillow and resettled her head.

An intense light appeared in Kyle's eyes.

Ignoring their exchange about his nephew, he went on,

wanting to finish the queries and get to something more important. Much more important. "Your Uncle Jacob has been out here for years. All your life, in fact. And Miss Mary—who also knows all about the weather here in Colorado—and he are safe, snug, and happy in their very sturdy abode Charlie gave them on the ranch." With the distinct air of one ending a conversation, he told her, "Fang, too."

Something in Kyle's tone stirred a response in her. She sensed that her husband of only one month was losing interest in her questions. When he feathered kisses along the side of her neck, she was certain of it.

Twisting so that she lay on his chest, she looked deep and long into his eyes. With grave deliberation, she took his face between her hands and slowly brought her mouth down to his, her gaze never wavering. Then, as the touch of her lips to his drugged her with languorous sensation, her thick lashes fell to veil her eyes and the love that shone in them.

The kiss was long and sweet. She lifted her head and smiled down at him. "I love you, Kyle Devereaux."

Adoration in his eyes, Kyle rose lithely and pulled her up and against him, quilt and all. As the wonderful scent of burning piñon wood swirled out of the fireplace to surround them in a fragrant draft from the storm, love for the woman in his arms surged through him. Kyle groaned with inexpressible pleasure and lowered his mouth to her own. A single deep kiss left her clinging, her arms entwined about his neck, trustingly to him, weak with sweet surrender.

Kyle swung her up into his arms. Moving effortlessly, the quilt trailing after them like the robes of royalty, he carried her out of his study and toward the impressive circular staircase in the wide front hall.

As he mounted the stairs two at a time, surefooted in the gathering darkness, his heart felt as if it would burst with happiness.

His voice husky with the strength of his emotions, Kyle bent his head down and said very softly the words that he'd so long feared he'd never be privileged to say. "I love you, too, Mrs. Devereaux."

Now, at last, because of his cherished French, he knew that never again would he have to endure a winter of longing.

Outside, the blizzard began to sing.

*If you enjoyed this book,
take advantage
of this special offer.
Subscribe now and get a*

FREE
*Historical
Romance*

No Obligation (a $4.50 value)

Each month the editors of True Value select the four *very best* novels from America's leading publishers of romantic fiction. Preview them in your home *Free* for 10 days. With the first four books you receive, we'll send you a FREE book as our introductory gift. No Obligation!

If for any reason you decide not to keep them, just return them and owe nothing. If you like them as much as we think you will, you'll pay just $4.00 each and save at *least* $.50 each off the cover price. (Your savings are *guaranteed* to be at least $2.00 each month.) There is NO postage and handling – or other hidden charges. There are no minimum number of books to buy and you may cancel at any time.

*Send in
the Coupon
Below*

To get your FREE historical romance fill out the coupon below and mail it today. As soon as we receive it we'll send you your FREE Book along with your first month's selections.

—————————————————————————————

Mail To: **True Value Home Subscription Services, Inc., P.O. Box 5235
120 Brighton Road, Clifton, New Jersey 07015-5235**

YES! I want to start previewing the very best historical romances being published today. Send me my FREE book along with the first month's selections. I understand that I may look them over FREE for 10 days. If I'm not absolutely delighted I may return them and owe nothing. Otherwise I will pay the low price of just $4.00 each: a total $16.00 (at least an $18.00 value) and save at least $2.00. Then each month I will receive four brand new novels to preview as soon as they are published for the same low price. I can always return a shipment and I may cancel this subscription at any time with no obligation to buy even a single book. In any event the FREE book is mine to keep regardless.

Name _____

Street Address _____ Apt. No. _____

City _____ State _____ Zip _____

Telephone _____

Signature _____
(if under 18 parent or guardian must sign)

Terms and prices subject to change. Orders subject to acceptance by True Value Home Subscription Services, Inc.

11811-7